THE ABNORMAL SPIES SERIES

TREASURER OF SKULLS

TREASURER OF SKULLS

ISBN Kindle: 978-1-9168887-8-4
ISBN Paperback: 978-1-9168887-9-1

This book is a work of fiction. Any references to historical events, real people, or real places are used fictitiously. Other names, characters, places and events are products of the author's imagination, and any resemblances to actual events or places or persons, living or dead, is entirely coincidental.

Cover Design: Enchanted Ink Publishing
Editing: Sydney Hawthorn - Little Daggers Editing Guild
Book Design and Typesetting: Enchanted Ink Publishing

First printing, 2025.

For the readers that wanted to be pirates.

Flee with this treasure. Try to not get cursed.

Other books by Lauren Jade Case

The Creature Chronicles:

The Starlight Trilogy:
Starlight
Starfall

The Abnormal Spies Series:

Bearer of Masks
Treasurer of Skulls

My intent with this book and this story is never to harm and I don't want to risk someone's health by not disclosing that which may cause such things – even if some triggers may only appear in one chapter, in one line, in large or small quantities.

Below is a list of what the following book does contain and so now please be aware that these things are present in the story of TREASURER OF SKULLS to some degree.

This book contains the following content warnings:

Adult language
Blood/ Gore
Depictions of anxiety/ anxiety attacks
Fainting/ Unconsciousness
Injuries/ injury detail
Kidnapping
Mental abuse
Mentions of drugs
Mentions of childhood neglect
Prejudice
Mentions/ scenes of a sexual nature
Violence
Vomiting

THE ABNORMAL SPIES SERIES

TREASURER OF SKULLS

LAUREN JADE CASE

Case File: #508
Written by: PRAXIS ███████
Date: 40th day of Winter 2407
Location: ██████████████████████

Log type: MISSION
Status: CLOSED/ COMPLETE
If Complete, to what level: ████████████

The nature of this case it rather a joining of two: ████████████████████. This is not a first for ████████, just as it will likely not be the last, such is the nature of this job. However this connection of missions is rather unusual but also quite ████████.

I am aware that noting personal opinion is not required, but I will provide such things as I see fit in the way of keeping record for ██████████████.

Case #████ started with █████████████ setting out in ██ They searched the ██████████████████████████████████ No sign of them could be found. █████████ were █████████ from ████, however they were severely ███████████████████ that had ████████ ██████████. Another █████████ was called in to ████ in ████████████████████████████, allowing the ████████████ to ████████ ████████ again.

Case #██████, another given to ████. This one more ████ ████. They were sent to ██████████████████ that had recently paid █████████████████████, in full, to ███████████████████████ they were owed, and their ████████████████████ were rising. They were ███, edging even towards ██████████████████████ as a high-brow ████████████████████. The mission here was to ████████████ ███████████████████and to █████████████████ that which had made this possible.

Outside factors made ██████████████.

Later another recruit, one who was on ████████ ████████████████ he was cleared for ████████, located the team ████████████████████████████.

Thankfully, in regards to ██████████, there were no issues. In fact, those were the easier parts to manage for this machine to keep running. Which in itself was surprising considering the nature of ██████████. The █████ we have now also █████.

The █████ had quite a dense, hot climate and atmosphere. That led to one recruit falling dangerously ██ – not that their █████ will admit the full extent. Both they and another ████████████████████████████ for ██████ after stumbling upon a ████████████ ████████. They were seen to be ██████ when the one ████████.

Once past initial emotions, such as shock and awe and confusion, the ████████████. The ██████████ did ████████████████████████████, but it worked and was a sensible choice made by those present. A █████ who is fine-tuned with the ████████████ and another █████, discovered the truth behind ████████████, giving answers. However only one could ████████████ said █████, as they were ████████████████████ █████, to a certain degree, otherwise the supposed █████ would've taken another █████.

Due to the nature of this specific case, no time limit had been set for completion as it was a culmination of █████.

Providing each member gave an accurate account, this file is to document the proceedings of case number #508.

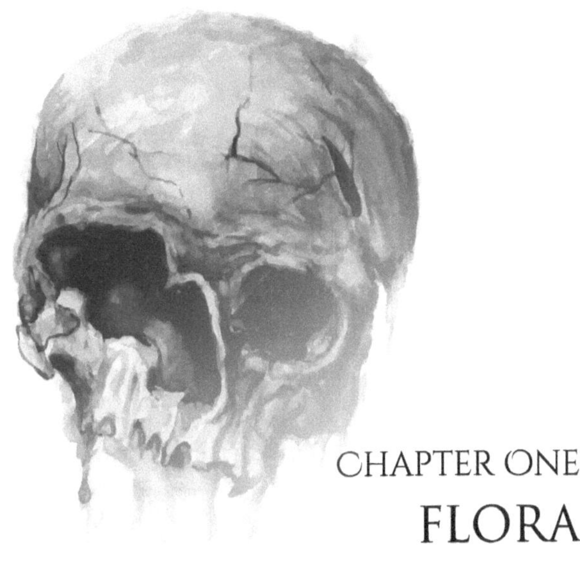

For as long as Flora Waite could remember, she'd been in love with Preston Tolhurst.

On a near daily basis, their paths crossed. His room was just down the hall from hers and they'd pass one another sometimes on the way to bed. Or they'd sit near each other at breakfast. Sometimes he'd purposely slow his run time around the garden just to jog alongside her when she couldn't keep up with the rest.

He snored. His birthday was on the 51st day of Summer and he would bring her a small iced cupcake for hers every year. He would compliment her yellow raincoat or her dull copper hair, sometimes even her smattering of freckles.

But she'd never tell him.

Tonight, Aleema's piano playing made Flora think of him. She pictured the way Preston's hair curled when wet or damp, how his eyes would water in spring because of the pollen, the half-awake smile he'd try to wear at breakfast.

Flora turned away from the melody. Playing the piano was Aleema's way of letting go; she pushed every thought, every emotion, every *everything* into it. Her abnormality melded with it. She couldn't help it, that was the way of abnormalities sometimes – but Aleema's was powerful. She could play music anywhere, on nearly anything she could form to be an instrument, and it would toy with people and their emotions. Aleema could use that however she liked – she could twist someone like a piper.

Thankfully, Flora didn't have to endure much. Dalton, the third person in their trio, burst into the attic. The grin on his face spread from ear to ear, wide and dazzling. Aleema's music cut off on a single low note.

Aleema turned on the bench to face him. "You're smiling," she pointed out as she adjusted her sage green hijab.

"Actually, it's a grin," Dalton corrected unnecessarily. "And a shit-eating one!"

Flora interlocked her hands in her lap. "Are you going to tell us *why* you're grinning like that?"

Dalton practically started to bounce on the spot. "I'm going on a mission!"

In one swoop, both Aleema and Flora were on their feet. They crowded into Dalton, sweeping him into their arms together. It was a warm hug, full of many emotions as if Aleema was still playing her music and the noise carried through their blood.

Going on a mission was a big deal. Right from the start, the correct qualities needed to be hand-picked by those in charge to ensure a success. That meant, for some, they weren't picked for *years*. Others could be chosen for every other mission. It all depended on the abnormality and how it could work for the benefit of all.

Dalton had a 'good' abnormality. He could connect with computers physically. It didn't matter which ones, all of them were accessible to him. But not every mission required that skill for the whole thing. Sometimes he was pulled in to others, maybe to hack a security camera or an electronic gate system. From how excited he was, it seemed he would be in it from the very start. *His* mission.

After a moment, the trio pulled back though they didn't unlock from one another.

"What's the mission?" Aleema asked, breaking the silence first. "When do you leave? Who are you even going with? Or is it solo? I didn't hear the news break for a mission? When were you even called in? I thought you were going into town for the dentist?"

"I did, go into town I mean," Dalton answered. "Maggie caught me on the way back." His fair blond hair fell into his green eyes and Flora reached out, pushing it back for him. "It's some sort of cyber mission."

"Should've guessed," Aleema huffed.

Dalton's grin didn't falter. "It's something to do with high school hackers. The schoolboard think some students are trying to access upcoming exam papers. They want to change the questions to suit themselves or to get them early to cheat the answers. We have to go put some walls and codes to secure things."

Dalton always tried to explain the tech stuff to Flora and Aleema in a way they might understand without being conde-scending or insulting to their lack of intelligence in that specific area.

Flora felt her left cheek twitch. "Who is *we*?"

For the first time since arriving in the attic, Dalton's grin faltered. "It's nothing dangerous. He'll be keeping *me* safe more than I'll need to protect him."

"Dalton?" Aleema pressed.

He pulled his gaze away for a moment before returning it directly to Flora. "It's Preston," he said, lowering his voice.

Flora's cheek twitched again. "Preston? You and him, on a mission together?"

"It's a cyber mission," Aleema reminded her. Her hand felt heavier on Flora's shoulder now, like she knew Flora would need the external balance. "They'll hardly be in any danger, if at all."

Slowly, Flora nodded. She'd never mentioned aloud her attraction to Preston, but she knew her friends knew about it. How could they not? She tried to catch glimpses of him or would mention talking to him if it happened. Maybe once, she would've been embarrassed by that. But Aleema and Dalton were her best friends.

Though Dalton would have Preston as back-up, it didn't alleviate her worry. Dalton hadn't been on a mission for years, not since the two he'd gone on within the first year he'd arrived at Redwing Mansion. Frequently he was called in to aid others, but he hadn't needed to leave the safety of the mansion to help. And he'd never had to leave without Flora or Aleema before.

Flora's insides squirmed at the thought. She always worried over her friends even though this was their *job*.

"It's a four day trip," Dalton continued. "I'll be gone and back within four sleeps, maybe less. You know my skills."

Aleema laughed. "They're more trouble than they're worth sometimes."

Their second mission – which was really their first true mission since they weren't being judged for a lifelong job – had involved locating a missing high-brow celebrity. Flora remembered all too well the way Dalton had walked over to an electrical socket, shoved his fingers inside, and grabbed onto a computer tablet with the other hand as he manually and literally hacked his way into every camera within a fifteen mile radius in the time it took for him to let out a little yelp. He wasn't immune against electricity, so he often got shocked – one time he'd been thrown halfway across a room because of his methods. But because of him and his extremely helpful gift they'd completed the mission, handing back said missing celebrity after rescuing them from the kidnappers, all anonymously, within two days.

Dalton squeezed them both. "I know you'll miss me." He slid his hand from Flora's shoulder to her cheek. "Try not to."

"You're making it *so* difficult," Flora joked back.

"To leave?" he questioned. "At least you'll get a good view of my arse as I walk out."

Flora scoffed. "Somehow I don't think so."

"I *know* my arse looks great in these." He spun for emphasis, showing off his bum with a wiggle. Flora laughed and Dalton's grin returned. He then looked to Aleema. "Have a syrupy coffee ready for when I return?"

"Six full sugars in a tall tower glass," Aleema promised.

Flora's light amber eyes fixed onto his face as her friend's words sank in. "You're leaving? Now?"

"Once my bags are packed," he confirmed with a nod. "It's not a high priority thing but we're heading into exam season for most schools and colleges. It needs fixing."

"Why can't the boards sort this out themselves?" Aleema asked. Flora had been wondering the same thing.

Dalton wiggled his neatly shaped eyebrows. "We're not sure if they're innocent either."

Both Flora and Aleema exclaimed a "*what?*" at the same time.

"Some board members have kids within the schooling system still," he explained. "Wouldn't you do anything to help your kids if you could? Even if it meant potentially screwing everything up? So if you had access to something, wouldn't you give them a leg up to make sure they got what they wanted so they could go on to have a life you think they've earned by being born '*normal*'?"

Power and wealth had always driven the world. Those who were considered elite would always do what they could to provide the best for their young. The added divide between the people – those who were 'normal' and those that weren't – gave them an extra edge to push them. They already thought they were better than those that had less; they ultimately thought they had been given the overall gift and were owed for being unmutated and having to live in a world of freaks and horrors.

Simply, the world didn't appreciate Abnormals – those with a mutated gene that resulted in a power. Most of the public population didn't know those very Abnormals were risking themselves to help keep humanity afloat, however they could, on a day-to-day basis. So while the 'normal' people thought they were owed the world, really it was the Abnormals who mostly deserved it.

"Wrap up warm," Flora said as she dragged Dalton into another hug. Dalton kissed her cheek.

"She's right," Aleema agreed. "You can't go everywhere in self-styled cropped jeans."

Dalton pulled back to peer down at his legs. Flora's eyes followed. He was indeed wearing a soft brown corduroy pair of trousers he'd taken a pair of scissors to. The ends were fraying rather well at his mid-calf.

"Everyone wants to see my beautiful body," Dalton joked.

"I'm sure the sickness you'll suffer from the cold hands of the *winter* will be worth it," Flora said.

Dalton's green eyes lit with amusement. "Right, right. Warm clothes, I promise." His grin dulled to a smile, and Flora's heart cracked a little at the sight; they were drawing closer to their final goodbyes. "This might be the first time I *ever* listen to either of you about fashion. The first and the *only* time."

Flora glanced down at her floor-length orange skirt. "There's nothing wrong with how we dress."

"What was that about winter?" he mocked.

"I'm perfectly toasty right now!"

"I wish I had your confidence and delusions, dear." Dalton pressed another quick kiss to Flora's cheek. "Be good."

"When are we not?" Aleema challenged.

Dalton laughed, then pulled Aleema into another hug before he backed off. "When I'm here."

Flora knew what was coming but she still had to glance away as Dalton waved a final goodbye and fled the room like he suddenly had a countdown clock hanging over him.

The trio was down to a duo.

In all the years they'd been at Redwing, the trio had never been parted like this. Their previous two missions had been done together. They came as a package deal. Where there was one of them, the other two followed. A triangle of Abnormals.

Why did Maggie split us up? she thought, eyes prickling at the corners.

Of course, Flora was delighted for Dalton. He constantly needed something to do. And she was proud of how much he could and would do. But it still stung. Being left behind, left waiting for someone else's return, *hurt*. And knowing he was off with Preston of all people…

It was as if the universe wanted to send her scattering.

Flora reached out for Aleema's hand. She was glad she still had *someone* she loved nearby.

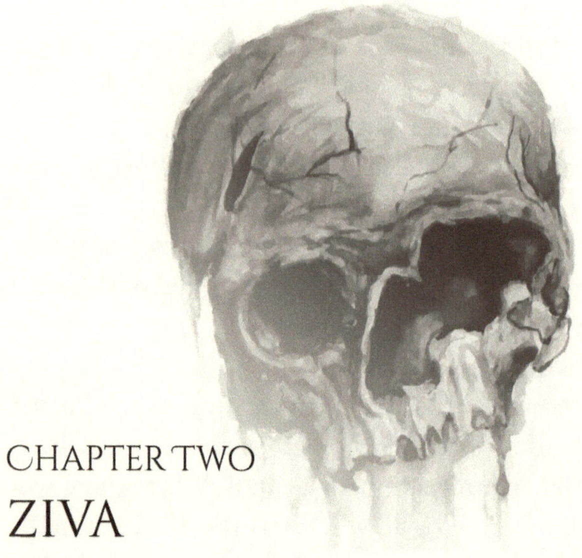

CHAPTER TWO
ZIVA

15th Day of Winter 2406

Violette had been pushing them since eight AM sharp. It had to be somewhere near nine, somewhere near the end, by now. An hour had to have passed.

Ziva watched as a breath of air puffed out of her mouth, and then she ran through it a split second later. Her lungs burned and her throat scorched against the cold winter morning air. Gretchen ran past her on the right, and Ziva spotted the clouds puffing from her mouth too.

Horn after horn signalled each lap completed. Ziva trotted past Violette and received her fourth toot that day. She tried to smile, it was her best record so far, but it dropped off her face as quickly as it tried to rise. She had no energy left inside her, even for the small things.

Frosted grass crunched underfoot. The group was small this morning. A new mission had been started last night, sending four recruits out at once. Ziva also noticed Dalton was missing, and she wondered if he had been included in the group.

The track Violette had laid out with orange flags and cones today was more gruelling than the previous few days. Ziva wondered if it was some form of punishment to them all, but she didn't know the crime they had supposedly committed.

She pushed her legs harder but her speed didn't seem to increase.

Nearly an entire season had passed since Ziva had joined Redwing. Every time she dwelled on that thought, she couldn't believe it.

The bedroom she'd first been assigned too was still hers, and was gradually being made *into* hers. She knew most people's names and even some of their powers. Morning training and the big breakfast afterwards had become a normal routine. Even better, she could now find her way around the mansion without the map *and* could journey into town and back without help.

Her legs finally wobbled, forcing her to slow up to a pained walk.

Though she could see the effects of the cold air this morning, she couldn't feel it touch her skin. She was too sweaty.

She wiped a hand across her forehead, pushing aside the damp fringe she'd started to grow out.

"You alright?"

Ziva peered to her left. The mist on the grounds added to the ominous flair this place seemed to carry. It was thicker than yesterday, but not so bad that she couldn't make out Ommin jogging towards her, not a bead of sweat in sight.

"I'm fine," she said, hoping she hadn't wheezed despite feeling her lungs ache.

"You're walking." His eyebrows always looked like they were permanently set in a downward slope in the centre, something like a scowl but without the anger or judgement to match in his dark eyes. "Are you injured? You looked like you were doing well."

"I was," she agreed. A tightness started to swell on her left and she resisted the urge to attempt to grab and hold her side. "Just tired now."

Ommin nodded, and the tiniest little bead slid down from his forehead. Ziva watched it run; the only indication he was being forced to run laps around an enclosed field. There was no wheezing, no sighing, no stopping in him. How long had he been doing this morning training? Ziva was somewhat jealous.

Will I be like that one day? Ziva wondered, looking at him.

Even in the early morning and despite the winter settling in, Ommin looked good. His umber skin was flawless, not a blemish in sight. His eyes weren't streaming from the cold and the air didn't seem to touch a whisp of black hair to steal the tiniest piece from a single tight braid. Worst of all, the beginnings of a smile appeared on his lips as if he was enjoying this torment that kept being called 'exercise'.

"We should be done soon," he said quietly as if the universe might jinx things if it heard.

Usually, Ommin didn't talk much. Yet morning training seemed to bring his voice out. Something in him seemed to crack wide open whenever exercise was involved.

It had become hard to tell if anyone else was nearby, but Ziva couldn't hear the rumble of feet close by. "Hopefully," she breathed. "I beat my record, but at what cost?"

Ommin finally seemed to give in to the smile. "That's always the question. But that's good. You're improving."

"What's your best?"

"Laps? Twelve."

"*Twelve?*" Ziva grimaced. Her four-lap best didn't seem quite the success anymore.

"I've been here since I was fifteen," he told her. "I'm twenty-nine now. That's fourteen years' worth of improvement." With a single nod, he ran off again, disappearing way up the field.

Having been at Redwing for nearly a season now, Ziva had learnt some things and knew she there was still far more about others to be found. One thing that didn't stick was how big the age range of the people here was.

Within the first week of being a permanent resident, Ziva had been told that Ommin was the oldest living and working member, and Helen, the one-eyed girl, was currently the youngest, coming up to fourteen. There had apparently been older people once, but before Ziva and Chandler had been brought in, there had been a major incident that had taken most of them out. That very incident had led to Ziva and Chandler's recruitment.

No one talked about the incident or what'd happened, only that it had, and there used to be far more people about to occupy space in the halls and kitchens.

Ziva tried to zone back into running. *I wonder what the record is,* she pondered. *How many laps has someone run in a day here? The record for an hour?*

Running laps was a timed challenge. Some days the clock could be set for ten minutes, and others it could be three hours. Training could last until lunch or until someone ticked all the correct boxes first. Any other challenges were added or taken away; the only consistency was that running would be happening no matter what.

Yesterday, a pull-up challenge had been added to the routine. Wane Grittal, the youngest brother of the twins Seamus and Doug, had beaten his own previous personal record. But had it really been a challenge? His abnormality was strength itself. It seemed like cheating.

Thinking of Wane made Ziva momentarily lose concentration, and her feet stumbled. She didn't fall, sticking her arms out for balance in time, but it had been a close thing.

As she righted herself, she thought of Chandler.

Her friend had knocked on her door last night, explaining she'd be leaving on a mission that very same eve. Both her and Wane were heading to some sub-zero climate place far north of the globe. It would be the perfect place for Chandler, and Ziva wasn't upset staying behind, but she had been a little sad to say goodbye to her best friend.

They'd hugged quickly in Ziva's doorway. Neither of them had expected to be called away so soon after their first mission, but there Chandler was, bags packed and ready to leave by the midnight hour.

Ziva found the energy to smile to herself as she picked up her pace once more.

Her first mission had cemented her place at Redwing, alongside Chandler. They'd had to locate and retrieve a well-known mask that could grant the wearer a change of face. They'd been given ten days to complete their mission, and though there were several hiccups and moments where time had felt like it was being pulled from underneath them, they'd succeeded with the help of a another – Quinton Eichner, an Abnormal who'd been at Redwing long enough to know the ropes.

Not long after arriving back at Redwing, once completing the mission, Quinton's half-sister had stopped at the doorstep. Apparently, no one had any idea that he even *had* a sister. Chandler hadn't mentioned knowing of one and she'd been to one of Quinton's family homes during their first mission.

That very sister had also claimed she could see through the bubble, the very *shield,* meant to be hiding Redwing from the world.

Just one day later, Quinton left. He'd said nothing to Ziva or Chandler before going. Nor had he said anything to Gretchen, his supposed best friend. Ziva wasn't entirely buying that she'd been left completely in the dark though.

No one had heard from him since. No clue to where he'd gone or when and if he would return.

Ziva sighed and fought against the urge to walk again. She just wished Violette would call the final horn so they could stop, and so Ziva could go shower and eat something.

A lap later, Ziva's prayers were answered. She paced past Violette who had her favoured expression – a solid scowl she was never without or ever far from – seared into her features like marble venom.

Those ahead of Ziva stripped off their muddy shoes as soon as they reached the doors, and the Helpers immediately picked them up to carry off and clean.

Ziva followed suit, slipping out of her trainers a little haphazardly. She went to neaten them but a Helper stole them away before she could untie the laces.

Biting her lip and trying not to look back, she moved on upstairs.

Back in her room, she trudged achingly to the en suite. She stripped down the rest of the way once the door was shut and slipped under the near-instant warm water of the shower. It dragged down her spine to her throbbing legs. She let it cascade like a waterfall until she felt numb, then chased the water with orange scented soap.

It wasn't until the water had fully gone cold that she stepped out. She wrapped herself in a towel and picked out the easiest clothes she could find – plain underwear, a scrappy jumper, and the pair of jeans she'd acquired when she'd first arrived at Redwing.

Part way through dressing, she had to sit on the edge of the bed. Her spine protested as she bent forward to lace up her new white trainers. But for once the strain felt *good*, like she'd accomplished something.

Quickly, she tied her new haircut into another low ponytail and blasted the ever-growing fringe with a drier. When it laid right, she darted from the room.

She stopped at Chandler's door, hand raised and poised to knock.

Chandler wasn't there.

Ziva lowered her hand again. She had grown so used to one of them collecting the other for breakfast – whoever dressed first went to find the other – it had become just another part of the routine she'd comfortably found herself in.

Both of the two people Ziva had found she could *really* be herself around were gone. She could message either of them at any point – though she doubted Quinton would respond since he hadn't so far – but messaging wasn't the same as seeing their faces. Even Abel, the guard she'd met her first day here, was momentarily occupied.

Taking a steading slow breath, Ziva pulled back from her best friends' door and headed down to breakfast alone.

CHAPTER THREE
CHANDLER

16ᵗʰ Day of Winter 2406

If you keep holding the reins like that, he'll buck you off," Chandler warned.

Wane twisted awkwardly in his saddle to look at her. "Why do you think that?" he asked. "My horse seems fine to me."

"He keeps huffing out his nose." As if hearing them perfectly clear, Wane's horse let out a heavy breath from his nostrils. Chandler fixed Wane with a pointed look. "Plus, I *listened* when our instructor was telling us about what to do and what not to do."

"I listened too!"

Chandler pulled her reins and her horse adjusted accordingly. "Sure."

"I did!"

"What did her chest tell you exactly?"

"You don't have *sight* powers," Wane hissed ungracefully.

"I don't need them to know where you'd been looking the entire time." Their instructor had indeed dressed to impress despite the frozen landscape. Wane had nodded along but Chandler knew nothing had been heard; he'd just nodded along with the bounce of her bust as she'd clapped. Chandler sighed. "Just be gentle, and at least act like you *might* know what you're doing. The horse will sense otherwise."

Without letting go of her reins, Chandler cracked her knuckles before picking up the pace.

Midnight had just passed by the North Pole. The visual ahead was poor and the temperature had slipped well below freezing hours ago, not that it increased much during the day.

Before they'd first set off, Wane had wrapped himself in at least five layers. Two damned hats covered his usually vibrant ginger hair. Even Chandler had to admit how deeply the cold sank inside her skin; she'd worn two pairs of gloves and a thicker jumper beneath her thermal fur-lined coat.

The route to their destination, a little outpost just past a secluded ice village, lay beyond the enclosed mountain pass they'd started to travel through. There could be no flights overhead and no sailing ships on high seas to reach it. There was only land and it couldn't even be walked. Special Snow Beasts – horses bred to become twice the size of normal ones that would not suffer under such harsh conditions – were the only mode of accessible travel.

Chandler had always wanted to ride. She'd listened to the entire safety briefing with open ears and had itched the entire time to just mount up.

The Beasts were as white as the snow around them, with a thick coat for protection against the harshest winds and ice storms and a mane tightly plaited to keep it from flapping about. Their ears and eyes were left unshielded since there was nothing in this such remote location to distract them from their job. Saddles had to be worn when riding, and those were white too. Everything was designed to blend in here, to be seen as natural elements.

A small group of experienced travellers led the way; Wane and Chandler brought up the rear of their six person group. They were here under false pretences; they'd given an excuse for needing guides to the remote village when really their mission was to travel *past* it. They'd find a way around that when the time came, Chandler was sure.

The group of four travellers often passed through this mountain range to hunt or scavenge, preferring to live freely off the land. Though, it was difficult to get that information out of them. Partly because they were so private. The rest was due to a language barrier.

Most of the world spoken Common Tongue – a century-old variant of what used to be known as 'English'. Other languages had also come along and survived – Japanese, Chinese, Russian, Spanish, and Tamil. Unfortunately, most of the other languages had fallen away over the years. That was either due to countries remaking themselves, or from the land having divided or reforming in some way that required a rebirth of itself.

However, this group of travellers spoke Polean and barely a word of anything else.

Wane had thankfully recognised it. Chandler couldn't speak it but Wane had basic knowledge to communicate. It was enough though.

Wane shifted in his saddle again to turn from Chandler. She didn't mind. He seemed nice enough, and she knew she could've been stuck with someone worse, but they weren't *friends* by any means. They lived in the Mansion, ate breakfast at the same table, and trained together every day. But outside of that? Not a lot required their paths to cross.

Chandler was forced to grip her horse's reins tightly and squeeze her legs until her thighs burned as the path sloped downwards suddenly. She looked at the others and found they were having to do the same.

Her horse slipped a little but quickly righted as the ground evened back out, and Chandler released her death grip.

Slowly but surely they cleared the mountain pass. She had no idea what time it was, all Chandler knew was that the night sky had grown so pretty. Stars upon stars twinkled against the navy and black backdrop. Even the crescent moon hung perfectly. It looked like a scene from a movie or a piece of long forgotten art.

Chandler lost all sense of direction once the mountains disappeared. She couldn't see anything beyond the stars and the snow after a while. The openness almost scared her. She'd never been to many places – before Redwing, she'd barely been outside of her city – let alone having traversed somewhere so untouched.

After more time where Chandler had to keep adjusting her legs so her arse wouldn't go numb, Wane pulled back from the group to trot his horse alongside hers.

"Are we going to sleep once we reach the village?" he asked quietly. Though they hadn't *spoken* Common Tongue, it was unclear if the travellers could at least understand it.

"I think we should," she said lowly. Even a whisper sounded loud here.

"My arse definitely knows we've been on horseback for a while," Wane grumbled. "It's both numb *and* sore somehow?"

Chandler shifted slightly again and her whole body protested. "Fuck, that does not feel good."

"That settles it. We're resting for a while."

Wane shivered and Chandler peered at him. Where the scarf had fallen from his face, she could see his fair cheeks and nose were burnt red. That would take time to reverse. She briefly wondered what her face looked like or if she had an advantage against that too. She'd never tested the idea before, but she certainly wasn't feeling the cold like he was. That she knew for definite.

"I'm thinking about hot drinks now," he whined. "A warm alcoholic apple cider would toast my insides up perfectly."

"I've never tried it," Chandler admitted, half-heartedly shrugging.

Wane found it in himself to glare at her in surprise. "*Never?* You've never had warm apple cider? Or never had an alcoholic one?"

"No?" She covered one hand with the other, popping her knuckles. "To both?"

"Have you ever had a basic cider?"

"I've never really drank."

"*What?*" His gaze shifted from surprised to disbelief. "You're... how old?"

"Twenty-two. Twenty-three by the end of Winter."

"And you've never had alcohol?"

I've never really had a lot of things, she thought. She wanted to say the words, but she couldn't bring herself to do it despite how true they were.

"I've had a drink before," she said instead, shrugging it off and cracking the knuckles on her other hand. She could feel the snow shift around her, the crystals of ice within them waking. "I worked in a youth nightclub before this."

"But you've never had *cider*! It's, like, every young person's beginning *thing*!" He scoffed loudly and his horse mimicked him. "If this place has cider, I'm buying. If it doesn't, I'll owe you that drink when we get back home."

"Wane—"

"No one turns a Grittal down when they offer to buy something."

She scowled. "Why not?"

"Because it's a rare thing to occur in the first place."

Chandler nodded, not knowing what else to say. She tried cracking all her knuckles again, and they indeed set off with a series of little *pop, pop, pop*s. The noise settled her racing heart slightly which in turn calmed the ice around them all.

Her life before Redwing hadn't exactly been a happy one. She'd worked to earn money that her mother would end up stealing from her, so she'd had to hide pieces just to make sure she got some of what she'd earned. She'd had a father that had vanished and supposedly died years beforehand. Her only close connection had been her uncle, and he was gone now too. No friends existed because who would want to be friends with the quiet girl that had to be poked and prodded by medical professionals and their machines because she had an Abnormality? She'd tried to escape it all several times, trying to find better places to live or other jobs, but her Abnormality had made her an outlier, an outcast, from the start.

Most of the world didn't want anything to do with an Abnormal.

Such a depressing mess to look back on.

Redwing had, essentially, given her what she'd given up dreaming of.

After finalising the paperwork to say both her and her best friend, Ziva, were going to stay long-term, they'd gone into the local town together and had returned with commemorative tattoos. Ziva had the date stamped in print on her right wrist. Chandler had a masquerade mask on her inner right arm, just above the elbow, designed around the Lost Mask of Iris without being the obvious thing itself.

The light didn't change much in this part of the world, but Chandler caught the snowflakes twinkling with minimal shifting effects at different times, proving that were was a tiny switch happening.

Chandler managed to wrestle her slouched, aching body into a somewhat flatter upright position and, as she did, spotted a few deep brown wooden huts up ahead. Smoke from the huts clouded out of chimneys into the sky above them.

She glanced at Wane as he spotted the huts too. His entire face illuminated with hope and the promise of somewhere comfy and *warm*. Chandler wasn't unenthused, the idea of getting off her horse made her happy, but if there was smoke there would be fire; she didn't exactly do well with extreme heat since her abnormality was one at the opposite end of the temperature gauge. She just hoped it would be enough to melt their bones and not scorch her insides.

The group cut across the final distance to the huts, and dismounted once they were outside the carved front door of a specific one they'd been led too. Wane nearly fell off but by pure luck he caught himself before he smashed face-first into the ground. Chandler had to look away so she didn't laugh at him.

Together they were ushered into the building where they were each given a bed roll upon entering.

Chandler turned and immediately realised the whole hut had been designed to be nothing but one bedroom. The space wasn't big, but several mats were spread over the floor and soft orange light created a gentle atmosphere around the room. A tinier light at the back of the space showed the open doorway to a small avocado green bathroom. There also appeared to be a metal urn stacked on a small table and a few off-white mugs beside it, hopefully provided to guests who needed a warm drink.

"Here," one of the guides said.

Chandler and Wane immediately looked at each other in surprise. They had their confirmation that at least one of them had understood Common Tongue enough to express something in it.

"Is it just for us?" Wane asked, glancing about.

The guide nodded and pointed to themselves, then the other travellers. "Have home," they said, words slightly muffled by the scarf still covering their mouth. They gestured to the room. "Spare."

"It's like a hotel hut," Wane gathered. The guide tilted their head, questioning. "Thank you."

The travellers seemed to take that as a dismissal and a cue to leave. Cold swept into the room briskly as they opened the door. Once they were gone, Wane began to strip the layers from his body as he stalked towards the old fashioned wood fire to the side of the place. He unrolled his bed roll and dropped it onto the mat nearest the fire.

Taking off her woolly hat, Chandler unhooked the haphazard braids she'd thrown her brown hair into that morning. She ran her fingers through it and there was barely a kink to show it'd been up at all.

She took a quick peek in the little make-up mirror she'd brought and though the edges of her hazel eyes looked a little crusted, they thankfully weren't red raw from windburn. Her pale skin wasn't too blemished either, despite the lack of general protection she'd used to cover it.

Chandler closed the mirror and repacked it as Wane took his hat off. His vibrant ginger hair summoned the room's light to it, making it look like a fire on top of his head.

He threw the hat onto the pile of clothes he'd made, then made an effort of taking his gloves off and scrubbing his bare hands over his flushed yet still relatively pale face. Without bundles of layers around him, he looked like the solid man he was; his huge muscles flexed when he rolled his shoulders and he stood so tall it was a miracle he didn't knock his head on the ceiling. He stretched and his t-shirt slid up his hairy but well-toned stomach.

"Are my lips chapped?" Wane asked suddenly, dropping his arms again.

Chandler met his gaze in surprise at the question. "What?"

"Are they chapped?" He pouted at her and there was indeed red splits along his lips. "They feel like they're breaking."

"Do you have anything to put on them?"

"Like what? I thought I'd be fine!"

"In frozen temperatures?"

"My scarf covered my face, I thought that would be enough."

Chandler sighed and dug around in her bag. She pulled out the spare lip balm she'd brought along. "Use this," she said, handing it over.

"How often do I have to use it?" he asked as he applied it.

"Some now, some when you wake, and then whenever." Chandler shrugged. "There's no *real* rules but you don't want to overdo it. And it's not an immediate magical fix, your lips won't heal overnight, but that'll help protect them and shouldn't let them get any worse while they do heal."

"Were you going to use it?" He tried to hand it back.

"I have another one." She pulled her fresh one out to prove it.

Wane dropped down to his chosen mat after unlacing his boots and slid inside the bed roll. "This feels *good*," he groaned. "Who knew a wooden floor could feel like clouds?"

Chandler chose a mat halfway from the door and the fire, and sank into her bed roll there. She could feel the warmth of the fire from this distance but she knew she wasn't likely to melt. If she had to, there was still plenty of room and other mats she could transfer to if the heat became unbearable.

"Clouds glorious clouds," Wane sang. "Oh, I love this flooring."

"We need rest," she reminded him, hoping to cut off the awful tune he'd started.

"All of me hurts." He groaned again. The noise was less sing-songy and instead somewhere between sleepy and a grumble of pain. "I hope you don't want a bedtime story 'cause I don't think I'll be awake much longer. My eyes are already closed, Icy."

Though he wasn't looking, she still rolled her eyes at the nickname. She had no idea who at Redwing had started calling her that first, but it'd happened. There were other variations too, but she knew Quinton had been the first one to really call her that.

Chandler shifted over, rolling to face away from Wane as he started to snore softly. She tried to find her own peace.

The orange light above wasn't intrusive and the crackle of the fire popped pleasantly in the background. No windows captured the outside world, not that there'd be much of it besides snow.

After a while, the snoring and the fire grew quieter. Only when they both faded, turning into nothing, did Chandler let herself drift away.

CHAPTER FOUR
GRETCHEN

17th Day of Winter 2406

Gretchen wrenched her arm free from Maggie's grasp. "Bloody ground beneath me!"

Maggie, old as ever, sat back like she'd exerted all her energy. "There's no need for the language," she scolded.

"You hurt my arm!"

"*You* hurt your arm first," Maggie reminded her. Her piercing eyes dipped to Gretchen's left wrist as she cradled it in her right hand. "It's not broken, just sprained."

"Thank bloody goodness I 'ad you 'ere to tell me that, doc," Gretchen mumbled.

Even though Gretchen's power over bones – the ability to break or heal them – didn't extend to herself, she could tell if she'd done damage. She'd hurt herself enough before to remember the pain. This hadn't felt like a break, but it still *hurt*.

As soon as the pain had reached her brain, causing her to hiss and clutch the wrist to her chest, she'd needed a second opinion on how bad it really was. Out of the three adults in charge, she'd sought out Maggie specifically. Praxis was just useless with anything outside of paperback and managing. Violette was a royal *bitch* who wouldn't help anyone except herself it was a wonder she'd been chosen as one of the three charges of Redwing at all. But though Maggie might've been old, she was kind to everyone without judgement, and she'd been around enough to have studied most injuries during her tenure as an Abnormal here.

Maggie interlinked her bony, saggy-skinned fingers. "How did you do it?"

Gretchen rolled her heavily lined eyes. "Lifted somethin'." There was no point lying, but it was still stupid.

"Which was what?" Maggie pressed.

"I tried movin' one of the little tables in my room when I felt it pop. It ain't no one else's fault."

"I didn't say it was." The old woman sighed. "Have you still got your brace?"

"Should 'ave, yeah."

"Good. You'll need to wear it for a while again. But leave it off at night."

"And you'll assess me in a few days?"

"More like a week."

"*A week*?" Gretchen stood abruptly enough that her chair scooted on the floor. "Righto, doc."

She didn't try and hide her annoyance as she dismissed herself from the office.

Back in her room, she shoved a middle finger towards the offending table for good measure. She even kicked it too, and the awkward angle she'd drop it at got worse. In defeat, she hunted through her bedside cabinet and found what she needed.

Strapping herself into the brace felt like she was somehow giving up. But nothing else could be done. No one had a medical or healer power in the building, only her, and that never worked on herself. Not that a sprain was a bone issue, but still.

She'd only wanted to rearrange her room. How it looked had bored her and she'd finally given in to fix that. She'd wanted freshness. Moving the bed a few inches across hadn't screwed her over, yet one poxy table had. The ridiculousness of it wasn't lost on her.

Gretchen slumped to the floor at the foot of her bed. Quinton should've been here to help move the table. He'd helped her last time she'd needed or wanted to do something; that's what best friends were supposed to do, look out for one another in whatever way that was needed. Or maybe even Wane would've since he had strength unlike any other.

But neither of them were around.

Wane was on a mission somewhere North with Ice Girl. Like always, he stood as the mission's muscle. Gretchen hadn't heard much about the mission, only that Wane and Chandler were looking for evidence of missing researchers.

Gretchen wasn't too worried about Wane though. They weren't *together*. Yes, they hooked up if they were free, but she didn't think it was anything serious – there was no indication to say it was. Wane was a decent person, certainly better than his twin older brothers, and definitely a good screw, but nothing tied her to him. No emotions, nor feelings. But he still would've helped her rearrange her room because she liked to think they were something close friends.

Quinton, however, had left during the last season with his half-sister. He'd had enough time to say his sister's name, Darlene, and where they were going, before they'd just *gone*. No promise of return had been left and every message she'd sent him had gone ignored.

Gretchen and Quinton were supposed to be best friends. They'd spent all their time at Redwing together. And he had just *gone*.

Despite her better judgement, knowing it would be pointless, she pulled out her phone. She huffed at the sight of the missing "Z" button – her phone had fallen from her pocket the other day and broke a little.

> **Gretchen:**
> I sprained my wrist. Again.
> I can't be left alone.
> I'm a danger.

The message sent. She didn't know if Quinton even got them or if he'd binned his phone or something.

Whatever the reason, it hurt a little.

Of course she understood that there were bigger things for him right now, that his illegitimate sister turning up at Redwing and could potentially see *through* the barrier that protected it was *big*.

But she was also allowed to feel like a ship with no sail at sea when her best friend was so far removed from her. She would've been there for him if he needed her. And though she didn't exactly need him, she did want to know if he was at least ok.

She threw her phone onto her bed behind her. A message wouldn't miraculously appear if she just sat and stared at the screen all day. Quinton had already made it perfectly clear he wasn't going to respond.

They each needed to do their own thing.

Gretchen clambered to her feet and left her room empty-handed. She needed to do something, anything. Her wrist throbbed like it was trying to sway her decision on what to do, telling her whatever she decided on needed to be something easy. She wasn't usually the type to do *anything*. But today she wanted more than to lie on her bed all day.

On her descent down the main staircase, she passed Violette. Gretchen sneered but the perfectly designed woman didn't seem to notice. It angered her a little. She'd never found out all the details about what'd happened between Quinton and Violette – their romance or dalliance, whatever it was, had been short – but something had occurred, and it'd come crashing down and not in a blaze of glory.

The kitchen was bustling with activity. Helpers were carrying bowls and scrubbing dishes and chopping vegetables. Some were simply cleaning the floors or counters or appeared to be carrying laundry to hang out on lines.

Gretchen bypassed it all to get to the back gardens, stealing a piece of carrot on the way.

Sunshine blinded her as soon as she stepped out the tiny backdoor. She shielded her eyes until her vision adjusted. When her eyes settled, she spotted a few other recruits who had clearly had the same idea as her; despite it being winter, they were lounging on soft chairs or blankets down by the lake.

Skidding down the mostly-dead grass embankment, Gretchen trudged towards them.

Even when there was nowhere for her to be, she still dressed as if there was. That meant drawing on her eyebrows, lining her blue eyes in thick black, straightening her blonde hair which now had stripes of neon green throughout, and putting on the chunkiest black boots she could comfortably walk in.

She'd had to swap her style out on her last mission to Old Cairo, and she'd come home deciding that the desert, or any sunny climate, really wasn't her thing.

"Hey, Gretchen!"

Gretchen peered over to the group sitting on blankets that were splayed out on the grass. On one, Flora and Aleema sat comfortably alongside Helen. Aleema had clearly been the one to speak; her hand was stuck in the air mid-wave and her accent from before Redwing had slipped out, giving her away.

"I'm surprised you're outside," Aleema joked.

Gretchen played along, peering down at her arms. "I ain't gone up in flames yet, but there's still time."

"Even in winter?" Helen asked, curiosity written into her overly wide brown eyes.

"What can I say? I'm the sun's favourite target."

Gretchen had come back from Old Cairo with burns in places she didn't know she could burn in. The worst bit had been that she'd worn the heaviest sun protector cream she could find, yet her skin had still flared up red all over.

Flora patted the space on the blanket beside her. "We can keep an eye on you if you want?"

With no excuse not to sit with them, Gretchen relented.

Helen seemed pleased at the company and pulled out a wooden basket her body must've been concealing, placing it in front of her. She took out four mugs and started pouring hot chocolate from a flask into them. How she knew to bring four, Gretchen didn't know. Helen didn't have future-seeking or psychic powers as her gift. Maybe she'd simply brought more just in case?

I don't really want to be here, Gretchen thought. Selfishly, she wanted to be anywhere else, with no one except herself.

She didn't voice that, however. She sipped the overly sweet drink and let the cocoa warm her insides. Mostly she drank to occupy her mouth so she wouldn't have to talk. She might've lived with these girls for years, but they hadn't spent *that* much time together before.

"How is it?" Helen asked after a moment.

There was still a babyish look about Helen – the slightly rounded cheeks, the short height, the constant pink flush to the tip of her button nose, the wild gleam of joy in her brown eye, the endless curls in her dark blonde hair. But that might've also been everyone's permanent perception of her because she was still the youngest around. The forever baby of Redwing.

Gretchen nodded. "Too sweet for me, but still good," she admitted.

Helen beamed. "I made it myself!"

Aleema took a drink, then asked, "Did you use real chocolate?"

"Yes!" Helen's smile shone brighter than the sun, and Gretchen turned away from it slightly.

The girl's single eye blinked rapidly – the other eye, everyone knew, was missing and the lids were sewn shut, but all was hidden underneath a skin-tone patch.

"The staff helped. They still won't let me near the stove on my own."

"You're thirteen," Flora said.

Gretchen wasn't sure if that was meant as a positive or negative statement.

"Exactly!" Helen exclaimed, taking Flora's words as backup to what she wanted. "I'm fourteen in a few weeks."

Gretchen smiled awkwardly, sure it was coming out strained. "The drink is good either way, Helen."

Helen drank deeply from her own small mug. Not much was known about her, just that she'd been left somewhere along the path to Redwing when she was a babe. Maggie had found her, brought her in, and given her a name. It was still undecided if she even had an Abnormality, but she belonged here anyway. No one else was close to her age here, but everyone accommodated her, talked to her, let her join in on their things if they could.

Gretchen tried to take in the conversation as it happened around her. They were talking about Helen's baking. But her attention simply couldn't be fully kept.

Gradually, the sky overhead darkened. The others around seemed to shrink from it, but Gretchen watched eagerly. Her mind cleared whenever there were storms.

"I think it's probably time to head inside," Flora declared, climbing to her knees.

"Yeah," Helen agreed as she started packing her things back into the basket. "Thank you for letting me sit with you!"

Aleema's smile was all charm. "You're always welcome to come hang with us."

"I know," Helen nodded. "But I like being invited."

"You're *always* invited."

Flora glanced at Gretchen then. "That goes for you, too."

Gretchen quirked a brow. "Well... Thanks."

What else could she say? Things had nearly always been just her and Quinton. Mostly because she avoided others. When they *had* been apart, she'd hung around the Grittals', but they were all out on missions right now.

I can have more than three friends, right? she wondered. *Or just hang around more people.*

She hadn't thought about how closed off she'd been, but maybe it was worse than she'd realised. She did live side-by-side with these people after all.

Maybe I'll try?

They headed inside together. Just as Gretchen stepped back into the kitchen, she heard the familiar *pat, pat, pat* of the rain on the stone patio behind her. She turned to watch it through the door's window. It started slow, then began to fall from the sky like it might never stop.

She watched for a few more minutes before walking off, smiling to herself for the first time in days.

CHAPTER FIVE
QUINTON

17th Day of Winter 2406

11th Winter
10:22
"Gritty":
The twins just got sent on a mission? Them two? TOGETHER.
Disaster waiting to happen!

12th Winter
19:19
"Gritty":
You're missing out on a pretty bitchin lamb stew here.

22:04
"Gritty":
Dyed some of my hair green.
Its bright.
Thought you might approve? You do like your
colours.

22:49
"Gritty":
I look like a lime.

23:01
"Gritty":
Ok. I like it.
Call me Bony Lime.

23:04
"Gritty":
Want to see a HIDEOUS photo?

15th Winter
02:21
Wane and your vision girl just left for the
fucking North Pole???
What is there besides snow???

> **04:09**
> Did I ever tell you I fucked Wane?
> I like girls. Obviously. What's not to like?
> They're HOT.
> But...

> **04:26**
> I don't have feelings. But... Wane's cute.

> **04:32**
> Not that it's any of your business really.
> Just keeping you updated on the Lime's daily
> business.

> **17th Winter:**
> **10:17**
> I sprained my wrist. Again.
> I can't be left alone.
> I'm a danger.

Quinton scrolled up and down, reading over and over and over again the messages from his best friend from the past few days. He smiled at each one, though he felt the smile get sadder every repetition.

"Who you texting?"

He looked up from his phone as his little sister casually strolled into the room and plonked herself down opposite him at the dining table.

Darlene both looked like him and didn't. Her eyes weren't stormy, but forest green, yet they shared the same naturally light hair – even if his was currently dyed a deep-sea blue. She stood tall, probably taller than most her age. Quinton had also noticed she smiled the same way he did and laughed in the same tone too. The whole thing was a tad scary. Like they were some kind of copies of each other, just a few years apart.

"I'm not texting anyone," he told her.

Darlene scowled. "But your phone—"

"No phones at the table!" Darlene's mother cut in as she rushed into the kitchen herself. Katia glared softly at Quinton. "You know I don't have many rules here, but that's one."

Quinton tucked his phone into his trouser pocket. "Sorry."

"S'alright, as long as I don't see it again." She smiled sweetly.

He smiled back. "Yes ma'am."

Darlene groaned and rolled her eyes like any twelve year old would, but her mother shot Quinton a quick wink before settling in to finish dinner.

Quinton couldn't grumble about the rules. Katia had welcomed him happily when he'd first arrived, and kept letting him stay. She'd given over her spare room to him, cooked most meals, and even made him coffee in the mornings. She treated him as if he was her own.

When Darlene had appeared at Redwing, Quinton had gotten the shock of his *life*. She'd admitted to leaving home on her own, scribbling a note to her mother in crayon to tell her where she was going. Somehow she'd found her way to him; he still wasn't sure *how* she'd travelled that way on her own. But she was young, and he saw it as his duty to get her back home where she really belonged.

Then he'd stayed.

Katia never once liked him helping out, constantly telling him he didn't need to, that he was a welcomed guest in the house and he could stay as long as he liked. But he wouldn't stop earning his way. He'd mow the backyard, do some washing up or fold laundry, clean parts of the house or cook on the nights Katia had to work. He even walked Darlene to and from school so she wouldn't be lonely.

Quinton watched the older woman peel potatoes. She hadn't been surprised when he'd turned up on her doorstep – a lovely two-story house on the outskirts of Texi, New America – with a reluctant and tired Darlene behind him, nearly one season ago. She'd welcomed him in easily and the rest was done.

That was why he stayed. He couldn't just leave now that he had a family that had found him. Not when they'd gone through so much trouble to bring him into their lives, and brought so much joy and love into existence.

For years, he'd wished he'd had siblings. Now he really had one. Even if she was technically only a half sibling. He only ever called her sister, however. She deserved that much respect. And she equally treated him as her full brother.

Twelve years ago, Quinton's father had had a fling with Katia at one of his weekend work conferences. Katia had been a waitress at the bar and had been startled but pleased by the attention of an older, richer man. At the end of the weekend, Quinton Senior had gone home to his wife, grovelling and confessing to all his wrong-doings, and she'd forgiven him – Quinton didn't understand how, and sometimes he wondered if his mum really did forgive his dad, but then she'd always been too good for his father.

It had turned out though that his mother had known about the consequential baby too.

Katia had gone to Quinton's family home to admit she was pregnant, and had found Quinton's mother home instead. Katia didn't want anything except to explain. She was going to keep the child, she'd already grown to love it and the idea of being a mother, but wouldn't expect Quinton Senior to treat the child as his own. Quinton's mother had accepted the decision and had been giving Katia money every month since Darlene was born to help support her. They even met up every so often.

Darlene had grown up knowing Quinton's mother, and subsequently Quinton.

Unfortunately, Quinton had been a little late to the party, not knowing of his half-sister until a few years back.

One day, when Quinton just come into the city for a break between duties at Redwing and holidays for his mother, they'd met up. She'd invited him to a back-water seeming café. The owner surprisingly knew her and had given her things without having to order first. Quinton had asked how the owner knew what she wanted, and his mother had explained everything.

Sometimes Quinton wondered if his father ever even *knew* of Darlene, or if his mother had simply taken care of everything herself. Not for her father's sake, not even for the tabloids sake. But because Quinton's mother, and Katia, were women who would use everything in their power to look after their young whatever it took to keep them safe, however that looked.

Darlene would sadly never be entitled to the Eichner name or fortune, so things would still fall onto Quinton's shoulders in time. But mostly he was glad for her because she could have the life *she* wanted.

Yet, despite his knowledge of his sister's existence, they hadn't officially met until last season.

After his last mission, Darlene had shown up at the secret and what should've been *very hidden* front door of Redwing. She'd claimed she could see through the shield that kept it out of the eyes of anyone who didn't already know of its existence.

Quinton had spent hours with Praxis and Maggie, going over what to do. They had simply said he should do whatever he needed to.

The rule for Redwing was, if someone left, they were gone. Yet neither Maggie nor Praxis had said he couldn't return when he'd decided to leave with Darlene – she was still young and needed her mother, and he refused to just ship her back to her home on her own. They had wished him well and hugged him goodbye, but there had been no final farewell or something alluding to one.

Could I go back? He'd thought about that over the past few nights now. But even if he could, would he choose to?

Quinton now had something close to three full families: his official birth one, the one at Redwing, and also his sister and her mother. He knew his birth family, his father really, had let him go years ago, but they would expect him back one day. That made him feel split down the middle about the other two parts of his life and where he belonged.

Darlene's claim to be able to see through things seemed to hold up. She'd first mentioned Redwing's barrier when she'd first arrived there, but a few weeks back she'd spied through what had appeared to be a wall to Quinton. When she'd walked through it, he'd followed instantly, only to find himself stood in a small rum lockup with his sister grinning wildly at him.

Knowing of its existence now, Darlene would probably be accepted into Redwing if she wanted to go. It was clear she could see *through* things – to what extent, he didn't know. She had to have an Abnormality though.

He'd thought about having his sister at Redwing with him too. But what would Katia think? Darlene was her only child, and she wasn't very old. She couldn't just be swept away in the middle of the night.

Except Darlene had already done that. She'd squirreled herself away, just to find a brother she'd heard stories about, and Katia hadn't seemed *too* surprised by it when they'd returned together as if she vanished often.

Regardless, Quinton still felt like he was trying to splice himself in half.

Katia's voice broke him free from this thoughts. "It doesn't get too cold around here in winter," she said as she moved the pot of potatoes over the stove. "It gets cooler, but never close to freezing."

"Do you get snow?" he asked.

"Do you get snow?" Darlene mimicked, laughing. "No. We don't get *snow*. Snow means it's cold and Ma just told you it doesn't freeze."

He looked at his sister. "Have you seen snow before?"

"Once," Darlene answered, almost pouting at the idea. "Ma and me went to Snowdonne a few years back."

"Snowdonne," Quinton repeated quietly.

"Have you been there, Quinton?" Katia asked. "It was wonderful for us. I was *exhausted* when we got home. Put my feet up for days. We did too much, but I wouldn't have done the trip differently at all."

Quinton nodded slowly. "I was there last season."

Since he'd left Redwing, Quinton hadn't stopped thinking about his last mission. From the moment Ziva and Chandler had filed into the mansion, to the end where Darlene had appeared. He replayed every moment, repeated every word he could, until each thing started to blur together like he was forgetting the details.

Thinking about it all made him long for his sketch-pad. Currently, it was tucked in his room upstairs, though he'd not used it once since arriving. There had been no need. No visions had come because no one had touched his crystal necklace, and no dreams had plagued him either. It seemed strange to have a clear mind for once, a brain lacking in visions. It didn't feel bad but neither did it feel good.

"Darl?" Katia called. "Hand washing time!" Darlene stomped her feet but left the room; Quinton heard the stairs creak as she climbed them. Katia turned to face Quinton, a soft look upon her soft face. "Are you alright, Quin?"

Katia had taken to calling him Quin. At first, it'd been odd. His own biological family had never called him anything other than his name. Probably because, to them, he was nothing *but* a name. Yet Katia had given him more, something of his own even if it was simple.

"You're awfully quiet," Katia continued. "You didn't even ask to peel anything for dinner."

He smiled. "You wouldn't have let me."

"That hasn't stopped you from asking before."

"Maybe."

"Until tonight." She waggled the end of the wooden spoon at him. "What's eating you and that seaweed hair of yours from the inside?"

Quinton touched the top of his head. "The bottle called it *deep ocean*."

"The bottle lied. It's closer to a damp seaweed."

Quinton laughed, one tiny little gasp of air, but it passed on quickly. Shaking his head, he admitted out loud what had been eating at him; truly admitting it to himself as well.

"I don't know what to do."

Katia stayed silent for a moment. Then, slowly she folded her arms. "About what?"

"I like it here. Day is wild and you're wonderful! You've both become a proper family to me."

"I'm glad you feel like that." Katia turned the stove off without looking at it. "But that isn't the whole story or problem." She wasn't phrasing it as a question, but instead like she already knew.

Quinton grimaced. "Where Day found me..."

"You had a life there," Katia finished. "And you want to go back."

"I don't know."

"Quin." He glanced up at the woman who had treated him as kindly as his own blood mother. Her deep-set eyes were already focused on him. "Be honest."

"I am," he said.

"With yourself."

He had to look away. "I've always wanted fun and adventure and something *interesting*. And I have that. Here or there."

"Darl said you were surrounded by hundreds of people."

Another half-laugh escaped him and he looked back at her. "There wasn't hundreds. Barely fifty. Doubt that's even the right number."

"You're stalling, Quin."

"I was just clarifying facts."

"Have you spoken to any of those fifty or less people since you left?" When he shook his head, she nodded. "Some people are lucky to have one family. Sounds like you had two." She turned back to the stove without another word. "Maybe you should try and reach out?"

The phone in Quinton's pocket suddenly felt like a brick. His heart weighed him down too.

Katia turned back to him as if hearing his thoughts. "How about we set the table?" she suggested, changing the subject and quietening his mind for now.

Darlene reappeared just as Katia scooped dinner into orange bowls. They sat together at their small, wooden table.

Before they ate, they linked hands and closed their eyes as Katia called a prayer – she still believed in the old ways and the Old Gods. Darlene followed, and out of respect to them, so did Quinton.

Quinton couldn't focus on the words as Katia spoke her blessings. He could only think of one thing. If he was truly being honest with himself, he wanted the best of both worlds. He wanted there *and* here. He just couldn't see how he could have that.

At the end of the day, he couldn't split himself in two.

CHAPTER SIX

CHANDLER

19ᵗʰ Day of Winter 2406

Two days passed before Chandler and Wane began to really think about leaving the small village to continue on their mission.

During the third night, somewhere before midnight, Chandler woke when something like a tree branch crashed on top of their hut roof. Her eyes cracked open, crusty with sleep, but alert. High winds had probably torn it from its perch, sending it smacking into the wood.

Wane continued to snore in the corner.

Annoyed that she'd been the only one to wake at the noise, Chandler slipped from her roll and crept over to him. Pushing ice through her fingers – definitely more than necessary – she pressed her palm to his shoulder. He startled awake with a satisfying yelp and a fist ready to punch. When Wane spotted Chandler though, he pulled back.

She stepped away from him. "We have to leave."

"*Now?*" he asked, surprised. "It's the middle of the night."

"And there's a storm."

"Why would we be stupid enough to leave during a storm?" He didn't bother to cover his mouth as he yawned dramatically.

Chandler rolled her eyes. "Because, a tree branch just fell on the roof and who knows what else might fall? Might be something heavier next time, and it might come *through* the damn roof."

"Is there something heavier around here?"

She ignored his question. "*And* the storm will give us cover to get away."

"A storm might kill us!"

"We'll be fine. I can manage parts to let us through."

"Like pathways?" He pulled out his newly acquired lip balm and applied it rather sloppily. "Are you sure?"

No, she wanted to say, because she'd never tested the theory. "Yes."

Wane sighed and glanced longingly at his bed roll. "I was having such a nice dream."

Chandler didn't give him a response and just started shoving her feet into her snow boots. Even though Wane groaned, he began to dress in his many layers too.

Their mission was to travel further north and investigate why a group of scientific researchers suddenly lost communications with the main group of scientists back in a less dramatic climate. There had been no storm the night of their supposed loss, no news of Abnormals or vigilante anti-government groups in the area, so something else had happened. Chandler and Wane weren't told what the research had been about, only that now the scientists were seemingly gone. They needed to establish if only the communications were down or if the scientists themselves were – if so, why and how.

Fifteen minutes or so later, Chandler stood by the door, preparing to open it. Wane gave her a nod, so she yanked it.

Freezing cold wind immediately slapped her cheeks and nose. She'd braced for it and her body reacted accordingly, drawing in some of the coldness so it didn't feel as heart-stopping. Wane, however, couldn't do that and his teeth began to chatter loudly.

"Are you *sure* we have to leave now?" The scarf Wane had tied back around his face muffled his words and the added wind blocked more sound, making it seem like he was whispering.

Chandler stepped out into the ice storm.

If they didn't leave now, when the storm could cover their tracks, the group here might never let them leave. They might've been accommodating, giving them privacy in the evening, but they'd barely left Chandler and Wane alone otherwise. Even now, she was wary they might be watching. But the storm was strong and visibility was poor even for Chandler, who could manipulate some of the ice to her whim to make it easier. Hopefully, it would obstruct them from view for a while.

Wane seemed to realise how heavy the ice and snow was as he left the hut behind, attaching himself to Chandler's sleeve as if he feared losing her. Normally she would've shook him off. Not this time. She didn't exactly want to lose him either.

A few steps into the walk, Chandler decided that she couldn't move efficiently with Wane dragging behind. She linked arms with him instead. That way they could walk side-by-side and wouldn't get separated. Her vision and the power she could wield would guide them both.

They would need Snow Beasts eventually, but Chandler remembered from the briefing that there was a ranch not too far from here. Just a little further west, then north a bit. They could walk that distance.

Ice and snow slammed into them thick and fast and hard. After a while, even Chandler started to struggle. She couldn't feel the freeze but being repeatedly beaten by something, by *anything,* couldn't be ignored for long no matter who or what was facing against it.

At her side, Wane mumbled something she couldn't hear. She shook her head knowing he couldn't see it. They were stuck out here but here was where they needed to be.

All they could do was move on.

Just when Chandler's feet started to drag from the sheer lack of energy she had remaining, she nearly tumbled overtop a dilapidated wooden fence. Wane caught her in a vice-like grip.

Chandler nodded at him and he adjusted his hands, though still not letting go. She tried to lean in closer to the fence and noticed how the snow had mostly buried it completely. Glancing along where other parts of it may be, she saw a few more spikes sitting barely above the snow-drift.

She lifted her head and her body went rigid. Wane's did too.

"The ranch," Chandler whispered.

The few buildings she could spy stuck out as dark shapes in the otherwise barren place. White followed by white covered every inch of ground, even blending with the sky towards where the horizon might meet it.

"We're here already?" Wane panted.

What do you mean already? she wanted to ask but couldn't find her voice.

They'd clearly been walking for hours. She could feel the exhaustion of fighting the storm back for at least half that time everywhere; inside her body and out, all at once.

Chandler glanced behind her. Though the storm was passing here, the winds lessening by the minute and the snowfall dragging away, the footsteps both her and Wane had freshly just made were already covered and buried. But the longer they stood there, the quicker they were running out of time to create distance between themselves and the group they'd barely managed to leave behind.

They didn't know *why* that group hadn't let them leave despite knowing they needed to, but they'd tried everything to keep Wane and Chandler in their sights for some reason.

And she could also feel the storm's ice dwindling in power like it was exhausted too.

"We need to get in," Wane said, cutting off her thoughts.

"Hop over." She gestured to the jagged and broken fence around them.

Wane unhooked his arm and hopped over easily. His hat slid back slightly and the shock of orange hair was brilliant against the all-white surroundings.

There was another, bigger fence they needed to cross over next. Chandler didn't understand the need for two defence layers, and yet she had nearly tripped over the first.

Chandler and Wane walked together up to the second fence layer. This one wasn't as hidden beneath the snowy background, leaving it appearing somewhat tall in the landscape.

Wane went across first this time, hauling himself over with a little more struggle but otherwise easily. Chandler followed, climbing onto the rungs to then swing over.

Halfway, however, her foot slipped. And then she was falling forwards.

For the second time in minutes, Wane caught her before she hit the ground. She glanced up at him. "Thanks."

He removed the scarf from his mouth, revealing a smile. "It's kind of my job," he told her.

"To make sure I don't fall over?"

"If that's what I'm needed for." He shrugged casually. "I'm the muscle. Whatever that requires."

As if that settled some sort of debate, they started through the ranch, keeping lower to the ground where possible. It was an expansive, exposed area.

"You don't sounds too pleased by that," Chandler mentioned a moment later.

Wane fixed his hat and hunched lower. "I'm a *little* tired of only being needed for my strength. I'm more than just my ability. Despite how universally helpful it can be for these things. I'm *worth* more."

Chandler gave him a long look. She knew how he felt. All Abnormals did.

The problem was, the world only ever saw them for their abnormalities, and so after a while, they did the same to themselves. What was the difference, really? Chandler constantly had to remind herself that she was more than just her abnormality alone.

While she'd been fixated, Wane had slipped away. Her head popped up higher in realisation, her back ramrod straight in panic.

Then she saw him leave the nearby barn – when had they gotten so close to one? – with two Snow Beasts geared up, one on either side of him. The Beasts seemed to come willingly with Wane as their guide.

Wane helped hoist Chandler up onto her Beast, his strength alone setting her into the saddle. He shrugged at her when she'd laughed unexpectedly. Wane was more than his power, they all were, but his power was incredible all the same.

Wane groaned as he climbed onto his own Beast. "My arse hasn't missed this," he groaned. "How can I *still* be sore? I'm going to have bruises for days after this."

"Hopefully we won't be on them long," she tried to reassure.

"This better be the last time we need them."

Chandler agreed. Her body also ached with the memory of their last ride.

Once situated the best they could be, reins in hand, they set off again.

Is that it?" Wane narrowed his eyes. "It doesn't look like much."

He was right. The research base looked more like a run-down tin shack than a scientists' dream station.

Metal upon metal built the walls, the roof, and even the steps up to the partially rusted metal door. There appeared to be no windows on any side and nothing else stood out from the structure.

Both of them circled it several times – both by Beast and by foot – before approaching closer.

The storm had completely vanished behind them now. They stood out in the vast blanket of white snow like flares in a cloudless night. They needed to decide what to do and fast. They tied the Beasts' reins to a nearby wooden post – something the Beasts could easily pulled themselves free from – and looked around for a moment.

Wane made the choice himself and stomped up to the front door. He wrapped against the metal several times with his glove-covered knuckles.

No one responded.

He looked back at Chandler and shrugged, then barged his shoulder into the door like a cannonball. The whole thing un-hooked off the hinges. Wane caught it mid-air, propping it up just on the inside somewhere out of sight.

"Oops," he said flatly.

Chandler walked up to him. "Did you forget how strong you were or did you not realise how weak the door was?"

"Bit of both?" he answered. At least he sounded guilty.

Chandler rolled her eyes and stepped inside first.

It took a moment for her eyes to adjust to the new light, but once they did, she realised how oddly clean the room was.

She hadn't thought about what to expect, but tucked in chairs and neat piles of paper weren't it. She had a tiny expectation of seeing bodies – either bloodied or frozen, or huddled together for warmth. But there were none. It was as if a cleaning crew had swept through to purposely make the place appear brand new and unused. Especially with how the metal looked freshly polished and the grey walls seemed to have been recently painted.

Still unsure if anyone might be inside, Chandler remained cautious and on high alert. She'd had some training, but she'd only been at Redwing for a season. Her skills were no way up to scratch for a fight of any kind.

Tip-toeing as best she could in snow boots, she made her way around. When she picked something up, she made sure nothing else was attached to it that might trigger an alarm.

Nothing appeared to be amiss though. Even Wane seemed stumped. But the lack of dust and the fact that nothing was out of its supposed place was highly suspicious. More suspicious than if everything had been thrown everywhere.

Where was everyone?

Deeming the coast clear, they took to opposite sides of the room for a more thorough search.

Chandler thumbed through files and shifted chairs out the way. *What were you doing here*? she wondered. *What could you have been researching? Where are you?*

The more she tried to unearth, the less she found. Until she reached a single stack of papers that'd been tucked away from others.

Chandler took the top sheet off the stack and studied it. The more she read, the more the confusion grew. Several times she had to retrace the words just to make sure she'd taken them in properly.

The paper talked of a man with an extreme skill. He could apparently find gems and jewels and riches buried anywhere.

He'd lived in the north; having moved here from a city to try and get peace because the more remote the area, the less people tended to travel to it, so the less any riches fell away from their persons. He claimed he could hear the items talk to him and he wanted his mind to be quiet. The paper said he was being tested by scientists, that perhaps he was using a special kind of detector to find these riches or that maybe *he* himself was the detector. The writing on the page transcribed that the man was deemed to be valuable either way.

"They were researching a *pirate*?" Wane questioned. Chandler jolted in surprise; she hadn't heard him come up behind her to read over her shoulder. For someone so big, he often made the smallest sounds.

"I don't think he's a pirate," she told him, heart still racing.

"Sounds like a pirate."

"I think he was an Abnormal."

"An Abnormal pirate?"

"Just an Abnormal."

"And he could just *find* pirate treasure?"

Chandler turned to scowl at him. "There are no pirates."

"Can you really be so sure?"

Wane seemed so innocent sometimes, like a child. His eyes were small and brown, yet blown wide with joy. Recently, Chandler had had to remind herself none of them were really that old. She herself was only just coming up to twenty-three. Wane might appear big and muscular, but he was still young.

She moved her gaze back to the paper she still held. "These researchers were studying him," she said, choosing to move on rather than to further argue. She passed him the page.

"Does it say anywhere where they are now?" he asked.

"No." Chandler grabbed another sheet, then another, and then one more. There were no answers, just more of the same thing she'd already read. "There's nothing."

"Our mission is still the same?"

"We find them," she agreed. Though she didn't know *how*.

Wane's eyes met hers and a gleam inside ignited. "Maybe we'll find pirates along the way?"

Chandler simply sighed. Wane seemed content enough, if his laugh was anything to go by.

Shoving scraps of paper into their inner jacket pockets – anything that seemed interesting made its home there for now – they made their way to the hole that had been a doorway before their arrival. Outside was still cold but at least it had cleared up.

This stop hadn't provided much besides a reason for what the scientists were doing. Their tracks were still missing and it wasn't the snow that had covered them. Where had they gone and why?

Wane unwrapped the Beast's reins from the post. Chandler struggled her way back onto hers, this time doing so on her own, and watched as Wane heaved himself up with ease.

With no true direction and no leads on the missing researchers except the potential for a powerful Abnormal to be in their company, Chandler didn't know where to search next. But they were all important. The world couldn't lose the unknown man *or* the scientists. So they needed to be found.

"We're all dressed up and have nowhere to go," Wane joked.

"But we have to go somewhere," she said.

"How about we keep going away from where we've been?"

That seemed as good of a plan as any.

Nudging the side of her Beast with her heels, Chandler set off towards what she hoped was further north.

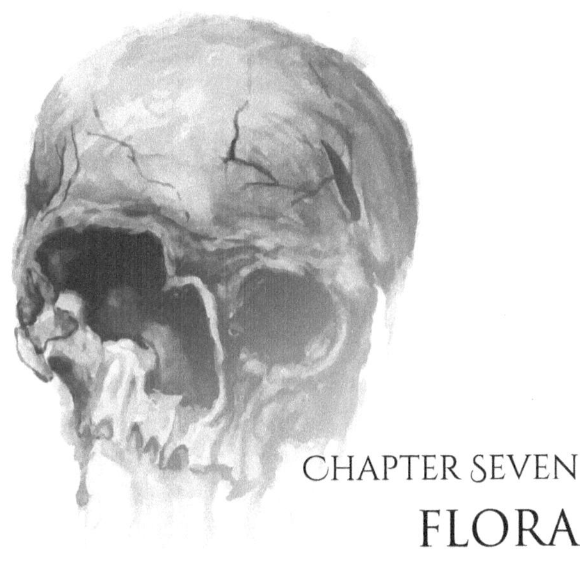

CHAPTER SEVEN

FLORA

20ᵗʰ Day of Winter 2406

Dalton and Preston were supposed to be returning from their mission tonight.

Flora waited within sight of the front door all night, camping out in the first-floor common area. It overlooked the main entrance and foyer perfectly. She had clear areas to see and, since it was the middle of the night, there were less people to disrupt too.

Aleema kept her company for as long as she could, but eventually her eyes drooped enough that opening them again proved difficult so she took herself to bed. Tiredness had abandoned Flora though.

Any time there was any sort of movement near the front door, Flora's attention snapped to it immediately. Several times it opened and closed, and each time she nearly threw herself over the first-floor balcony in excitement. Even when the Helpers passed by, her brain latched onto the figures and warped them so she could see what she wanted to see just for a brief moment.

It was never really her friends.

Those same Helpers brought Flora warm drinks and some snacks without being asked. They didn't speak to her – it was rare for them to ever be heard speaking at all – and simply moved on after. Flora accepted each thing, smiling, and saying a thank you. Her parents taught her some manners, if nothing else good.

Close to midnight, the front door groaned open again.

Flora was slower to her feet as if her body was pre-emptively expecting to be disappointed. But she shouldn't have been. Her heart leapt into her throat as two figures stepped inside from the growing cold. As her brain caught up with the true image before her she sprinted down the stairs without a second thought.

Dalton clearly spotted her first, dropping his bags and opening his arms wide for her approach. Giggling, Flora launched into his space. They staggered backwards slightly but somehow managed to stay upright. He kissed her temple and squeezed her, and she fisted the back of his shirt as she tried to pull him tighter.

Pulling back a few inches, Dalton examined her. "Miss me much?"

"*Yes!*" she exclaimed gleefully.

"I thought so." He planted another kiss to her head. "But I haven't been gone long."

"You've been gone long enough."

"What about me?" Preston suddenly asked.

Flora turned to him slowly. She hadn't forgotten he was there, but if she had focused on him, he would've stolen all her attention from the start.

He stole it anyway.

Preston's black hair had been swooped back, exposing his dark eyebrows and lashes. His half-smile remained on his lips and Flora felt her cheeks flush at the sight of it, yet she couldn't quite tear her gaze away.

"I missed you too," she admitted meekly.

They were close, *friends*. But she'd always wanted more than that from him. She didn't know how he perceived all this, what he thought of them – if they were only friends or if he shared her wishes of *more*. But, because she'd never tell him of her own feelings, too scared to admit aloud in fear of rejection and getting hurt, she wondered if she'd ever know his.

Preston's laugh cut through the silent hallway. A second later, Flora rose inside the circle of his muscular arms. She shrieked in surprise.

After a moment, he gently lowered her again. "I'm glad you missed me," he whispered.

She gazed up at him, her light amber eyes meeting his coal black ones. "You are?"

"I missed you too."

"You did?"

"I really did."

The room around them disappeared. Nothing remained but them.

Flora wanted to stare at his smile forever. And she thought she might. But then his hand came up to cradle the side of her face.

Warmth spread across her body, inside and outside of her skin. She didn't know what was happening. She *did*, but she didn't know whether to believe it was or not.

Her eyes narrowed on his, on his face, on his *lips*.

She mentally begged the universe to not wake her up and say this was a dream.

Preston's smile slipped into something smaller but still present, like it had become somehow private and only for her to see. The edge of his thumb stroked across her cheek at the same time. It took every ounce of patience Flora owned not to just yell at this man to kiss her already – if that was even his intention.

All the air in her lungs escaped as he lowered his face towards hers.

Their lips grazed.

But Flora never got to find how he really felt as the mission alarm fired off around them.

Flora nearly jumped out of her skin in surprise, the daze broken. Preston removed his hand from her, almost like he didn't want to let go yet still did anyway. She reached out to take his hand but he moved out of reach; something in him had definitely changed in a split second.

Had she imagined what'd just maybe occurred? Or had he really been about to kiss her?

She still didn't know how he felt and something definitely felt different between them now, especially since he wouldn't meet her eyes again.

To hide her disappointment and rising sadness, she sought out Dalton who had turned his back on them as if that was the best privacy he could offer. Flora smiled awkwardly when he turned back to her, a question in his gleaming eyes.

She couldn't say anything though.

All at once the foyer was full of recruits. Most appeared tired and fresh out of sleep; rumpled hair at all angles and mouths stuck open mid-yawn. Maggie and Praxis entered the space last, a little wide-eyed themselves, as if they too had been asleep and the alarm had woken them with a slight fright.

"I just came back," Dalton groaned next to Flora as he reap-proached her. "There's no way I'm going anywhere again."

"We'll be deciding that," Praxis said, carefully unlocking his office door. He slipped inside the room with Maggie, leaving the recruits in the figurative dark of the Mansion. They returned moments later, and Praxis' eyes wandered around the space carefully. "Ah, yes. Gretchen? Flora? Please follow."

Flora blinked, her left cheek twitching in surprise. The crowd parted for her expectantly and her legs moved on their own. The hairs on her arms rose at the attention of the other recruits but she wouldn't look. She wasn't exactly aware of what was happening until the office door shut behind her, the lock turned with finality.

Gretchen had moved with her, and she had been even quieter than normal.

No one had ever been entirely sure on how missions came to exist or were decided. Who could select what was important in the world to save or surrender? There were plenty of theories – technology spying on the world and deciding what needed help or didn't, that aliens had come down from the stars to interfere and that's where the real gene change that caused Abnormalities had come from, or even a group of humans or ex-members of Redwing who kept their ears and eyes open at all times – but no one was ever given a clear answer when asked.

Only the leaders of Redwing knew more than basic recruits but that secret was one destined not to be shared with anyone, ever. *If* they knew anything more. It wasn't even clear how much they knew.

Layers of secrets existed to bury and hide it all, and probably to keep them all safe.

However it was done, Flora was just surprised she'd been summoned for something. Her Abnormality was specific in its uses and applications.

Praxis sat behind his desk, now fully alert. Last season, he'd tried to grow a beard. Now the ginger curls overpowered his entire face, hiding most of his mouth. He scratched at it, the same way he always did when he was thinking.

Maggie paused behind him as he pulled a piece of paper from a pink file on his desk. Whatever it said, they read the contents together in silence. Flora tried to not look too interested. She peered over at Gretchen instead, who appeared almost *bored*.

As if sensing the silence wasn't entirely comfortable, Praxis glanced over the paper. "We read the print quickly to choose you both for this mission," he explained. "We're just scanning the fine print."

"It's fine," Gretchen said, waving her working hand nonchalantly. Her other hand was strapped into a brace. "Come back to us whenever you're ready."

Maggie glared, but not unkindly, much like a mother would. "We'll need a few more moments and then you'll have our full attention," she promised.

"All the time in the world 'ere."

"Enough," Praxis warned, his tone stern yet calm. Gretchen raised an eyebrow, threatening to meet him in the silent challenge he was throwing her way. Flora didn't want there to be a confrontation at all. He ignored Gretchen's attitude, continued reading, and then released the paper to the desk. "We chose right. You two will be the perfect fit for this mission," he announced, eyes flicking between Flora and Gretchen equally. "*If you can work together.*"

Flora glanced at Gretchen nervously, heart thumping in her throat, but found the girl still glaring at Praxis as if her cold blue eyes could burn him from beneath the heavy black makeup she still wore despite the late hour. Despite that expression Gretchen still appeared bored, or indifferent at best.

"I think we'll be fine," Gretchen decided.

Flora couldn't exactly disagree. She didn't know enough about the other girl, but she had never had personal problems with her. They'd shared a hot chocolate in the gardens the other day. But that didn't make good working partners.

Maggie nodded. "Good."

Gretchen kicked her booted feet up onto Praxis' desk. "Wha's the mission then, big P?"

Praxis glared, his own eyes matching the fire of Gretchen's.

"How many times have I told you to *not* call me that?"

She rolled her eyes. "You can tell me as many times as you like."

"But you don't listen, Gretchen."

"I listen well enough, thanks."

Flora sank further into her chair as if she could physically hide from the confrontation.

"Back to why you're *here*. Your mission," Praxis continued, resigned to the fact that Gretchen wasn't about to drop her attitude. "The world's economy is a staggering mess of a cycle. All countries are locked to forever borrow money from one place and give it back to others because everyone owes everyone, and no debt is ever really paid off. Money just bounces around from here to there and back round it goes.

"However, it has come to our attention that recently one of the newly formed Caribbean Islands has paid off *all* their debts to any country they ever owed money too. They paid it *in full*. They now owe nothing to nobody. They've somehow broken their cycle. And we need you to find out how."

"Where you're going is small and the population is minimal," Maggie added. "We can arrange for an air-shuttle to take you to mainland New America, but you'll have to boat across the rest of the way to the island you need. You'll be out of reach from even us when you get there, so you'll have to rely on only each other."

Flora's throat had become dry. "There will just be the two of us?"

Gretchen removed her legs from the desk, her heavy boots slamming onto the ground. "Are we *really* the best fit for this?"

Maggie nodded again. "We think you are."

Everyone knew Gretchen's abnormality centred around bones. She could heal or break them but never her own. Flora's abnormality allowed her to control and manipulate *gold*.

It didn't matter how concentrated or pure the element was, or how much there was of it inside something, she could twist and control however much there was for whatever she wanted it for.

How could the two of them really be the best for this mission? Was no one else suitable? Flora supposed not. Redwing wasn't full of Abnormals for every situation, so the leaders would sometimes have to pick the best option out of a bad bunch. Like now. This sounded like one of those missions where anyone could go. That still didn't fill her with much appreciation or joy.

At least if gold or money was involved in paying debts, Flora might partially be useful.

Gretchen groaned heavily. "Back into the sun I go. I thought I was done with it. I *wanted* to be done with it."

"Pack some suncream," Praxis advised, a mocking smile plain on his face.

Flora didn't need to look across at her companion to know Gretchen would be glaring hatefully. Gretchen began to seethe, "I'll shove that suncream right where—"

"We should go pack a bag," Flora suggested, cutting her off.

As she stood, she noticed her hands shaking. She tried to bite down on the emotions threatening to overwhelm her.

She'd just gotten one of her best friends back, *and* Preston, who she remembered suddenly she'd been about to *kiss*. And now she was required to step away from them both. She would also be leaving Aleema. Aleema who had suffered from more nightmares since Dalton left and would suffer again with Flora gone.

Flora's entire body began to shiver.

Maggie trotted round the side of the desk. "We'll make the travel arrangements right away."

"Remember," Praxis called out once Flora and Gretchen reached the door. "You need to find out how their economy grew so wealthy, and, if you can, make sure it doesn't develop further. If it does, it would possibly cripple the world with wealth it has no business having. The world, unfortunately, moves with debts and fluctuations to that debt."

Flora knew from her old life that money didn't buy happiness and it could do far worse than topple something. It could entirely destroy lives if there was enough of it and someone's greed had no limits.

Still trying to hide her profuse shaking, Flora turned to Gretchen who was still smouldering. "I'll meet you down by the doors in ten minutes." She opened the door and threw herself out, eyes burning with threatening tears and heart still unprepared to say goodbye.

CHAPTER EIGHT

GRETCHEN

20th Day of Winter 2406

Gretchen stomped, deeply annoyed as sand slithered inside her shoes. She was far from the regular mud and grass of Redwing.

For once, she'd worn light material shoes, the type people typically wore on beaches when they went there on holidays. They did nothing for her. If anything, they irritated the skin on her feet more than any hard-shell boot would. But boots definitely wouldn't work here. It was too hot to wear something all-encompassing and the sand was too thin to wear something that heavy.

Even her blonde and green hair had to be constantly pushed out of her face. The more she tried to tuck it back, or flapped her lighter coloured t-shirt to get some self-made breeze to tickle and cool her skin, the less she thought of herself as Gretchen and more as an imposter in her own body.

Everything about this place was unbearable already, and they'd barely started.

Gretchen, half-way to being entirely and extremely miserable, followed a rather disturbingly silent Flora.

On both the air-shuttle and boat crossing here, Gretchen had been surrounded by children that'd kicked the back of her chair or tapped her shoulder repeatedly. Flora had brushed those things off with a light shrug, but Gretchen hadn't. She'd shot one child a glare and it'd backed off hastily. The parents had tutted like she was the problem in that scenario, and she'd wanted to tell them rather loudly that they needed to train their spawn better.

It was safe to say she'd been irritable from the moment Praxis had called on her during the middle of the night and her mood had only soured further since.

Sweat started to build across Gretchen's brow as the sun beat down upon them, and the weight of moving sluggishly below it began to take its toll. She covered her eyes with her hand to look where they'd stopped.

The Island they stood upon was a partially newly made landform. In the same way humans evolved, so did the Earth. It shifted and reshaped itself regularly and constantly, all over time and never stopping. The process definitely appeared more 'natural' now, rather than a messed planet trying to cope, which meant the Climate Talks – where group leaders came together to discuss the state of the world and how everyone could leave it in a better place for the next generation and animals – were working.

Tiny specks of the Caribbean stretch had come apart and new landmasses had risen out of the ocean in past years. This Island had been around for only a handful of years– the name escaping Gretchen entirely – and neither her or Flora had heard of it before Praxis' mention in their ride to the port.

Flora turned away from the scenery, uncertainty written into her own shielded eyes. "Where should we go first?" she asked. "There's so much here and we don't really know where to go."

All that lay ahead was sand. A small patch of what seemed to be trees stood in the distance, and if they could grow here, then there had to be some sort of fresh water source. At least that was Gretchen's thinking.

"Towards the foliage," Gretchen decided. "I'd live closest to clean water."

"Not the beach?"

Gretchen shook her head. "The tides all around the world are still unpredictable. You know that. One high one and you're washed away. You can be close to the sea and sand without living on top of it."

"So, the trees?"

"The trees."

Gretchen hoisted her bag and they started making their way towards them.

Some time later, Gretchen found herself yearning to stretch her aching limbs under the shade of the trees, for her clothing to not stick to her tacky skin anymore, and a land-rocking thunderstorm to cool the baking and humid air.

She only received one of those wishes.

The mass of trees she'd spotted from the beach created a dense area of shade. As soon as she staggered beneath them, she flopped to the ground. Heat exhaustion weighed her down on the inside. It ran deep, deeper than any type of exhaustion she'd felt before. And she knew it wasn't done beating her. There was still no civilisation in sight.

"I don't want to know what'll climb down these trees in a few hours."

Gretchen glanced over at Flora who had also dropped to the sandy ground. No breeze travelled through the space and Gretchen wondered if this was what it would be like if she shoved her entire body inside an old-fashioned fire oven.

In all honesty, Gretchen hadn't given a fleeting thought to what might reside in the plants above her. "Neither do I," she agreed. "We need to move again."

They'd been dropped off with their usual affects and some supplies each – large water canteens and food sachets – but none of it would last long, maybe a day, day and a half, at a serious push. And that'd been from the moment they'd stepped out of Redwing, almost thirteen hours ago.

"Do you think we're going in the right direction?" Flora asked. She sounded like she was trying to gulp the air into her lungs.

"Is there any other way to go?"

They'd both studied the map of the island before leaving Redwing. It was a long and somewhat curved expanse of land, like a crescent moon. A few pieces, depending on the tides, would get cut off from others at times, but it wasn't entirely *huge*. Just reasonably large. The width from one curved side to the other in the middle section was a different matter. But people were here. They knew that.

All the research had been done on the shuttle and boat ride over here.

"I wish one of us had the power of a compass," Flora grumbled.

Gretchen rolled her eyes. "That still wouldn't get us to where we need to go. It would only tell us North or South. Not where to head."

"The power of a homing pigeon?"

"If we've never been there, we can't 'ome in."

"A map built into our brains?"

"We could've just asked for the one back *there*." They both knew Gretchen was referring to Redwing.

"And information on where to go."

"We got all the information they 'ad."

"They could've—"

Finally done with her companions shit, Gretchen cut in. "Enough! We 'ave all we *could* 'ave. Praxis told us what we needed and we studied the rest. There wasn't anything else on paper. That's why we're 'ere. To figure out the gaps."

Flora's amber glare cut across the space between them, but it quickly softened as she sighed. "I'm sorry."

Gretchen glared right back. "What for?"

"I'm missing home and I'm taking it out on you."

Gretchen fought the urge to roll her eyes. "We only left a few hours ago." It was definitely more than *a few* but she didn't exactly want to point that out and rub the real time into the wound Flora was clearly suffering with.

"We did," Flora agreed.

"But you miss it?"

"I don't leave much."

"*How* can you be missing it already though?"

Flora shrugged pathetically. "I don't know."

Shifting her entire body, Gretchen fixed her full attention on her companion. "Yes, you do," she argued.

"I know most of us never had a good time *before*," Flora dropped her head against the tree she leaned back on, "but Red was the first place where I felt like I belonged. I had friends. A *family*. No one was scared of me or wanted to use me. I wouldn't disappear if someone left me in a corner and no one wanted that to happen either. I could just be me. Quiet and content."

"You do realise they *do* want to use you, right?"

"No—"

"Where are you right now? Out in the world, *being used*."

Flora shut her eyes. "It's not the same."

"How is it not?" When no response came, Gretchen rolled her eyes and reached into her pack for her water. She took a deep swig before recapping it and throwing the bottle at Flora's feet. Flora opened her eyes to peer at it. "If we share, we won't have two bottles likely to leak at once."

Flora took the bottle and took two, long gulps. "It's warm."

Gretchen let out a surprised, unbelieving laugh. "Everything 'ere is."

Unsurprisingly, silence stretched out between them, only the caw of nearby gulls cutting through it.

"At least here, I'm using my power how *I* want to use it," Flora eventually said, her voice barely above a whisper. It didn't seem like they were in danger of being overheard but no Abnormal could ever be too careful. "I'm choosing to go out into the world and help with a wider reach. Within reason anyway. We can still deny a mission, though I don't think any of us really would. Has anyone ever?"

"I don' know," Gretchen admitted. She'd never heard of anyone at Redwing denying to go on a mission. They all went on them, even if they complained the whole time.

"Back *before*, things weren't like that for me."

Gretchen watched Flora closely. "That bad?"

"Worse."

While she might've complained about her life before Redwing, Gretchen had grown to realise that she might've actually had one of the best *befores*.

Her home life hadn't been the best, but both her parents had supported her at a minimum. She hadn't been prodded and probed and poked full of holes by medical professionals. Her parents had even supported her when she'd left them behind, the promise she was going to do something with her life uplifting them all to varying degrees. Gretchen even wrote to them on occasion – Praxis had to read the letters before sending, just as he had to assess letters arriving in case of information leaks. They believed the lie that she'd gone to study how to help fix people. It was close enough to the truth.

It had been everything else outside of her parents that made her feel like she'd been dragged through the lowest dirt of life.

"As much as I want to stay in the shade, the sooner we move on..." Gretchen climbed to her feet, snatching her water bottle and repacking it again. She'd never been good at emotions, and she was reaching her limit on them now. "The sooner we move on, the sooner we can get you 'ome again."

Flora wiped her palms on her thin trousers and stood too. "I never thought I'd have a welcome home."

"I think almost all of us feel that way."

"And that's why I think I miss it so much already."

Unlike Flora and her seeming outward optimism, Gretchen knew to not get too comfortable in one place. She knew of a few others who shared that sentiment too, and could guess others' beliefs in the matter of a permanent home. Abnormals never had easy lives and it wasn't great thinking to start to trust something would stay. Anything could change, even if it looked like it wouldn't.

Gretchen tried not to huff in annoyance. "Come on."

Flora grumbled something about hoping she wouldn't be going on many more missions for a while, but Gretchen tuned the rest out. She didn't know the girl, and didn't really want to start hearing Flora's internal monologue when she couldn't control herself to keep it in.

While walking further into the trees, Gretchen dug out her phone. On the screen she saw she had a single bar of signal.

Since it was there, it encouraged her, and she typed.

Gretchen:
Im on an exotic island full of sand and sea and
sun. Ew.
Another sandy mission.
If you wanted to join? Feel free.

She sent the message, then typed another with her coordinates, and then pocketed her phone just as the signal died for good.

CHAPTER NINE
QUINTON

ith one hand behind his head like a pillow and the other tucked just below the waistband of his trousers, Quinton should've been relaxed enough to close his eyes and attempt to find sleep. He'd already showered, eaten a full meal, and had drunk his evening cup of tea with one less sugar than the normal three scoops.

So why couldn't he slip away into dreams?

He went through the normal practices. Counting sheep to twenty-five. Turning his pillow over to the colder side. Humming a droning tune he'd heard someone whistle a few days ago. When the tune bugged him, he listed off all the names and places he'd travelled to in the world.

But nothing wore him out.

Despite the darkness of night, he could still peer up and see the ceiling clearly. Above him a mosaic of white shapes slotted together like a jigsaw. He tried to move the shapes and create pictures with the pieces in his mind. And even that didn't work to tire him.

He slipped his hand lower inside his trousers; the warmth of his palm surprising against the rest of his skin. His fingers travelled all the way to his thigh and then gradually back up.

Back at Redwing, he would've explored and touched himself more in an attempt to burn the restless energy thrumming through his veins. But with his sister asleep just across the hall, he hated the idea entirely and threw it from his mind.

Withdrawing his hand, he flipped onto his stomach with a silent sigh, face planting the pillow. It became an effort to breathe but he managed well enough after a slight shuffle.

Truthfully, he knew *exactly* what was keeping him awake.

He wasn't unfed or unwatered or even missing the touch of a hand.

He missed adventure. He craved intrigue and drama. Even a little danger. *Fun.*

His mind easily slipped into memories of his last time at Redwing, of the few weeks before he left. He could see Gretchen laughing and then leaving for her mission in Egypt. He could hear Aleema's piano music flowing down the halls and under cracks in doors, and the way Flora, Dalton, and others danced to it. He felt the stare of the Grittal twins' as they tried to rope him into bets or started random play fights with people for their attention.

Clearest of all was Ziva and Chandler, two girls who had walked into Redwing early last season, and had been companions when they'd gone on his last mission to recover a missing famous mask of power.

Groaning, he rolled back over.

Since leaving Redwing, Quinton had tried to not think about them. He always failed. Just as he did when he tried to push thoughts of Gretchen away. She was his best friend, but there had been a connection to the girls – somehow Ziva and Chandler had grown on him more so than some of the others he'd lived with for years.

He launched himself upright, sitting at the edge of the bed. He didn't want to get stuck down *that* avenue any longer, because he would.

Someone knocked softly on his door as he ran a hand through his hair. Quinton let the duvet fall off him as he went to answer it.

Quinton had been expecting to find Katia on the other side of the door. Instead, he found his sister.

Darlene looked sleepy with her eyes half scrunched and light brown hair in two braids that were coming undone. The hallway nightlight illuminated her face and the yawn that followed.

"You're making a lot of noise," she complained somewhat quietly.

Quinton grimaced. "Sorry, Day." He tied his hair up with the band on his wrist.

"Our walls are thin." Darlene rubbed her eyes, clearly not noticing her brother's discomfort at that comment. " I can hear you sighing a lot. Why are you in a mood?"

"A mood?" he questioned.

She peered round him as much as she could. "Your room is a mess. Have you been throwing things around?"

The room wasn't that bad. Just some messy pillows and a duvet that'd fallen to the floor. Maybe some clothes strewn about. The curtains were mostly drawn, but not fully. A few hairbands had fallen to the carpet and had bounced around.

"Maybe you should dye your hair a new colour?" Darlene continued.

"Why would I do that?" he asked, not keeping up.

"That's what people do when they're sad."

Quinton shook his head, grinning. His sister might be only related technically by half, but there was no denying they were blood when she said things like that. "Why don't you come in?" he offered. Darlene didn't move. "Or should we keep standing in the hallway? Oh. Maybe you're tired and should go back to bed instead?"

"I'll come into your room."

Of course you will, he thought, his grin widening as he stepped aside.

Darlene strolled into the room with all the confidence a twelve-year-old could muster. She happily plopped herself on top of his bed after picking his duvet back up for extra padding to sit on.

Quinton threw a spare blanket around his sister's shoulder as he joined her. She snuggled into it, and it made him thinking about the last time he threw a blanket over someone.

He shook his head. The circumstances were different. The *people* were different. One was his sister. The other...

He cut himself off. Chandler hadn't been anything except a work colleague and possible friend.

Quinton flicked on his bedside light and then leaned back, trying to appear casual. "Where did you learn about people dying their hair when they're sad?"

"Do sad people not dye their hair?"

"Some people want to express themselves with their hair. Some people just want a change. Many do it when they get older to hide the fact that they're ageing. It depends on the person, but no, you don't just have to be sad."

"Why did you do it?"

He smiled to himself. "At first I was trying to stand out and annoy my parents."

"I wouldn't be annoyed at coloured hair."

"You don't know your father very well."

"I'm glad." Darlene lent against him, tucking herself so her head rested on his shoulder. "If he doesn't like simple things like hair, then he can't be very nice."

Quinton snorted loudly. Darlene tilted her head to stare at him, and he shook the look off.

From what Quinton knew, as much as Katia had taken Darlene to see his mother, Darlene had never once met her real father. Quinton Eichner the seventh wasn't a nice man. Nor was he a terrible one. Honestly, he wasn't much of anything, because most of the time he didn't care about anything outside of himself. But it was still probably for the best Darlene hadn't been introduced.

"I had red hair last season," he continued. "Then white."

"And now blue." Darlene reached out, dragging a strand out of where he'd tucked it back to inspect. "Why?"

"I'd never had blue before."

"That's it? No cool story?"

"Not really."

She nodded and let go of the strand. "Are you going to tell me why you sounded like you were angry now?"

He felt his eyebrows furrow. "I sounded angry?"

"You were huffing and sighing and I'm sure you hit your mattress with your fist." In the dark of the room, her face looked even more childlike. "That sounds like anger."

I hit the mattress? he wondered. He sighed out loud and wrapped an arm over Darlene's shoulder, holding her to him. "I wasn't angry. I'm just..." He wouldn't lie and say he didn't know the issue, because he did, but saying it outright made it somehow more *real*. "I just can't sleep tonight."

She glanced away, using the darkness to shield her eyes. "I heard you and Ma talking a few nights ago," she admitted quietly.

"Oh?" He squeezed her closer to prompt her to continue.

"Do you miss the place I found you at?"

"How much did you hear?" he asked back.

Darlene's eyes found his again, her dimly-lit gaze full of guilt. "Enough."

"How much, Day?"

"Ma said you'd been quiet and you said you like it here."

"I *do* like it here."

"She also told you to be honest. You miss that big place where I found you too."

Quinton couldn't contain his heavy sigh. "Sometimes."

Darlene tilted her head, innocence disappearing and getting replaced with something far beyond her current years. "Be honest."

It was Quinton's turn to look away. "I do," he whispered.

"Can't you go back to it?"

"Probably."

"Then why don't you?"

He returned his gaze to his sister. Sat there, in his borrowed room, he'd never seen how much they were really alike before. It was like peering into a mirror, and not just in their features. Her sharp facial angles matched his, as did her daring smile. But also her questions and intrigues were much like his. The genuine concern over the questions and their answers was all his worry too.

Quinton hugged her even closer. "Going back would mean leaving you behind," he admitted, hating how the words sounded.

Darlene stuttered for a moment. "But I can see that place! I could come with you? They'd let me in, right? They did before!"

"But Katia couldn't come too."

Quinton expected Darlene to start crying. The way her eyes glazed over seemed to suggest she would. Yet, no tears fell. If anything, Darlene's resolve came back to her stronger as she pulled out of his grasp slightly.

"I could still talk to Ma," Darlene tried to reason.

"Maybe," Quinton agreed.

Letters would be an option and *maybe* phone communication would be open, even directly from Redwing, but only because Darlene was so young.

"And I could see her!" Darlene pressed.

Quinton said nothing to that. Most, once they came to Redwing, didn't see their outside families. Again, Darlene's circumstances might've be different if she came along because of her age. But most others didn't have contact, even if there wasn't a rule strictly against it. The rules only stated that their lives at Redwing couldn't be shared outside of it.

Tiredness found him at last as they spoke, and a yawn expelled itself from his mouth. He wanted nothing more than to finally lie down and put his head on the pillow. He honestly wanted to be done with this conversation entirely.

"But it's not a house, where you found me," he added.

Darlene tilted her head again. "It's full of special people. Like us!"

When they'd come to Darlene's home last season, Quinton had tried to explain what Redwing was without breaking any rules. He'd explained that everyone living there had abnormalities – like him and Darlene maybe did – and it was safe for those people because they were away from the public who often despised them for their one mutated gene they didn't ask for.

However, Darlene still didn't know about missions or the job that came attached to living at Redwing. But Quinton wondered if she'd be able to put two and two together if he said much more. She was intelligent and obviously resourceful for her age.

"It's not that easy," he told her. "Or simple."

"But being here is making you noisy and sad."

He chuffed half-heartedly. "Sorry about being noisy."

"*And* being sad?"

"I don't think I can help that."

"Yes! You can!" Darlene unwrapped herself and sat up on her knees, staring at Quinton like she could outline him perfectly. "I know you like it here. I see you smiling," she told him. "But you need to do what makes you happy. Nothing is better than happy. That's what Ma says."

"Your Ma is a smart person," Quinton said.

Darlene flicked a braid over her shoulder dramatically. "Of course she's smart. She had me." She rolled off the bed and walked away with a tiny wave, leaving Quinton to watch.

Mouth slightly agape, like he'd been left in the wake of a passing hurricane that'd changed course, it took Quinton a minute before he shut off his bedside light and laid back down. How could Darlene be so young yet so intelligent? Katia really was a strong and smart woman, and she was raising a stronger and smarter girl.

Quinton watched as his phone screen illuminated, lighting up the dark room. He snatched it from the bedside table to read the message, and he smiled.

Darlene and Katia were right. While he did like it here, in their home and their familial warmth, he missed being at Redwing equally, if not *more*.

Clambering out of bed for the second time that night, he reached under his bed for his bag and started to shovel the thrown about clothes inside. This wasn't going to be a goodbye for good. He could stay in contact. He *would* stay in their lives. He'd make it work.

As he dashed about, whirling round and round the room, he wondered if he could have both lives in part.

But right now he needed to make a choice. And he needed to choose what really made him happy and run for it.

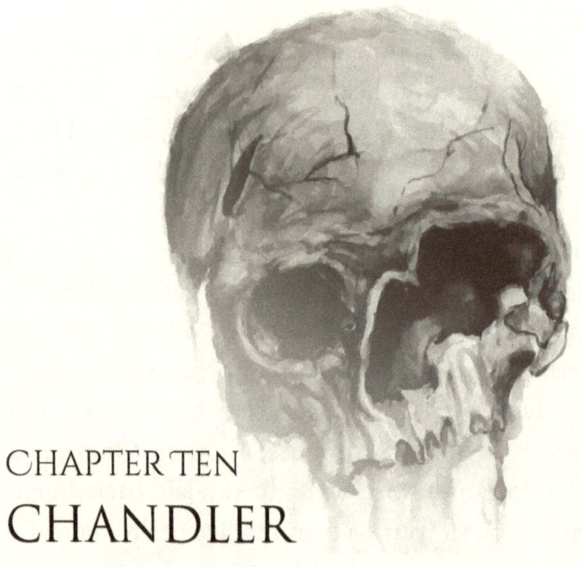

CHAPTER TEN
CHANDLER

21ˢᵗ Day of Winter 2406

Oranges and golds smeared their way across the horizon to intertwine and replaced the blues and purples as they receded with the dying moon.

Chandler and Wane had travelled another day and night with next to no direction to make it this far. They couldn't tell how much distance they'd covered, but they'd travelled anyway.

They slowed their Beasts when a sign appeared out of the clear ice ahead. The pole was buried beneath snow, and the metal of the sign seemed to be *burnt* somehow, but it was there, just warped slightly. Who would've met the sign with a match out this far? *Why?*

Wane slid off his Beast and rubbed a hand across the sign. FURTHEST NORTH RESEARCH LAB had been printed in big, bold lettering. He smiled back at Chandler rather smugly, like finding this had been his intention.

Rolling her eyes, Chandler and her Beast trampled past him.

Further up the path, Chandler unzipped her jacket just to feel the cold better. There was no ice-storm today and the slow air felt refreshing. She'd tested years ago to see if any sort of coldness would kill her – she hadn't met one yet that could even touch the sides – but she could still get ill. It took a lot, and she'd only get some sniffles or a runny nose, but right now it was a risk she was willing to take on.

Chandler took several deep breaths. The air was crisp and clean in her lungs. Pollution didn't seem to reach here; not where the world still lived as naturally as the day it'd been formed. It was peaceful and quiet too.

Slipping her gloves off, she raised her hands and wiggled her fingers. Using her power so openly had never been something she could even think of doing before now. But here, surrounded by no one and nothing but *her* nature, she could.

Ice flakes layered over the fresh snow rose into the air before her at her command. They danced in the daylight like crystals. It made her spine tingle to watch. The ease with which she could reach out and call to her power had never sunk so deep into her before. Maybe because she'd never tried, or never had the power to try.

For one second, her brain emptied itself of all thought and let her have a moment to herself in blissful silence.

"That still freaks me out," Wane's voice cut through her peace as he caught up. Chandler waved her hand, sending some flakes to flick the end of his nose. He waved them off. "I *meant*, I'm not used to people having such *physical* powers."

More flakes rose in place of the others. "I wouldn't call it physical," Chandler argued.

"You move things. That's active enough."

She looked across at him, and his dark eyes seemed to hold such joyful lightness. "What would you call yours?"

Wane thought for a moment. "Physical," he agreed. "I think most of us can be split between physical or mental."

"There's a few that could cross over."

"Oh, for sure! Like Bony's."

She scowled. "Bony?"

Wane tore his gaze away suddenly. "Gretchen," he murmured, but it was loud enough in the desolate space. "You met her, right? Before we left? Tiny thing but vicious and could cut you with her heavy make-up or a knife?"

Chandler nodded slowly. She'd met Gretchen at the end of her last mission. In Quinton's room. The girl had strolled in while he'd been giving Chandler a piece of premonition artwork.

Chandler had never mentioned or told anyone what she'd done with Quinton's drawing. Not even him. Outside the Helpers, only Ziva had been allowed into her room to see that she'd carefully picked a frame for the piece and had nailed it to the wall beside her window. She was drawn to the artwork as much as the real-life scenery outside. There was no answer to *why* she felt so attached to it – maybe it was the memory of the occasion, of how free she'd felt or how she'd been on her first mission and one step closer to finding a true home for herself – but *something* in her had grown attached.

She shook her head to free her mind. She needed to focus on her current mission, not one of the past.

Yet the Quinton in her mind wasn't so easily dispelled.

He'd left with his sister, off to who-knew-where, and no one had heard from him since. Chandler had cursed his name once he'd left. It'd taken her a lot to consider friendship with him, it'd made her feel vulnerable in a way she'd never felt before and he'd pulled away. Not that that was his problem or fault. But it reminded her that she shouldn't get attached or make friends. People always left or disappointed her. Ziva excluded.

The next time Chandler lifted her gaze, she forced her Beast to stop quite harshly. If she hadn't, she would've smacked its nose on the front entryway.

She slipped down its side carefully. She could easily reach out and touch the stone door. She didn't, choosing to walk *round* the door.

It stuck out of the ground like the top of an elevator shaft but someone had forgotten to build a building around it. Concrete sealed it in behind, meaning there was one way in and that was it. And there was no way to see how deep it sank underground because clearly this was the top level it could reach.

Chandler scowled. *Why build a sign and then hide the building?* It didn't make sense.

Walking back to the front, she found Wane already pulling the two halves of the door apart; the noise of stone grinding on stone made her want to crack her knuckles. He peered over his shoulder at her when he noticed her return, and she shrugged. There was no sense in stopping his advancement now.

There was no elevator on the inside, but a single staircase that descended steeply.

"Are we going in?" Wane asked, stepping back.

"We're here," Chandler shrugged again. There'd been nothing about a "furthest" research lab, yet they'd stumbled upon one anyway.

Holding onto the rail cautiously, Wane went first. Chandler slipped her gloves back on before following.

Minimal lighting showed their path. It glowed a soft lavender rather than pure white which was unusual for a lab. Though Chandler was beginning to see that nothing about this mission was normal.

"Watch out," Wane said. He'd gone further than a few steps ahead and had sunk into the darkness. "I think there's some water down here."

Chandler's grip on the handrail instinctively tightened. "Water?"

"*Something* sounds sloshy." Wane paused. "I *hope* it's water. Please let it be water."

"I don't want to know what else you think it could be, do I?" But she could guess already.

When Wane said nothing else, Chandler continued down the steps until her foot sank into something that was indeed sloshy. She winced. The liquid wasn't hot or cold, nor were her boots new and about to be ruined – old habits had made her buy some second-hand – but her reaction was because there was a slimy sense to whatever she'd stepped in, a sticky sensation whenever she tried to lift a foot.

Luckily, there was no smell other than that of stagnant water.

"Any chance you can freeze this stuff so we can skate over it?" Wane asked, looking back at her curiously.

They still weren't at the bottom of the complex. The hand-rail continued lower and Wane was already a few steps ahead of her downwards. The lighting made it hard to see what they were doing, or what they could be surrounded by.

Oh, what the hell, she thought, and tried to reach out. She waited and felt the temperature around her dip. But the liquid didn't react to her invisible touch.

Chandler looked back at Wane and shook her head. "I can't do anything."

"Fuck," Wane grumbled.

"It doesn't feel like I'm being blocked," she tried to explain. Chandler could *feel* the liquid, but it wasn't cooling. She took another soggy step and realised the liquid barely moved despite the disturbance. "I don't know what this is."

"So we have to swim through it?"

"I don't think we need to swim. We can probably reach the floor."

Wane stepped down fully, letting go of the railing, and the liquid came up to his mid-thigh. He was taller than Chandler, but it still shouldn't cover her completely. She briefly considered asking for a piggyback just to avoid the mess but quickly dismissed the idea. Plus, she was already wet with this *stuff* sticking to her clothes. It was too late to turn back or change tactics now.

"Through the puke water we go," Wane sang.

Chandler's insides squirmed as she followed him.

Thankfully they only took a few more steps into the weird water, the level of which kept rising higher to their midsections, before the flooring levelled out.

Once more an open space greeted them.

Besides light fixtures which still offered the same soft lavender glow, nothing stood. Some of it could've been partially submerged and hidden. But the light made it hard to see down into the liquid. Nothing stood out on its own.

Wading further into the room, Chandler could see the only way to go was left. To the right sat a blank concrete wall, maybe a place where a desk would've once been. Or a coffee table and chairs. Or a vending machine.

Chandler's stomach revolted at the thought of food.

"Why flood this place?" Wane asked as he waded in the other direction.

"To flush away traces of what had been here?" she answered, though she wasn't certain either.

They began to follow the curve of the place. "Why?" Wane dragged his hand along the wall. "We knew about the last lab. It was on maps and buildings. It wasn't impossible to reach, just bloody difficult."

Chandler's foot skidded on something she couldn't see. Her body tumbled. She caught herself before falling fully into the murk, but not before her left arm sank into the water as she tried to catch herself.

She stood upright and shook her sopping arm, scowling. Now the liquid was closer to her face, she could smell the undercurrent of something rotten. She fought the rising gag and immediately shoved her arm away from her body.

They needed to find something, *anything*, and get out. Then Chandler would get a decontamination shower, burn her clothes, and send a demand that Praxis should pay for therapy or a spa day to recover.

"Why a second lab?" Wane continued, clearly not having noticed her devastating stumble. "And why keep it so out of the way, remove everything from it, and then flood it? What was here that needed to be kept so secret?"

"The other one was probably a decoy," Chandler said. She stripped off her gloves again; there was no point in them anymore. "Or it did function as a lab. But the real work was done here."

"And we stumbled across it!" He turned to her, grinning. "What *luck*!"

It *was* luck. They'd only headed this way to avoid having to go back the other. When the last place had been a bust, the plan had been to keep going until they found safe space to be lifted out from.

But there were still some researchers missing. And they still had a mission to find them.

At the sight of a doorway, Chandler pushed her way into it. The water was somehow shallower inside; she couldn't tell where it was draining, but at least it sank back to ankle height.

Filing cabinets and bookcases littered the room. Chandler blinked at them. Surprise coursed through her at the sight or *things*. Though they hadn't explored much here yet, she'd expected this room to be no different than everywhere else they'd trapsed through.

Chandler took to one side of the room, Wane the other. He began to practically throw things off shelves, items falling into the liquid at their feet with soft splashes. Chandler dug through drawers and file holders with more care. Though, every time she came up empty, she'd slam the drawer shut again.

If this had been a real lab, and linked back to their theory of the last one being a decoy, it had to be for a reason. It was so secret – signpost out front ignored – and underground.

Most labs these days are linked to—

"Got it!" Wane yelled, cutting off Chandler's thoughts.

He trudged over to her, waving a piece of paper. She immediately saw the symbol at the bottom of the page and didn't fight down the urge to crack her knuckles.

"The New World Government," she spat.

The New World Government, a group of people from each existing country that sat and debated things on a global scale. They were responsible for Summit Talks – things affecting the climate and such – as well as sporting events, trade deals, and many other things too. Seemed they were also now responsible for this lab.

"Can you read it?" Wane questioned, shifting the paper this way and that.

"There's too much damage." Chandler shook her head. Whatever was in the water, it caused the ink to fade, but also the lighting wasn't helping clear things up either. "But... It's still sturdy paper." She took the page and shook it a little. It didn't tear or rip, but a drop of water slid off the bottom corner. "Maybe we could..." She drifted off.

"We could, what?"

"We need to get going."

Wane's eyes started to dart around. "Did you hear something?"

"No. But I have an idea."

"About what?"

"The paper. I think we can find out what it *did* say."

"You having an idea is more dangerous than anything I was thinking of."

Chandler glared at him but the intensity dropped from it when she spotted the playful grin every Grittal brother had apparently been given at birth. When he pulled a face like that, all rosy cheeks from laughter and ginger hair wild from the outside elements, it was hard to take him seriously.

She rolled her eyes. "Come on." She began to fold the paper into her upper coat pocket, wading away again. "We'll get out of this *water* and rest for a bit, even warm up and dry off. I might not feel the cold, but you will. Illness is not on my cards of things to collect from this mission."

"How are we going to warm up and dry? It's not exactly paradise here. And there's not a lot of space either."

"I'm sure we'll find a way." Chandler regretted the words as soon as her own ears heard them.

Wane laughed loudly. "I like some of your dangerous ideas," Wane teased.

"That's not what I meant."

"But that's what you just said."

"Oh, fuck off."

"I can't do that. You *just* lectured me on staying dry! Fucking off would mean walking in more goop."

"Then follow me to the top of the stairs where we will sit in silence while we wait for this shit to dry up. And if you don't, I'll find a way to switch powers and set you on fire. That'll keep us *both* toasty." She turned and started the trudge back.

Wane laughed behind her. "Yes, Ma'am!"

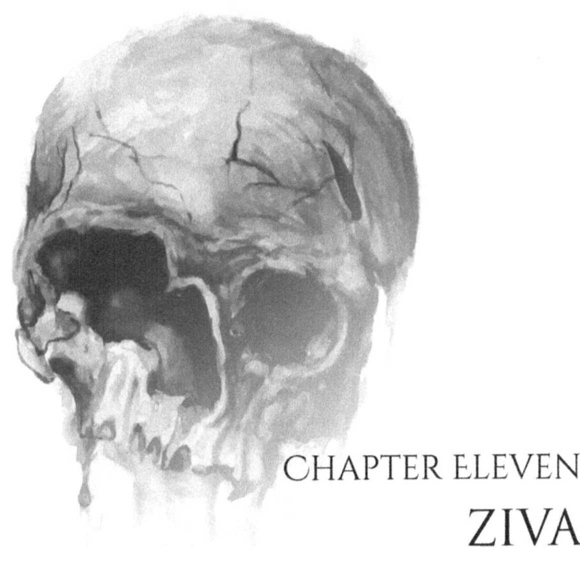

CHAPTER ELEVEN

ZIVA

22nd Day of Winter 2406

Ziva knew her Star of David necklace still hung from her throat, just as it always had, but her parents kept eyeing it suspiciously. Since meeting them outside the Hotel, they'd stared directly at it no less than seventeen times between them so far – Ziva had been counting. Even her grandmother had leaned on the table for a better examination.

She didn't know why they kept doing it. She fought the urge to tuck the star away, shielding it from their scrutinising glares.

Ziva had been the one to invite them here, to *EICHNER GRAND HOTEL*, for afternoon tea. A treat on her. A chance she was offering for them to catch up together. Yet they were treating her as if she didn't belong among them.

The hotel hadn't changed since the last time Ziva had been here. Including the front reception and the person occupying the welcome desk. She'd never seen this far in, however, so couldn't tell if this part was different in anyway. Last time, she'd been swept into an office with a job offer and then had been transported via private shuttle below ground.

Trying to hide her smile at what had become a fond memory because of what'd come attached to it – her joining Redwing – she peered around the room.

Lilac walls with what appeared to be real creeping vines – if the people going round spraying them with little bottles was any indication – spanned across the room. The ceiling had painted golden figures, but they were vaulted too high to distinguish the forms properly. Obscenely large gold and crystal chandeliers cascaded from the very tops to light the entire space. Round tables, clothed in white, had golden chairs tucked beneath them. Severs dressed in pressed white suits danced between those tables with golden platters or trays, offering delicate looking foods and small glasses to those currently taking lunch.

Just as Ziva watched one particular server swish through the doorway carrying a tray that had six odd shaped glasses perched on top, her grandmother's open-mouthed cough caught her attention. Ziva looked at her elders, part of her wishing she could've been left to watch the world in this room continue around her.

"How did you manage to book us a table here?" her grandmother asked. More than ever, her wrinkles buried her face behind all the years she'd lived. "And how did you afford it?"

"My new job pays well," Ziva answered simply.

It wasn't a complete lie. Working at Redwing *did* pay well; two hundred pieces a week to be exact. It was at least fifty pieces more than any *normal* sort of job. But she couldn't tell them that. They didn't know about Redwing, nor could they know.

EICHNER GRAND was just a hotel, however. Or so most were led to believe. But really it was just one more place secretly attached to Redwing. It also happened to be attached to Quinton's family – they owned the hotel and the franchise was named after the family itself. Whether Quinton's family were aware of what else their hotels were used for outside of lavish lunches and a good sleep was yet to be known.

Ziva's mother huffed. "As much as I know I will enjoy this," she said. "I would've preferred to have gone somewhere where my other children could've also joined."

Ziva now had to fight the urge to roll her eyes. She'd specifically chosen the hotel as a lunch spot because it had a strict "adults only" policy – "adults" meant anyone over eighteen. Not everything in her life needed to have her siblings attached to it, even if she did love them.

"There are plenty of other choices where we could've all been together," her mother continued. "A nice family meal, all of us!"

"We have them every day," Ziva said.

"But we could've had a *nice* one somewhere!"

"It's my money, Mumma," Ziva replied cautiously. "I wanted to treat the adults in my life to something special. Somewhere that offers us a grown-up afternoon so we can *all* treat ourselves."

"It's not nice to count them out."

"And it's not nice to always have to include them in everything either."

The table went silent. Ziva inwardly winced. She knew she shouldn't have spoken to her elders that way. She never would have done so before. But it was too late now. The words had fallen from her mouth and there was no stuffing them back in.

Her father sat back in his chair, an unimpressed gleam in his light brown eyes. "You've changed," he muttered. It was loud in Ziva's ears; a diss, an assessment, an acknowledgement that she wasn't who they thought she should be. "The way you talk to us. The way you exclude your family. The way you even *look*."

Her grandmother nodded along. "I'm surprised you still wear your necklace."

Ziva finally allowed herself to touch the star. "Why wouldn't I?"

"Why would you?" her mother countered. "We know you've never believed, we *try* at least. But... Look at you."

She didn't need to look, Ziva knew herself well enough.

Over the past weeks, she'd thrown out anything old and ruined and handed down that looked *wrong* on her – something she'd never have had the confidence to do before, because really she'd been lucky to get anything – and had replaced most of her wardrobe with things *she* wanted.

Today it was a knee-length red jumper dress with a silken white scarf at the waist for a belt. She'd paired it with the white boots she'd bought with her advance she'd received from before officially signing on to stay at Redwing.

Her hair had also been recently cut much shorter. The once long, black tresses now perched just onto her shoulders, her full fringe growing out slowly but surely. A tinted pink lipstick also lined her lips today, sharpening and defining her face somewhat. She looked and *felt* like an adult.

More than ever, she felt like herself.

That didn't stop the words from hurting though. Ziva felt the familiar burn of tears in the corners of her eyes.

"How am I different?" she asked, somehow managing to keep her tone level.

"A whole new person is sitting with us today," her grandmother scoffed.

Ziva swallowed a thick lump in her throat. "Is that really a bad thing?"

"Not always," her father conceded. Ziva knew he would say more, but he paused for a moment.

In the space her father left, a server approached their table. Bubbly drinks, hot vegetable soups, and baskets of bread were laid out. Everyone grabbed something in the silence. Ziva drank deeply and nearly choked on the fizz. It didn't stop her from doing it again though. She needed something else to focus on.

The server disappeared and Ziva felt herself deflate with their leave – it'd been her one moment of reprieve, when someone else had been here to block the onslaught she felt brewing.

Her father slathered a thick layer of butter onto a roll. "There is nothing of you left," he finished.

Ziva surprised herself by lowering her glass calmly; her heart didn't feel heavy, yet it also didn't feel light, just slightly hollow. "There is more than enough of me left. I'm still the same. Actually, I feel *better* than the same."

"You are not yourself," her grandmother argued. She sipped at her soup viciously; Ziva cringed and didn't dare look up to see how many eyes were on them.

"I am."

"Are you really? Could you really still be the girl who was born first? The girl who looked after her siblings on cold nights and during long days? The girl who respected her elders and taught her youngers to respect them too? The woman who went to provide for her family? A woman who looked up to her parents, watched them work hard, and aspired to do the same?"

"I'm still all of those things." Ziva felt like she was caught in a loop.

"Are you sure?" her mother questioned. "You don't *look* much like that girl anymore."

"That's because I'm not a girl. I'm a woman."

Her grandmother's laughter sounded cruel. "You are not."

"You yourself just said I was a woman. Am I or am I not? I can't be both or neither."

Soup splashed onto the tablecloth before her grandmother as she snorted. She scowled at the stain as if it'd been the soup's fault for jumping out of the spoon. "You are *far* from a woman," she chided. "You are barely a babe out in the new world. A little babe in a forest of wolves that *will* eat you alive if you continue on this damp and dark path. It's unforgiving."

"How do I stop being a little babe?" Ziva found herself asking.

The oldest woman at the table offered a mocking smile. "Once you have experienced the world we have, *then* I will consider you more. But while you're still acting like a child, I will call you one."

"But—"

"The way to walk is by keeping your head down and working hard. By listening. By doing as you're told, when you're told." Ziva's grandmother shook her head. "You changed your look and how you act, you no longer treat your family, your *elders* with the respect—"

"No," Ziva cut in. Her grandmother's eyes flashed with anger. "I refuse to scrub away who I am. I won't give up everything for the sake of everyone else. Just because I want to have something doesn't mean everyone else has to have it too and I have to be the one to share it all."

"How *dare you* show such disrespect!" Her father's words were hissed.

"I didn't—"

"Oh, you did!" Her mother threw her napkin onto the tabletop.

"No—"

"After this meal," her grandmother's voice cut right to Ziva, "you are to *quit* your job. Clearly it has muddled your brain and is the root cause of your destruction. Then you are to return home where you will be brought back and you will remember your values and promises. We will accept you back. If you respect us, we will help you back onto your feet, child. We will love you back to yourself."

"No."

All eyes fell on Ziva, and for once she didn't shrug them off. "What do you mean, *no*?" her grandmother gritted out.

"I love my job and I love those I work with. No one in my family is entitled to anything I do or make any longer just because we're related by blood. I still love you, I always will, and I get that you're struggling, but your financial problems aren't mine. I wasn't brought into this world just to look after whatever other kids you decided to have. And, above all, I *refuse* to give up anything more about myself, or suppress it for longer, just because you don't like it or won't accept it. You are not me and I am not you. I am my own individual person. Something none of you have ever seen because we all have to have the same thing, do the same job, walk and talk and breathe the same way. I'm sorry, but I can't do that anymore."

In one solid movement, Ziva kicked out her chair and stood. She was aware of other eyes in the room now on her skin, but the feeling didn't tingle. It just riled her up further.

She stormed from the room in silence.

From behind the front reception desk, the man she'd met before raised his bushy eyebrows at her. She drew out her bankcard, paid for the lunches, and left the building.

She waited by the curb for a few minutes until a private roadway shuttle arrived for her; she'd messaged ahead of leaving inside. She stepped into the shuttle without looking back.

"Everything alright?"

Ziva turned in her seat to face Abel, one of the guards of Redwing. He was supposed to be off duty today but had both dropped her at the hotel and had waited to pick her up again.

Her eyes welled instantly. "I just yelled at my family."

Abel pulled the car into traffic. "Oh."

She half-laughed at the absurdity. "Is that all you have to offer?"

"Is there anything I can say to make it better? Or do you just want to me listen as you rant?"

Ziva clasped at her own shaking hands. She'd never yelled or stood up to anyone before. Let alone her own family.

Everything felt wrong. Her skin itched on the inside. The guilt... The guilt had begun to build and was already starting to burn, the years of having to respect her elders no matter what finding its way through her body to make her squirm. An in-built response from years of never challenging the notion when she'd never once been given an ounce of respect in turn.

"I don't know," she whispered.

"Ziva." He only said her name, but it was enough.

"They are my *family*. I cared for them for years, did every-thing to help them however I could manage. I love them and I know they love me, even if they never say it and rarely show it. But I *can't*..." She choked momentarily on a sob. "I can't keep locking myself away, hoping they'll set me free one day like some pet. I have to steal the key and let myself out." She sniffed and wiped under her eyes on the ends of her sleeves. "It's ridiculous. It's *all* ridiculous."

Reaching across the space, Abel grabbed her hand and squeezed. Shocked, she looked directly at him. His eyes were still forward, his other hand still on the steering wheel, but she could see his knuckles were white and his brow was furrowed.

"I'm sorry," she whispered. She tried to slip her hand back but Abel held on.

"Don't."

"What?" she asked.

Abel still wouldn't meet her eye, even for a second. "You've already said you don't want to lock yourself up anymore. So don't. Don't apologise for *feeling something*. You're entitled to your emotions, especially in this moment."

She took several deep breaths. "I'm okay, I promise."

"I believe you." Finally, his green eyes turned to her for a brief glance. They were gone quickly, but a small smile crept onto his face. "You look lovely in that dress."

A laugh escaped her. "I've just been crying!"

"And you can still look lovely."

"I'm not an ugly crier?"

"I never said that." He winked as she laughed again. "Do you want to go somewhere else now?"

Instead of getting to answer, Ziva picked up her phone as it started ringing. Abel pulled his hand away then and Ziva felt conflicted about it.

"Hello?" she answered, not willing to feed *that* emotion right now.

"Z?" Chandler's voice was crackly, like the connection was poor. "You there?"

Ziva sat bolt upright. "Chandler? Are you alright?"

"We're on... back. We'll be landing... hour... need your help..."

"My help?"

"Can... meet?"

"Meet you? Where?"

"City... Maybe... *au Lait...*?"

Ziva smiled to herself. "I'll be there." She cut the call, hoping Chandler had heard her, and turned to Abel. "There is somewhere I need to go."

He nodded once. "Just tell me where."

After a rather awful start to her day, Ziva hadn't thought it would've picked up again. But she could accept being wrong, and after that call, she was open to believe that things might get better after all.

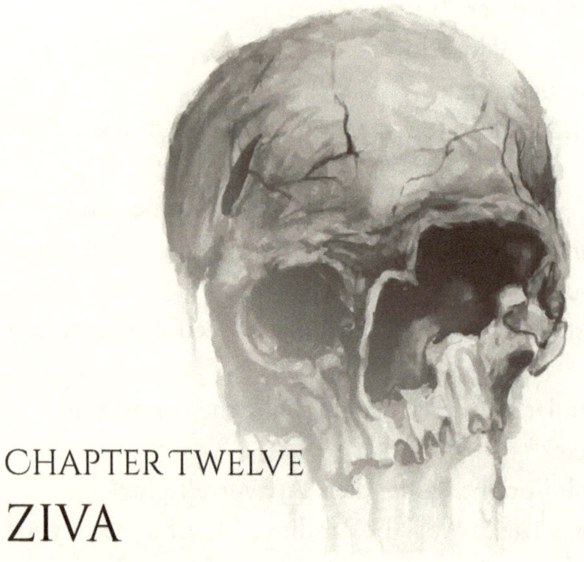

CHAPTER TWELVE

ZIVA

22ⁿᵈ Day of Winter 2406

You can't just sit in the car," Ziva argued.

Abel didn't look her way. "If I am obligated to, I will."

"You're not obligated at all! I haven't asked you to stay here." Even if he wouldn't look, Ziva stared at the side of his face. She hoped he could feel her stare and changed tactics slightly. "Have you eaten yet today? Drank anything? What about taking a simple moment *off* since it's your day off?"

"I offered to drive you around today."

"But that's part of your everyday role normally!"

"I like that."

"It's your day off. They're meant for *breaks* away from normal working life."

"And I don't mind helping you."

Ziva sighed; it didn't feel like she was winning this fight. "One tea?" she offered. "I'm buying."

Abel's green eyes finally found hers, and they narrowed. "You're buying?"

"If it gets you inside, yes."

He still seemed cautious, reluctant. "I don't normally hang around other recruits. I have a different job from you."

That was an ongoing argument. Abel thought he was on a different level to Ziva. He thought that he only protected the other recruits and their base, while those like Ziva did the "real" work. Ziva thought everyone was equally as important. Each role supported the next.

She let it go for today. "It's one cup of tea while I talk to Chandler. You don't even have to chat if you don't want. You can sulk in a far-off corner if you feel better about it."

A rare brief look of amusement crossed his face. "Sulk?"

"That face you pull sometimes?" She signalled to his face. "You're kind of doing it now."

"I'm a grown man. There is no *sulking*."

"Please? Just come inside?"

Another crack seemed to appear in Abel's resolve, except Ziva couldn't figure out its meaning. But he said nothing. He just motioned with his hand for her to lead on.

Ziva bundled out of the private roadway shuttle. She could hear Abel's footsteps well enough behind her to know he was indeed following – he still wore his heavy work boots even on his day off.

She turned briefly and tried not to laugh at his sulk, which he did have, and how the expression didn't match up with the overall towering size of him. When he looked at her curiously, she tried to blame her laughter on the naming of shuttles – they had once meant trains or trams – or roadway shuttles – which were once called cars. Abel didn't look like he was buying it, but it didn't matter as Ziva reached the elevator first.

The doors shut as soon as he was inside too and they began to rise.

Café au Lait hung over-top the street below. Shuttles of all kinds and people frequently went about underneath it. The last time Ziva had been here, it'd been with Chandler and Quinton last season. Quinton had been the one to introduce the girls to the place.

Ziva glanced around. It was funny how two things in one day related back to that first mission *and* Quinton.

The elevator stopped moments later and the doors creaked open. Abel motioned for Ziva to exit first, ever the protector and gentleman.

There appeared to have been no change in the place since the last time Ziva had been a customer here.

The six small tables were still round with white tablecloths but the green chairs were now a deep sunset orange. Two servers darted around, still in a uniform of dark jeans and logo'd t-shirts, while a third person manned the till at the back. New shelving had been put up behind the main counter to display the varying tins of tea for sale; Ziva debated getting more of the sort she'd been gifted by Quinton last time – Pink Rose Tea.

Ziva breathed in the smell of brewing tea and small, fresh pastries. Even if the outside world felt cold, the winter season beginning to draw itself in, this place felt warm. Like a blanket or a hug or a comforting ember of a still-burning fire.

With no sign of Chandler yet, Ziva found a table at the side and slid into a chair. Curiously, Abel chose to sit opposite and not hide in a corner. His brown leather jacket rucked up but he refused to take it off, settling for adjusting it as best he could. Ziva tilted her head at him.

On her introductory day to all this, just before her underground shuttle ride to Redwing that first time, they'd met because he had offered her an orange to eat. They hadn't talked much. Not until she'd gone for a midnight stroll in what would become her new home's gardens. She'd come across him on duty, patrolling the grounds closest to the building, and they'd kept each other company for a little while.

Ziva had noticed that Abel didn't seem to talk much to the other residents, but he would to her. Even if sometimes it was only a "hello". It was definitely more than most got.

She'd joined him on more of his nightly walks since becoming a full time resident at Redwing, even bringing out tea for him. He never shooed her away, appearing more than welcoming to her company. They would often stroll in silence, but whatever they did, it always felt comfortable to do.

She knew he had an older sister called Faith who was a dental nurse. He liked driving. He loathed having to wear his beret with his uniform. And he always wished he could paint but didn't have an artistic bone in his body.

Abel glanced around the room, and Ziva watched him. A pink flush adorned his ivory skin as the cold's touch lingered. The scar that ran through his right eyebrow and past the eye was visible under the café's lights. He didn't seem to care though, letting the world see it. His lips were plump and his throat bobbed as he swallowed, sending a ripple down his facial hair that was a shade darker than his head hair.

His eyes suddenly snapped to hers, the corner of his mouth quirking. She darted her gaze away, nervous.

There was no denying that he was physically pleasing to look at. More than once she'd wondered what it would be like to hug or maybe what it would feel like to kiss him.

But she'd never kissed anyone before. She didn't know if she truly even wanted that. She'd never felt the urge to bring herself close to someone in the past, but around Abel it seemed like she did want that. Like when he touched her hand in the car.

Ziva couldn't decide properly though. They were friends, her and Abel, weren't they? But did she want to change that? Did she want more than friendship with him? Was that even *allowed*?

It was all just confusing.

Today was confusing.

She needed to speak to Chandler about it all.

"Z?"

Ziva looked up at the call of her name. Like her thoughts had summoned her, Chandler came strolling into the café.

Ziva jumped out of her seat and dashed at her friend. Chandler embraced her back.

"Bloody skies above," Ziva cursed, pulling back. "You're *freezing*."

"I did warn her on the way over she was making everything colder," Wane said as he came up behind Chandler. He was dressed head to toe in an outfit perfect for an icy winter.

Chandler shrugged. "I feel fine." *She* was dressed in her green mushroom cardigan, boots, and dramatically flared black trousers.

"You're *made* of ice, Icy," Wane whispered carefully. There was a table currently occupied by on-break semi-rowdy builders, and another had an elderly couple slurping tea rather loudly. Those people were further into the café, out the way of their conversation, but no one could be too careful. "The rest of us? Nope. Plain old skin and blood and can feel the chill factor. And just because you *can* drag the stuff towards you doesn't mean you *should*."

Chandler glared at him. "I don't always do it on purpose."

Wane leaned round them both, clearly noticing something. "What's the guard doing here? Do we need protecting? Is something happening?"

Ziva didn't look behind her. "I offered to buy him tea for driving me over," she answered. "He picked me up from my family lunch."

"Did he." Chandler hadn't phrased it as a question, and when Ziva met her gaze, she could see that it hadn't meant to be one.

Ziva fake coughed and changed the subject. "Tea?"

"I'll take a hot chocolate if they have them?" Wane said.

Chandler rolled her eyes but Ziva pulled her away to the counter to order before she could comment on Wane's choice of drink.

A young looking server brought over the teas – one Pink Rose for Ziva, one herbal combination for Abel, and one jasmine for Chandler – as well as a hot chocolate in a bobbled glass. A little tower of sandwiches and plate of warm shortbread were also provided.

While they'd waited, Chandler and Wane caught Ziva up to speed.

From their far north travels, Wane and Chandler had brought back a piece of paper. Wane pulled out the document. It'd been tucked inside a plastic wallet, but Ziva could see the droplets clinging to the inside. She tried to not bite her lip.

"Can you do this?" Wane asked, handing it over.

The colour of the paper, the ink colouring specifically, was so faded it was hard to tell if it'd ever once even been written on at all. There were just a few marks that indicated that it had.

Ziva's abnormality revolved around colour. She could change it, manipulate it, even take it away or give some back. She could drain the colour out of an apple to make it stark white or tint the light in a room to complete blackness. Or she could illuminate even the smallest rainbow prism to blind, or just turn someone's hair a new colour.

Because of that, Wane and Chandler were hoping Ziva could revert the colour of the page they'd rescued to what it had once been, and hopefully restore the writing in the process.

"I think so," she wavered, sounding and feeling uncertain.

After a single nod, Chandler subtly touched the document. Whatever liquid had been trapped alongside the paper began to solidify slightly; it didn't appear like it would completely turn to ice but it shifted states of being enough.

Once she was sure everything had been successfully frozen enough, Chandler withdrew the document with her free hand and passed the rigid page over to Ziva who nearly dropped it. It was *so cold*. She hadn't been expecting such a vast temperature difference. But she realised she should have.

Abel shifted his body across the table, and Ziva realised that he'd been using his body as a sort of shield to block what they'd been doing against potential onlookers. He grabbed some napkins and slipped them around the paper's edge. Ziva took them from him, thankful for an extra layer of protection against the ice, though it wouldn't do much for long.

Ziva was aware that Chandler looked once between her and Abel. She could feel her friend's eyes, but Chandler said nothing.

Focusing on the task at hand, Ziva zoned in on the symbol at the top of the paper. It was the easiest bit to make out, so she slowly filled in the blanks in her mind.

On the page, the symbol began to form brighter.

Looking further down, Ziva could see faint markings and tiny scratches where the words should've been. She could see a completed document in her mind, typed letters fully distinct. She began to pull that image to the forefront of her mind, honing in on the black of the ink that would stamp each letter or symbol.

She watched in real time as the words refilled the page.

In her hands, the document returned to its former, colourful self.

Excited and brimming with renewed energy, Wane stole it. Most of the ice had gone and the paper was back to being limp without being soggy, so they let him read in silence.

Ziva worried about the other café patrons but Abel shifted again. In all the times they'd spoken, she'd never once asked about his abnormality and he'd never once offered it. All she knew was that it'd led to him being a protector, or guard.

Could it he be some sort of shield? He had used his body twice already to hide what they'd been doing at the table. It would make sense.

"I forget about your power sometimes," Abel commented quietly.

Ziva blinked, surprised. "What?" She'd just been thinking about *his* gift, yet here he was mentioning hers.

"You don't ever use it," he explained. "Or, hardly ever do. Especially compared to a lot of those..." He trailed off. "Compared to everyone else. Chandler aside."

"Thanks," Chandler commented blandly.

"I meant that you try to not use yours either," he said. It was the most Ziva knew of him to talk to others. "You don't show off. I don't know if that's because everyone else is comfortable or what."

Chandler cracked her knuckles but said nothing.

Abel acknowledged that with a single nod.

"I never have a need to use it," Ziva said, choosing then to respond to Abel. "Unless I'm dying someone's walls or hair."

"Or restoring a lost artefact to its true glory," Chandler added, smiling.

Ziva offered a shy smile in return. "That was once." She indicated to the paper to take attention away from herself. "What does it say?" She hadn't read it before Wane had taken it back.

Wane lowered the page, his expression gloomy. "They were researching us."

"Us?" Ziva asked.

"They had a second lab hidden away," his attention went to Chandler, "because they were studying Abnormals there."

"It says that?" Ziva heard the pitch of her voice raise.

Wane nodded. "Right here in black and white."

Chandler sighed and gripped her mug; the steam that had been rising out of it abruptly stopped. "Why am I not even fucking surprised?"

"This is a letter of approval for field tests."

"Field tests?" Ziva stared at the paper still in Wane's hands. "What does that even mean?"

"It *means* they've found one of us that interests them enough to study further. This grants the scientists permission, by the power of the *government,* to take the poor Abnormal sod out into the world and test their powers to see how they work in a different environment."

"Surely they must know how it works? They must know enough about our genes already?"

"Science makes new developments all the time," Chandler hissed under her breath.

"They determined they had the gene mutation, yeah. It doesn't say what abnormality either. But whatever else they had that prompted a grant on a field trip? It's not in this letter," Wane continued. "It does say they've gone to an island though."

"So our missing researchers are out galivanting and prodding the world with needles, and they're not actually missing?" Chandler asked. She let go of her mug and Ziva was sure if she touched it, her fingers would come away cold. "Fucking brilliant. Waste of our fucking time."

"Why an Island?" Ziva questioned.

"I don't know. Something to do with it being the best place?" Wane shook his head, uncertainty evident. "But it's in the Caribbean." He grinned. "Tropical air and suntans here we come!"

Ziva stilled. "The Caribbean?"

"Yeah!" Wane's smile slipped. "What? Is that a problem?"

"That's where Gretchen and Flora have gone."

"They're on an island too?" Chandler scowled. "Is it the same one?"

Ziva quickly read over the document as it was passed to her and nodded. "By the looks of this, yeah. They went a day or two ago."

"What for?"

Ziva shook her head, her hair tickling the side of her neck. "No one let anything slip."

"It has to do with gold," Wane blurted. He shrugged when Ziva and Chandler both looked at him in unison. "That's Flora's *thing*."

"Let me get this right." Chandler took a sip of her definitely chilled tea, grimacing. "Our supposedly missing researchers weren't missing at all, but have gone off to some island to experiment on someone like us," she drank again, "and our workmates have gone off, maybe to the same island, on a mission to do with something gold?" She took a bigger gulp this time. "Could these things be related somehow? Why *this* Island?"

Wane shrugged a second time. "We'll find out when we get there. Maybe we can meet up with them?"

Chandler grimaced again, this time subtly, and if Ziva hadn't been close she would've missed it; she didn't think the expression had anything to do with the tea this time though.

"I'll drop you at the port," Abel declared. Everyone visibly startled at his voice; he'd been deafeningly quiet up until then. He looked at Ziva directly. "I'm assuming you're going too?"

She opened and closed her mouth a few times. "It's not my mission."

"Of course you're coming with us," Chandler said instantly.

Ziva laughed weakly. "I don't have anything on me."

"We don't either. Not for a warm climate," Wane told her. "We'll do a quick drive home and leave again?" He eyed Abel out the corner of his eye. "If you're cool with that?"

Abel shrugged noncommittally. "It's my job to drive if that's what you need."

"It's your *day off*," Ziva argued back.

Abel rolled his eyes but it wasn't rude, rather like he was mildly amused.

"Won't Praxis and them get annoyed if we leave?" Chandler asked Abel.

"People come and go all the time. They have to." Abel dropped his voice low for what he said next. "You're on an open mission. When you have your debrief at the end, you can explain it all to them. You won't get in trouble for anything. Not unless you're causing harm or about to, which you're not. But if you're concerned, I can slip them a note or a relay a message?"

"I think that's settled that," Wane said. "We'll hop home, leave you," he nodded at Abel, "with a message in case anyone asks, and we *go*."

The group finished up before piling back into Abel's shuttle.

Quiet fell over the group but they didn't need to talk. Their coordinates were set. They were headed to Redwing and then the Caribbean.

Being upfront, Ziva could spy Abel. His sights were set almost forcefully on the drive. His knuckles weren't white on the wheel, but there was something distant about him suddenly. She didn't know why her heart slowed for a beat.

Like he'd done, she forced herself watch out the front window. She made a promise with herself to not dwell on anything that would confuse her right now.

She had a mission, something to pull her forwards.

And for now that had to be her singular direction and focus.

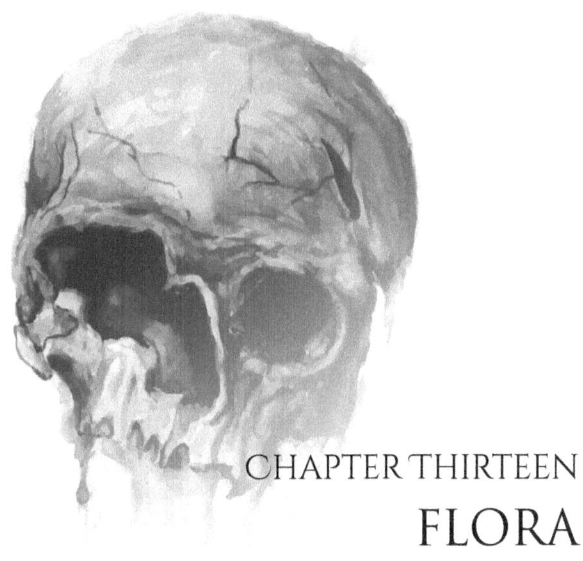

CHAPTER THIRTEEN
FLORA

23rd Day of Winter 2406

The island accepted visitors, just never many.

Flora and Gretchen stumbled across a small dwelling. Someone soon spotted them and they were ushered into an air-cooled building. Though slightly dazed, they quickly realised they'd been pulled into a small hotel. In the lobby, they were instantly supplied with lukewarm water and a fruit snack to replenish.

They'd been promptly shown to a room and had fallen asleep almost instantly, waking not long ago to a soft sea-breeze blowing through the three windows that had been opened at some point.

Flora stayed in the bed under the fresh crystal white sheets, gazing out across the pure blue water. She wondered how they'd missed it on their walk over. But then she remembered the awkward curvature of the island.

Last night, as they'd been shown to their room, Flora and Gretchen had been informed that those who came to the island usually only did so for a short break. Not many people stayed at any one time, hence the readily available accommodation. But it also wasn't a surprise for the residents to find people they'd never met wandering around either.

Finding this place had been pure accident. A good one, Flora would argue.

Eventually Flora moved from under the soft clouds around her. By the time she returned from her shower, her dripping hair pinned up with a single clip, Gretchen had rolled over in bed to eat a fresh thick slice of melon.

Flora walked right past.

If they'd been friends, she would've offered to put the rinds in the bin or warned her to sit up so she wouldn't choke or ruin the sheets with juices. But they weren't friends. And as much as they lived or worked together, some paths never really crossed. Gretchen had made it abundantly clear that she wasn't interested in getting to know anyone other than Quinton.

Like she could sense Flora's thoughts, Gretchen said, "I'm takin' tiny bites so I won't choke and die."

Flora slipped into her lightweight cotton clothes. "Good. I was about to warn you."

"Yeah, your face scrunches up when you're weighin' something up so I figured I better put you out your misery." Gretchen put another rind quarter on the plate beside her bed. "Which way we 'eading today?"

Flora finally turned to her companion. "Do we have a new heading?"

"Not really." Gretchen shimmied herself into a better sitting position. Her usually neatly drawn eyebrows and thick eyeliner were completely gone, making her look younger, *softer*. Flora had never seen her like that before; she wondered if anyone had.

"All we've got is the mission brief," Flora said, redirecting her thoughts. "Find where this island got enough money to pay off its debts. That's it."

"Tha's it," Gretchen grumbled back.

What could they even do? Money had been exchanged *somehow*. It had to have come from somewhere. But where? And where could they even go to figure this out? They couldn't just walk into a bank and request to see every transaction this island had ever made since it began.

"One island paying off all its debts," Flora mumbled as she adjusted her shirt. "A *new* one at that?"

"Wha' you thinkin'?" Gretchen raised a very faint thin strip of an eyebrow. "They're stealing the money from somewhere, maybe?"

"Money? Gold?"

Gretchen sat up to her full height. The covers slipped down to her waist, unveiling a tattered black bra, but she didn't bother to cover herself. "Gold?" she questioned. "Where would they 'ave stolen that from?"

Flora shuffled round to her bed. "I don't know. A shipwreck that was abandoned before this place became a thing? Maybe someone dived, discovered it, and took in the haul?"

"Your theory is a *gold thief*?"

"What theory have you got? What plans are *you* suggesting?"

A dark smile warped Gretchen's face. "*Whoa*, Florist Fancy."

Flora's cheek twitched in annoyance at the horrible nickname she'd been cursed with just because she dressed well and talked properly. "Don't call me that, please."

"I forgot you were sensitive to it," Gretchen said, showing no sign of an actual apology.

"I'm not *sensitive*. I don't like it."

"You're gettin' pretty worked up abou' it."

"I'm not."

"Tell that to your voice and tone and—"

"*You* are working me up! *You!*" Flora scrubbed her hands in the air like she could wipe away the conversation. She hadn't meant to be wound so tight, but Gretchen seemed to have the key to do so. If her power hadn't been bones, Flora would've sworn Gretchen could twist people. "Sorry."

"By all means, continue," Gretchen said, sounding entirely unbothered by the outburst. "You were on some sort of roll."

Flora sighed and tried to recentre herself. "We know the island paid its debts. We know money is now all one unit, we buy and pay for everything, everywhere, in *pieces*."

"It's the worlds currency," Gretchen agreed.

"But is it really that crazy to think of *old money*? Of old gold?" Flora continued. "Ships used to sink all the time. If we're going by *that* theory, is it crazy to think that one sank somewhere near the coast here, tipping gems or gold or *something* into the sea, and someone collected and claimed it?"

"Old money still exists," Gretchen said. "There's stories all the time about people findin' old coins or notes in their grandparents attics. Banks still accept it and exchange it."

Years ago, the world had converted to use all one currency called *pieces*. Leaders long dead now had brought down the order in a way to make sure there was no exchange rates or unfair pricings as the world changed. New lands forming as old ones merged or died meant there was a need for an upheaval in the system. If everyone went by the same rules, then it was a base fairness.

"Alright, Florist," Gretchen stuck a pale leg out from under the covers, "how do we go about *proving* this theory?"

Ignoring the reemerged nickname moments after saying she disliked it, Flora said, "We need to investigate shipwrecks. Maybe old shipping records? The island is *new* but they might have information about the area itself."

"Sure. I 'ave nothing better to do or say." Gretchen fully peeled her covers away and stalked into the bathroom, the lock on the door clicking slowly behind her.

Flora threw herself backwards onto her bed and covered her face with her hands. She'd only just woken yet exhaustion wanted to bury her.

This was going to be a long trip.

Hours later, Gretchen and Flora were still sifting through local news articles and history papers. Not that the history went too far back – the island was too new to have that much of a rich backstory yet.

But while the island had only recently been birthed from the seas compared to others, the technology was somehow still behind the rest of the world's.

Computers were still clunky and papers were still a printed item. Those things *did* still exist elsewhere, it just hadn't been the norm for a long, *long* time. At one point, the world had done everything virtually. That'd changed back when a few people who couldn't trust what technology might type became the bigger crowd. A system of screens and printed paper existed together again, but not to this *full* extent.

The island's library was small. One single floor covered the entire landscape. Shelves were jammed with books and papers and leaflets and files.

Despite the research they needed to focus on, Flora's mind kept wandering back to her family and Redwing. What had Aleema played on the piano these past few nights, or were her nightmares staying at bay without the music? Had Dalton hacked into anywhere he found fun just because, or was he keeping his mind intrigued learning some new skill? Was Preston out on another mission, or was he practising on the balance beams in the garden?

Her heart missed them.

With a deep sigh, Gretchen threw her stacks of papers onto the table hard enough that the top ones skidded off and slipped to the floor. "Look," she hissed, mentally pulling Flora back into the room. "The sooner we get this done, the sooner you can go 'ome again."

Flora blinked, caught off guard. "I wasn't—"

"You've been stuck in your own fuckin' mind all day."

"I miss them, okay!"

"So let's do the work and get you back."

Flora narrowed her eyes. "You say that like you don't have anyone to return to."

Gretchen snorted, hard and ungracefully. "I don't."

"That can't be—" Flora cut herself off.

It was too late though; Gretchen's eyes widened in recognition. "Can't be right?" She tilted her head, smug smile creeping onto her lips. "Use that pretty head of yours. You've seen me in that place. What *actually* do I have there? A single room of things? A place where the people talk so loudly around me I can't hear my own damn thoughts? People who cook and wash for me? Other people who let me join their afternoon picnic because they see me wandering around on my own?"

"There's more *there* than that," Flora tried to argue.

"*You* 'ave more."

"And you don't?"

"No."

"Quinton will come back."

Again, Flora saw the physical effects of her mistaken words as Gretchen's right eyebrow rose. Gretchen's whole demeanour changed, darkened, in front of Flora's eyes.

"Will he now?" Gretchen challenged. "He's been gone almost a full season. That's not usual mission time. That's him signing the fuck out."

"He wouldn't leave you like that. He wouldn't just *go*, not without a goodbye."

Flora knew how attached Gretchen and Quinton had been. All of Redwing had seen. They were each other's shadow. No one could touch them or invade the little space they had between them.

Gretchen rolled her eyes, feigning indifference. "Whatever."

"Fine. Shut down."

Flora didn't know why she was getting so upset over this, but she could feel her eyes beginning to sting and a ringing in her ears. Maybe it was because she was missing her own people and could sympathise on some level with the other girl. But at least *she* felt her emotions instead of stuffing them inside her chest in a locked up box.

"Ex-fucking-cuse me?" Gretchen asked.

"I'm just saying," Flora knew she needed to tread carefully, keeping her voice as steady as she could, "that it's okay for you to miss him. I miss my friends too. And you're right, the sooner we get done here, the sooner we can get back to them." She took a deep, steadying breath. "And I really do believe that he hasn't signed away from this, that he hasn't just vanished and given all this up. He would've said goodbye. You'll see him again."

Gretchen's eyes flicked up to Flora's. Emotion was written behind the stare but Flora couldn't pick up on what exactly the hidden text said. She studied her companion's face, trying to discover the meaning, but Gretchen lowered her gaze again too quickly.

Flora's heart ached. For one single second, she saw life as Gretchen would. With no family and now no real friends either. Gretchen had always come off as angry and wild, but closed off and alone too. Most of the reason why no one could get anywhere with her or Quinton was because she wouldn't let them in – he would, he'd tried to be friends with others at Redwing.

But Gretchen purposefully kept herself locked away for some reason. Something had made her that way. And part of Flora wanted to reach out to try and correct it somehow. She wanted to offer what she had so Gretchen wasn't so alone.

But that couldn't be done in one day.

"Tell me again what you were saying," Flora said lightly. "Then *we* can get back and you can kick Quinton's butt for making you come here with me." She hated the idea of violence, but something in her said Gretchen would appreciate it.

Gretchen's mouth quirked at the corners. "Did you really just say *butt*?"

Flora grimaced. "I'm not good with this."

"Clearly not. But it's a good thing I'm 'ere."

"Is it?"

"I can teach you how talk."

"I'm not sure I exactly want to learn."

"You'll pick it up by accident. It'll be *all you*."

The teasing continued as Gretchen went back to explain what she'd found, and this time Flora really did try to listen.

There was a dock on the beach, and apparently a small museum, too, that they needed to visit. Gretchen decided it might be able shed some light on the well-enough documented shipwrecks nearby. If they wanted to prove their theory right, that this island's debts were paid off by old money, then that was where they needed to head.

Closing up their books and putting them back, they headed out into the sweltering afternoon heat. A few locals passed them water – something they did for free just to make sure everyone stayed hydrated – and Flora thanked them as they went by.

It wasn't until she got to the beach, quietly coming to stand beside her grumpy again companion, that she realised she hadn't thought about her friends or Preston *once* since their rather heated conversation. She wasn't forgetting them. It was something else.

Unfortunately, Flora could also be considered closed off, just in other ways compared to Gretchen. But that one conversation with her companion had her sort of coming round to the idea of making room inside herself for the possibility of *more*. Maybe. Eventually. One day.

QUINTON

23rd Day of Winter 2406

Someone was following Quinton.

The further along he traipsed, the more footprints he laid, the more he became aware of a shadow at his back.

He tried to change his course a couple of times, but he knew he couldn't stray too far; he had a path to follow and if he lost sight of that he didn't know the land well enough to get back.

When he became certain his stalker took every circle-back or curve he did, he ducked behind a tree the first chance he got. He waited with baited breath. He counted the approaching footsteps though the stalker appeared to be trying to be quiet.

He turned the tables on his follower and jumped out on them.

The shadow yelped in surprise.

So did Quinton when he *realised*.

"What are *you doing here?*" he half-screeched. His eyes searched over Darlene with all the intensity of a worrying mother, or more accurately *brother*. The worry soured his insides, bubbling too hot and too fast under his skin.

"You disappeared," Darlene answered simply. She wore no concern on her face, and instead a concerning lack of care.

"Your *mother*—"

"Knows where I am."

Quinton was half certain his eyes had bugged out of his head and fallen entirely out of his skull. "There is *no way* she knows! You got on a plane and followed me, *here*. We are *so* out of normal life! How did you even get a ticket? What are you doing? *Why?*"

"I got a ticket the same way you did." Darlene pulled out a familiar looking silver card. "You forgot this."

Quinton stole his credit card back. "I didn't *leave* it anywhere!"

"Fine. I took it from your pocket. You really should keep a better eye on your things."

"How do you even know the pin to use it?" Quinton wanted to tear his hair out. "And what clerk let you use it?"

"I said I was with you and she accepted it. I had your card and do look enough like you." Darlene shrugged.

"I need to put in some *complaints*."

"Leave her alone! She was nice."

Quinton groaned and ran a hand through his loose hair. "Why are you doing this, Day?"

"You disappeared and left," she repeated, this time quieter. Quinton backed off a step and looked at her again. Now he could spy the flushed cheeks that didn't look like they came from the overall heat of the place, and the way her eyes had turned glassy. "And mum *does* know where I am," she continued. Reaching into her shorts pocket, she pulled out a square of paper. "I think she knew I'd follow you before I knew I would."

Quinton took the paper and unfolded it. Darlene's mother had written her a note, the handwriting messier than normal, but still decipherable as hers.

"I found it in my bag on the plane," Darlene told him.

Quinton tried to not crumple the note. "How did I not see you?"

She shrugged again. "I hid."

A startled laugh escaped him. "*Hid*? Where? The cargo hold? It's kind of my job to notice things and people that hide."

"You must be really shit at your job."

"*Hey*! Who taught you that word?"

"I've heard you and Ma say it."

"You're not allowed to use it."

"Why not? You can't have a different rule from me."

"I can."

"Why?"

"I'm older." It was a bad excuse and Quinton knew it.

"You're boring," Darlene huffed. "Well, except the bit where you snuck off and got on a plane. I was two rows behind you the whole flight, by the way. Your blue hair kind of sticks out a lot."

"Then you followed me onto a boat?"

"It wasn't difficult."

Quinton ran his fingers through his hair again, both out of habit and for something to do with his hands that didn't include throwing his sister into the water.

He glanced out to sea, at the bobbing boats on the soft waves. Could he somehow get Darlene to ride back? But that would mean leaving her alone. Even though he hadn't known she was with him getting here, she had been. If she stayed at his side, he would at least know where she was. Yet he couldn't promise she'd be any safer.

Two paths involving his sister's future were splitting in front of his eyes. The first led to sending her home on her own somehow. The second was bringing her on a secret mission that wasn't even his. A secret mission that involved a secret organisation he wasn't sure he was even part of anymore, an organisation Darlene had no idea of. Except, she had turned up at the Home...

Either way, both were bad paths.

Quinton needed a third option.

Darlene stepped in front of him, bringing her into focus. "Are you dying?" She jabbed at his ribs with several fingers at once. "Do you feel weird?"

He peered down at her. "What?"

"Your face is really red."

"It's hot here." The sun *was* beating down on them and Quinton could feel its sting already.

"It is," Darlene agreed. "But you aren't breathing right." She poked his chest next and he grunted. "Your chest keeps moving too fast."

"I'm not dying," he sighed, stepping out of poking range.

"Good. I'd hate to tell Ma you left me to die on an island."

"I'm not dying!"

Darlene held her hands up, her small rucksack dangling from one. "Fine, not dying."

"Listen," he dropped his voice, "we're not here on holiday. I can't tell you much right now, because honestly, I don't know much myself. But I'm here for my job."

"Your secret job," Darlene whispered back.

"Right, *secret*. Key word. So we need to lay low."

"We?" Her eyes nearly spread to double their original size. "*We?*"

"I'm not sending you home. I can't."

"I thought you would."

"Definitely considered it."

"Real hard? Because that would explain the weird not-dying breathing."

Quinton groaned; his sister was something else. "I'm here to find part of my team. My best friend is on a *thing* here. She sent me a message to come and help. I didn't want to leave you and—"

"Ma behind," Darlene cut in.

"I wasn't going to leave you."

Darlene glanced down. "I heard you and her talk." When she looked back up, the sheen on her eyes was brighter. "I knew you wouldn't want to leave. But you also didn't want to stay. Ma said some people are lucky to have one family."

Quinton reached out and tugged his sister into him, circling her safely in his arms like he could stop the world from getting to her. "They are."

"You have two," Darlene said against his chest. "I wouldn't want to choose."

His heart kicked hard. "I didn't want to either." He swallowed thickly. "I missed my other family though, Day. They make me happy as much as you and Katia do. I've spent the last few years with them and so little time with you and your mum, but I love you all the same. I just wanted to see them."

"Were you going to come back?" Darlene's voice was so tiny.

"I was," he nodded. "If I had the power to split myself into two, I would have. I'm a selfish man, Day. I want it all at once. I want you in my life, your mum too, and I want my other family."

Darlene's arms tightened round him and her head buried itself into his chest like she was trying to find space for herself inside his ribcage. Quinton cupped the back of her head to keep her there, even as her body began to shake. If anyone was to break this hold, it would have to be her.

Quinton had meant every word he'd just said. He loved both families he'd been gifted with, and not one of them more than the other. He was also so selfish that he wished to have both. He needed his heart to be happy and he would do what it took for him to get it.

After a while, Darlene pulled herself away. She didn't unlock her arms, just tilted her head to stare. A smile grew along her face. Quinton blinked; he knew that smile too well because it was his also.

"What do we do now?" she asked, voice clear as day again.

"We find my friends," he answered.

Darlene moved back further, unwrapping herself and reshouldering her bag. "How do we do that?"

Quinton frowned. "I have no idea."

"Are you sure you have a job?"

"Why?"

"You said it involved finding hidden things. But you didn't find me, and now you don't know how to find your friends."

Quinton sighed and stuck his hands in his hair, this time to tie it back. "Right."

"So what do we do?"

"If Gretchen's involved..." he trailed off.

If Gretchen was here, that meant there had to be something possibly involving bones. Bones in missions often translated to "dead things". *That,* paired with an island, maybe meant shipwrecks.

Quinton peered towards the crystal blue sea around him.

Without a word, he gripped Darlene's hand and he started walking. He remained conscious of his speed so he didn't force her to run, but he needed to move swiftly. They needed to be out of the heat soon *and* to cover ground to find the others.

The fine sand beneath their feet slowly changed to a burning white colour. Darlene almost started to hop, even on the boardwalk, and Quinton couldn't blame her. Even the tree cover had diminished, though there were a few umbrellas up ahead that would provide some shelter.

Just as Quinton stopped beneath one, dragging his hair up into a small ponytail, he heard something off to the right. He squinted into the sun. Then the voices grew closer, and louder.

Flora appeared first, aptly dressed for the conditions.

Gretchen looked like she'd been dragged out of an oven and through a bush.

Time slowed as three faces clocked one another.

Quinton stared.

Flora gasped.

Gretchen froze.

Quinton dropped his bag, and his sisters hand at last, and started to sprint at the same time Gretchen did. In a mess of sand and sun, they met in the middle like an explosion.

CHAPTER FIFTEEN
GRETCHEN

23rd Day of Winter 2406

Gretchen forgot she didn't like that much physical contact as Quinton lifted her in a circle, spun her round, and dropped her feet back to the sand again. It was bad enough that she didn't let go first, or complain how tightly he was holding her. She didn't even mention how *sticky* both of them felt because of the increasing heat.

"What are you doin' 'ere?" she asked, voice muffled.

Quinton let go, beaming like she was the sun. "Just visiting."

"No he's not." A girl, much smaller in height yet sharing similar features to him, appeared at his side. There appeared to be a backpack attached to her too. "He's here for work."

"Work?" Flora asked, creeping closer like a spooked animal.

The girl nodded. "Are you his friends he's looking for?"

Gretchen raised an eyebrow, though she wondered if anyone could tell since they were basically invisible when they hadn't been painted on. "Darlene?"

The girl straightened and looked up at Quinton. "You've talked about me before?"

Quinton had spent plenty of time mentioning his half-sister during late night chats back at Redwing. Gretchen had heard it all over time. From the moment Quinton had learnt of Darlene, Gretchen had known too.

"About how annoying you are," Quinton joked.

"Obviously you don't know me." Darlene rolled her eyes as dramatically as he would've. "I'm not annoying."

"But you are 'ere," Gretchen pointed out.

"A little hitchhiker," Quinton grumbled, though still managed to sound fond.

Seeing such a familiar face gave Gretchen life and made her ache for the *season* she'd missed without it. And seeing the matching face, but the smaller and younger version, patched up the tears.

Gretchen might not have a good family, but she would always understand those who went towards their own. Or, really, she'd at least try to.

"Are we going to stay out in the sun all day?" mini Quinton asked.

"I might not be made of gold, but I can feel myself melting like it," Flora complained. She wore light clothes and had tied her hair back, sweeping the rest away with a red headband. Yet even her freckles looked flushed.

Quinton looked at her curiously. "That's hot."

"It's hot *here*," Flora argued. For once, Gretchen was on her side.

The sand shifted beneath their feet as they all made a collective, silent move. They even started to stare towards the shade in joint silence. Cover and an iced drink sounded heavenly, and Gretchen wanted to drown in any of it.

But as Gretchen shifted again, she noticed something off in the distance. Her body moved until she was back facing the horizon. Something was floating out there. She shook her head. It wasn't just floating. It was *speeding* this way.

And it was getting close.

"Oh you've got to be—" Gretchen peered down at the young child among the group and coughed to hide the swear that almost escaped, "kiddin' me."

The boat bounced along with the waves, not against them, and started to steer towards the mini harbour at the beach where Quinton and Darlene had just come in from. Someone helped the newcomers rope up and disembark, bags thrown down at their feet.

Three passengers stood bewildered.

The four on the beach gaped.

Both parties stopped.

Then Quinton was suddenly running along the sand towards the guests.

"Well this is goin' to be fun," Gretchen grumbled.

"Certainly eventful," Flora agreed, making Gretchen jump as she'd thought the girl had taken off after the rest of them.

By the time Gretchen and Flora reached the edge of the beach, Quinton had Ziva in the air like a doll, swinging her round while both of them laughed.

Gretchen watched Darlene stare unashamedly between everyone, and she couldn't blame her. For everyone to be here, all on this one small island, it had to be either the biggest coincidence in the universe or something else was going on.

She spotted Wane among the group but didn't fully meet his eye. She couldn't. They'd left things off on weird terms. They'd been sleeping together, but neither of them had stayed the night in the other's bed. They had a no strings kind of relationship. Honestly, it was more like there was *no* relationship to speak of. Things just *were*.

Yet Gretchen still felt a little guilty for sneaking out of Redwing to hook up with a local girl a few times. There was no need for the guilt. It didn't make sense why it'd settled in her stomach like a load of stones, but she couldn't free herself from it either apparently.

Gretchen caught the moment Quinton realised Chandler also stood on the sand.

In the few hours Gretchen had managed to spend with her best friend before he'd disappeared, they'd talked. Or, Quinton had talked. He'd recounted his most recent adventure, as he called it. He'd said no less than five times how beautiful the Mask of Iris had been. But he'd also mentioned Chandler several times.

Gretchen had wondered if Quinton *knew*. If he was aware how his recounting of the mission twisted to keep including Chandler in it. It was clear he was at the very least intrigued by her. And even Gretchen could see that she was pretty too.

Ziva seemed to realise the same thing and stepped aside after Quinton lowered her, a secret smile on her face.

Slowly, Quinton opened his arms. And even slower, Chandler walked into them.

The moment was over in a blink. Quinton and Chandler moved away from each other like two magnets repelling, destined to be close but never meet. Gretchen narrowed her eyes at both of them and thought again. Maybe they were like two magnets who were destined to meet but the hands holding them weren't bringing them close enough yet.

Now Gretchen found herself intrigued by them both. And she'd never been *that* curious about people before. She blamed her proximity to Quinton. He was always so interested in everyone.

"Who are you?" Darlene's little voice carried through the group.

"We're friends." Surprisingly, Ziva was the one to answer. "We work with—"

"Me," Quinton jumped in, smiling. "It's good to see you. Even you Wane."

"Charming," Wane laughed. "I don't even get a hug?"

"Do you want one?" Quinton offered.

Without warning, Wane charged at Quinton and slammed him into a vice grip. Gretchen winced as something cracked. Wane had always been gentle with her unless she'd asked otherwise, and even then she knew he hadn't been using his full potential. His abnormality was strength itself. But watching him run for Quinton, Gretchen wondered if she'd need to fix some bones in a minute.

Quinton laughed as he backed up. "And this is my sister, Darlene," he announced, pointing to her.

"About time you introduced me." Darlene stepped forwards, her left hand extended.

Oddly, everyone formed some sort of semi-circle around Darlene to shake her hand. She appeared to be very pleased by the reception, even sticking her tongue out at her brother when he laughed.

"Technically, Quinton's my *half*-brother," Darlene specified after the hand-shaking was done.

"You're enough of my sister to count," he argued.

She rolled her eyes, just the same as he would've. "Whatever. *Now* can we get out of the sun?"

"Please," Flora nodded.

"Is there anywhere we can go?" Ziva asked.

"We're stayin' somewhere," Gretchen said. "We can 'ead inside and find somethin' iced to drink?"

Wane wasted no time lifting both Ziva and Chandler's bags. "We're following you."

Flora took off first with Wane not far behind. Darlene moved in line next like she had begun a march for her life, Quinton snorting behind her. Gretchen fell into step beside him. He peered at her and held out his hand, a small smile on his face, and she linked their pinky fingers. Chandler and Ziva brought up the rear.

Mild chatter carried the group on their walk all the way into the tiled and air-conditioned bar room. As they sat together round two pushed together tables, Gretchen realised Chandler wasn't speaking. In fact, she couldn't remember hearing the girl talk once on the way here.

Looking at Chandler, Gretchen noticed the girl's eyes were slightly glazed over. Drinks were brought out and the girl sipped from hers keenly, seeming to come back to herself again after a moment. Gretchen blamed it on the heat. This island's climate certainly wouldn't be kind and she herself felt like a piece of dried mud.

Before she could say anything, not that she was sure on what to say exactly, the meeting between them all began.

CHAPTER SIXTEEN

CHANDLER

23rd Day of Winter 2406

Chandler was starting to forget what *up* felt like.

She knew she was in a chair with a glass bottle of water between her palms – she'd drunk deeply already – and there was sand beneath her toes. But that was all she could distinctly focus on.

Voices flitted in and out around her. She couldn't pick out an accent and struggled with even some words. There was a faint whirring noise of a dying fan nearby. But the sounds all blurred together.

She was stuck. She was *drowning* in heat.

Because of her specific power, she knew there had to be temperature limitations. That'd always been a theory but one she'd never tested. One she'd never *needed* to test.

But now she was stuck on an island, surrounded by burning sun and sand, and heat throughout all hours of the day.

Ice couldn't survive above freezing-point. Chandler herself was made out of the stuff. She could control water and drag it to shards of crystalline solids, but the unfreezing wasn't always under her control. With the air around her unrelenting, she felt herself melting, her blood boiling around her bones.

She sipped the bottle and the relief came. But it didn't last.

Too quickly her tongue seemed to shrivel and grate against the roof of her mouth, her hands twitched, her knees jittered.

"Chandler?"

Chandler's blurry vision lifted. She tried to focus and after a slow blink she managed to see Ziva staring at her. Ziva's eyes were wide open and sweat dressed her forehead lightly.

"Chan?" Ziva whispered, leaning closer. "Are you alright?"

"I'll be fine," Chandler said. She couldn't really hear herself, so she didn't know how convincing she sounded. "Just a little tired."

"It was a long trip."

Chandler glanced over to the now blue-haired Quinton. He sat next to the girl he ran away for – his little sister. Chandler envisioned a glint in his eye, one of concern, but then it sparked out and she told herself she imagined it. He didn't care about anything. He'd left. Rightly so for his sisters sake. But it was the lack of *goodbye* she hadn't forgiven him for.

"It was," Chandler agreed, voice clipped.

"You should eat something," Ziva encouraged, pressing something into Chandler's hand. "It's a cucumber sandwich."

Chandler slid a slice of cucumber out from between the dry bread and popped it in her mouth. Again the relief came, and the relief fled within seconds. She didn't say anything though, just nodded and continued to chew on the slices she had the energy to.

The voices rose again, picking the groups next move. Chandler could focus a little more with each watery slice she consumed, but picking out specifics remained almost impossible.

All Chandler knew next was they were all clambering to their feet with fresh water being stuffed into bags and more cucumber being shoved into Chandler's hand.

Evening was falling outside. Either that or Chandler had gone blind. But she was certain she saw a twinkling star in the distance. Or maybe it was a far-off ship. Maybe a light somewhere...

"Hey." Chandler sidled up to the first person she found. Someone tall. Someone *big*. "Where are we going?"

The person stopped and large hands suddenly pressed into Chandler's shoulders. "Icy, you sure you're okay?"

Wane. It had to be him. Chandler hadn't lost all sense if she could still tell it was his voice.

"Where to, Wane?" she asked again, ignoring his question.

He sighed like he wasn't happy with her answer. "A cave nearby."

"A cave? Why?"

"Did you not listen in there?"

"I told you I was tired."

"And hungry, the way you're chewing that fruit." He sighed again, this time removing his hands. She might've swayed from the lack of sudden stability but couldn't be sure. "We're going to a cave, because most legends on this Island start in one, and we all seem to be hunting some sort of legend. We can't spend all our time in fancy hotels and spas."

"A legend? We're chasing myths now?" Chandler shoved more cucumber into her mouth and her eyes focused finally. Immediately she wanted to suck all the water out of another thousand slices.

"Flora seems to think so," Wane said. "We're looking for how this island got rich, and the only thing we can come up with is *gold*. That's her forte."

"So we find the gold trail, find the gold, and... then what? Find our missing Abnormal and researchers too?"

"We don't know how it ties together. But all our trails have led here."

Chandler stared. "We're chasing myths and legends and *hope*."

Wane's eyes refocused on Chandler's face like he had started to study her. But Chandler didn't care to be seen. She walked away from him.

The group seemed more than content talking amongst themselves, Wane even joining in once he caught up. Chandler didn't feel like doing much of anything except lying down in a cool puddle of seawater somewhere. The night hadn't yet provided much more coolness than the day, and if the entire night continued like this...

Chandler was worried.

Past more trees and some weird rock formations, they finally stopped. The two at the front, Gretchen and Quinton, scouted ahead for danger. When there were no signs of any, the rest of the group followed into the cave. The darkness turned everyone into faint blobs.

"We've got time for some of us to scout the immediate area," Ziva said. Her voice, Chandler would know anywhere.

"The gold isn't close," another girl's voice said. Chandler wondered if that was Flora. "It's not *far*, but nowhere we can see in the few hours of day we have left."

"What do you suggest?" Wane asked.

"We go back to the hotel and sleep," Gretchen's voice cut through next.

"No," Flora decided.

"If we have to sleep on rock floors, I want to go home." That was an unknown voice to Chandler. She couldn't picture a face to match either but she sounded young. Then she suddenly remembered it was Darlene.

"You can rest on me," Quinton told his sister.

"I still don't like it."

"We'll stay here for the rest of the day," Flora added. "Then move at dusk when the temperature drops again."

"*Is* the temperature dropping?" Chandler heard herself speak. She felt pairs of eyes find her but couldn't make out the colours of any. It was simply too dark. And her vision had gone slightly blurry again.

"It's dropped significantly," Ziva told her, her tone gentle and kind.

"Significantly?" Chandler glanced around and saw several heads nodding. She slumped against the cave wall and drew out her water bottle, sipping on the tepid liquid. "I don't think I've drunk enough today, and I'm just tired."

"Your power might be draining you too," Quinton suddenly said.

"What?" Ziva asked, almost desperately.

"Look at her, he's right," Gretchen said. "She looks like shit." Chandler raised her bottle in a *cheers* type motion.

"Her body's trying to overreact and count against the warmth here," Quinton continued. "It's a natural defence, and it's acting the same way it would if an illness was introduced to the body. The body would defend itself."

"How do you know that?" Ziva questioned.

"I'm fine," Chandler tried to reassure them.

"It's simple science," Quinton said. "Cold doesn't do well in hot."

"The cold here is doing fine," Chandler repeated.

Wane slid closer to Chandler, shifting the sand around them. "Stop trying to talk, and drink," he whispered. "They're right, you do look like shit, and you need to keep your strength here."

"We should send her home," Flora tried.

"She's a liability," Gretchen added.

"That's not what I meant."

"If she's overheatin', she's fightin' herself, right? So she'll only slow us down."

"Still not—"

"Stop," Chandler interrupted. She heard her voice echo back at her. "If you have something to say about me, say it *to me*. Don't talk like I'm not here."

"We *are* sayin' it to you," Gretchen said. "You look like shit and you shouldn't be here. You've been on this island a few hours, and you're only goin' to get worse. You're a problem and you need to leave."

Chandler wanted to reach out and pull the girl's hair, like a mature adult, but she couldn't. She simply rolled her eyes instead and drank another deep gulp then replaced the lid on her bottle. When it was back in her bag, she tipped her head onto Wane's shoulder. He didn't immediately throw her off, so she left herself there.

"And I'm telling you I'm fine to continue," Chandler argued.

"Fine," Gretchen conceded. "But the *second* you go to fuck this all up, we're sendin' you 'ome. I think that's more than fair."

"You don't have the right to pull that card," Wane said on Chandler's behalf.

"If it puts us or the mission in danger, any of us have the right."

Flora's voice of reason cut through the tensioned air a few breaths later. "We'll hunker down, sleep this mood and heat off, and move again at dusk like planned. We'll follow the gold trail and hopefully end up where we need to be. Then we can all extract immediately after."

"Sleep sounds good," came Darlene's little voice. Chandler had forgotten she was even there she'd been so quiet. What *was* she doing here? Had that been explained? "Can I have some sandwiches first?"

"Sandwiches?" Quinton asked.

"Ma packed them. They're in my bag."

There was the sound of a zipper being pulled. "Sandwiches," Quinton repeated, sounding bemused. "How?"

"I told you, she seemed to know I'd leave," Darlene told him. "They were in the fridge waiting for me. There was a little sticky note with a smiley face and everything. I'll share one if you're hungry?"

"No, no. I'm fine, Day. You eat them both."

"Don't have tell me twice."

Chandler couldn't fight to keep her eyes open any longer, nor could she fight the small smile on her face, she just hoped no one in the cave around her could see it.

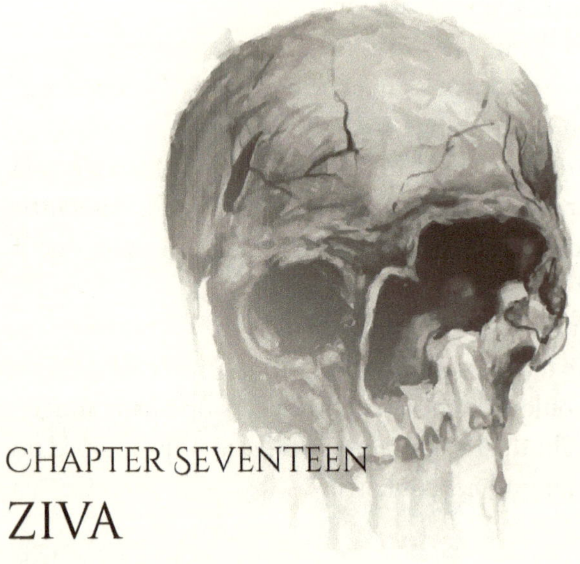

CHAPTER SEVENTEEN

ZIVA

24ᵗʰ Day of Winter 2406

lora led the way, with everyone else trailing behind like a group of lost sheep. Only Flora could see the supposedly invisible lines that led to the gold they were searching for.

"Orange slice?"

Ziva blinked down at Darlene and her open palm, indeed holding up a slightly dry-looking slice of the fruit. "Thanks," she said, popping it in her mouth. There was enough juice to tang against her tongue.

"I took some from the fruit bowl on the table before I left," Darlene said, eating her own slice. "I prefer red apples, but we didn't have any in the house."

Ziva smiled, and couldn't help but think of Abel.

To travel here and join this mission, Ziva had said goodbye to him back home. Abel couldn't simply take time away from his job – protecting the grounds and safe space of Redwing, and the recruits living there – to fly across the world. What was required of him was different than what was required of her.

But she thought of him anyway, and of how he'd offered her an orange the first time they'd met. That'd been before she'd even officially taken her role at Redwing.

Ziva took another slice of fruit when Darlene offered it.

"Does this group all hate each other?" Darlene said, cutting through Ziva's thoughts.

"No one hates anyone, Day," Quinton said, coming to Ziva's rescue.

Darlene stared at her brother. "No one's talking."

"We don't always need to talk."

"But you're not doing *anything*. No one's smiling or looking at each other. It's boring."

Ziva and Quinton shared a quick look.

"We're trying to save energy," she said first. "We know we have to follow Flora, so we're moving at her speed. We'll talk when we stop again, we promise. But we don't hate each other. It's just a complicated mission. It requires our full focus right now."

Complicated in the way that two missions had somehow combined into one. That had to be the case here. Scientific researchers wouldn't just disappear with an Abnormal and reappear on an island where they had outbid the world to run freely of it without there being links or debts. And that link had to be what the island had – gold. If Flora's detection was correct, there was a lot of it around.

The left two questions.

How did this island acquire so much gold? And what was this group going to do about it?

Darlene skipped off like the evening heat couldn't touch her. Quinton watched her go carefully.

"You can tell she's related to you," Ziva told him, wiping her brow with the back of her hand. "Asks about as many questions, too."

"Sorry," he laughed.

"What for? I'd rather a kid ask me stuff than be left to figure it all out on their own." Ziva glanced up at the stars that were beginning to appear. They were crystal-like, so bold and beautiful. "I remember what that's like."

For as much as her family had surrounded her, they'd still ignored anything Ziva asked as a child. She'd been left to ask classmates about how to do certain homework, online forums for hygiene and personal things, neighbours on cooking, strangers on directions. She'd wished her parents had been more open to answering questions – from those she needed genuine guidance on to those she had answers for but wanted reassurance about.

"She shouldn't be here," Quinton murmured.

"She's here now though," Ziva said. "All we can do is get her through this and then we'll figure out what to do with her after."

"Selfishly, I'm also glad I didn't have to say goodbye either."

"Not wanting to say goodbye to your family isn't selfish."

"If it puts her in harm's way, it could be."

"You didn't stuff her into a suitcase and drag her here."

"No. She climbed on the damn plane on her own. Then onto the boat."

Ziva looked up at him, at his bright blue hair and the crinkles of concern she could see around his eyes. "Sounds like something you'd do."

"But she has a big brother to fuss over her," he said, still focused on Darlene.

"And she'll be safer for it. Safer than any of us were a season ago, and probably better than anything you had when you first joined."

Quinton's gaze finally moved from his sister, who had begun to peel another orange under the starlight, and met Ziva's. "I was older than she is," he tried to reason.

"She turned up at *home*, on her own, didn't she? That means she's not defenceless either."

He sighed heavily, defeated. "When we get back, we'll have to debrief. That *includes* Day."

"It will," Ziva confirmed.

"They'll try and offer her a position, you know. She'll have been with us and succeeded, so they'll try and get her a place with us."

"And if she's Abnormal, that could be a safe space for her."

"But she's *young*, Ziva! Too young!"

Ziva stopped and touched his hand, causing him to stop alongside her. "Quinton, she'll be safe. You know that place better than I do, and you know their rules." She tried to speak softly, quietly, like he was a wounded animal she didn't want to spook or a child who needed consoling. "They don't yet send Helen out into the field—"

"Helen doesn't have what we do."

"That we know of. Hers might not have manifested yet."

"Day—"

It was Ziva's turn to cut him off. "*Does* have something. She found us, where we live. No one is supposed to be able to." She dropped her voice even lower. "But Darlene did. She saw right through it. So they might offer her a position, that might be inevitable. And, yes, she's young. But she does not deserve to be caged. Her own mother seemed fine with her leaving. Maybe she's concerned, as any decent mother would be, but she definitely hadn't chased her down to take her back. She seems to trust her own child and her choices. And staying, or going, *would* be her choice." Ziva rose onto tip-toes to touch his cheek. "Maybe you need to learn to trust your sister too."

Quinton leaned into the touch. "When did you get so smart?"

"The joker of the group left last season and never got to witness *me* growing up."

He laughed. "I'm more than just the joker."

"You are. Just as your sister is more than a little bird."

"I know. But she's everything to me."

"How about we worry about the debriefing and everything that comes with it once we're done here?" she suggested. "That's a *later* us problem."

"What else am I supposed to fixate on though?"

"Same as what we always do, the mission."

"Oh, the mission. How could I forget?" Quinton joked sarcastically.

Ziva removed her hand and started walking again. She could feel a shadow and knew Quinton was behind her.

Ziva could tell Quinton was a good brother and he had every right to worry over his sibling. That fear was always real for any older sibling about their younger. What danger would they come into? What harm might find them? What happens if they're on their own?

It was worse for anyone who had someone in their life with an Abnormality.

Those with the gene were hunted, persecuted, *hated*. Life for those who were different was never easy, not from birth or any time after.

Redwing had certainly helped Ziva, though. It'd given her stable grounding, a job, confidence, *safety* she didn't think she'd ever come into elsewhere. She'd started to treat it like home and a family.

Maybe Darlene could have that too. It would be her choice, and she *was* young, there was no denying that, but it could also be a better future for her when time came.

The group stopped at a cluster of trees that bowed away from the path they'd been walking. Flora held up a single hand as a signal for them to wait. Ziva couldn't hear or see anything, the darkness now deeply into night.

"What's happening?" Darlene asked, her voice not quite a whisper. Quinton shoved his hand over her mouth immediately, grimacing apologetically. She rolled her eyes.

"There's people," Gretchen answered anyway.

"A camp? Or hotel?" Ziva asked.

"Can't tell. I just know there are bones 'ere, and they feel fresh."

Ziva shivered at how creepy Gretchen had managed to make that sound.

"Is the gold here?" Wane asked. He didn't press forwards to the front as Chandler had seemed to cement herself to his side and he was comfortable staying with her.

"A large amount of it," Flora confirmed.

"What's the plan, here?" Wane questioned. "We charge in, take it and the people?"

"No," the rest of the group grumbled as one.

"Our mission is to find the missing researchers," Chandler slurred, though it was clear enough to understand. Ziva scowled at her; something was wrong, whether Chandler would admit it or not.

"Ours is to find how the island cleared its debts," Gretchen said.

"The gold has to be how," Ziva said.

"That's still a theory."

"It's not a theory is Floral can sense it," Quinton said.

"So we made one right guess about all this?" Gretchen threw her hands up. "Oh hurray. The mission's over."

"But Wane's right," Ziva continued.

"I am?" He looked back at her, a little surprised.

She nodded. "What're we going to do about it?"

"Debts and researchers, debts and researchers," Quinton whispered. "Clearly if you're to find the researchers, that means you need to retrieve them as well?"

Chandler nodded against Wane's arm where she'd fallen. "They're important to the government."

"The debt clearing just has to be reported on, right?" Quinton asked. "You just need to find out how it was being done?"

"That we know of," Flora said, nodding. "We weren't given much instruction on it."

"Any group have a time limit that we're working against?"

"Who put your blue arse in charge?" Gretchen sniped.

Ziva had been on the receiving end of that specific tone several times in the past season, and was glad this wasn't one of those times. Gretchen always reminded Ziva of a storm dressed up as a wild wolf; something unexplained altogether and something never to be replicated for how wild it truly was. She tried to avoid the attacks as much as possible, staying out of Gretchen's way back home, but some things were unavoidable when stressors were high and missions required close proximities.

"Is anyone else willing to step up?" Quinton challenged.

For a moment, silence. Then Gretchen's wild grin cut her face open. "I'm glad you're 'ere."

He laughed, full of joy but quieter than normal. "Me too."

"So do you have a plan?" Flora pressed.

Quinton's humour disappeared and he turned into the man Ziva remembered from last season as easily as he changed his hair colour. "I do."

CHAPTER EIGHTEEN

FLORA

25th Day of Winter 2406

So much gold, Flora's mind whispered.

She'd been around enough of the element in her life. It was often hard to escape since most jewellery was comprised of the stuff. But none of it had been in such volume, and in such a compact *state* before.

A plethora of objects gleamed under the light of dusk. Ancient warrior shields were half-buried. Plinths missing their exaggerated monuments stuck out of sloped sand dunes at odd angles. Even small glass bottles were piled together under towering palm trees.

Everything was gold.

And it was right there.

The group had been forced to take another night and most of the following day to rest up and gain back whatever strength the sun sapped from them. They'd hidden in another cave they'd found, keeping their ranks close and always with someone on watch.

They'd decided the best time to try and sneak into camp would be during the evening, close to dusk but not giving themselves away by using the dark. No one in the group had performed a heist before, but Wane had remembered his twin older brothers had.

Apparently, heists were easier to perform at night. Moonlight would provide cover but also some natural light to see by. Plus, being on a tropical island, night here would also offer a coolness that the day wouldn't, giving the group a little ease.

But this wasn't going to be a *normal* heist at all.

For this, they'd split into two groups to attack what they were still assuming was a camp from either side at once. Flora was with Ziva and Quinton. She was glad. They got along whenever they were in each other's company.

The other group had the stronger personality types all thrown together.

Not that Flora wouldn't deny Ziva or Quinton having a personality – Quinton definitely had one – but the other group had the one to clash with everyone, the one who wouldn't really talk to anyone, and the one who wanted to bridge the gap for all.

Darlene had been told to follow behind Quinton, but not completely. When things were to start, she would stay back.

A faint whistle cut through the evening crickets. It sounded like a bird calling for their partner. The group knew better. That was their signal to move.

The trio broke through the treeline and Flora's veins started to throb. She could've closed her eyes and sought out the gold just from the tension inside her body alone. She flicked her tongue out like a snake – something she often did when gold was nearby – and the familiar *tang* of it coated her tastebuds.

Flora's sandals slipped in the sand but she kept going. She needed to get closer. A desire to touch it wound around her stomach and lungs, threatening to cut her off if she didn't feed it.

There was a reason she didn't involve herself in missions if she could avoid it. While most Abnormals had powers that could be contained or brought out when necessary, Flora didn't quite have the same luxury. Hers manifested like a thirst. A *need* that, if not met, might be disastrous.

Gold called to her and she was helpless except to respond.

Her skin could absorb it, holding it tight within her own *blood* if needed, to then redeposit later. She could taste it like fine wine or fresh fruits. Her heart sang along with the same tuning. Her arms could lift the heaviest bar as if it weighed no more than a cloud.

Simply, Flora and her abnormality over gold could come and go as much as the rare element did.

She hadn't yet found out what would happen if she resisted the call though. She hadn't dared too.

On their own, Flora's hands extended out impatiently. As soon as her fingers wrapped around a pole, her whole body sighed with relief. She sank to her knees in the sand. Her tongue flicked out from her mouth again, tasting the air for more, and her heart thudded inside her chest heavily.

Quinton and Ziva shuffled around her easily. Flora watched from her position on the beach floor as they crept up to shiny surfaces and reached out towards them. Yet, unlike her, neither of them touched anything.

Clearly having met no resistance on their end, the second group appeared from the other side of the clearing.

Flora watched as Wane lifted a thick golden plinth, a dusting of sweat trickling down the side of his face; his abnormality was strength, but everything had its limits. Quinton joined him, and together they heaved aside an old-time historical clock that'd been half sunken.

The whole beached area was about halfway between the sea and trees. Maybe at one point, this had been the sight of a shipwreck; their assumption had been they'd need to find one to find gold. But right now it was uncovered and displayed up on the white sand.

"This is their treasure trove," Gretchen surmised, standing in the middle. "Bunch of greedy fuckin' dragons."

"Dragons?" Wane's expression perked up.

"It's an expression," Gretchen rolled her eyes at him.

"But where did it come from?" Wane asked, kicking a golden canoe with the toe of his shoe. "This can't all have magically washed up on the nearby beach? Everything's too random."

Refusing to let go of her piece still, Flora's eyes darted around. Wane wasn't wrong. Everything *was* random.

The canoe didn't match the running trainers, and they didn't match the old-style American football helmet. None of that matched the pizza box or the entire cutlery set inside a velvet case. And all those weren't the same as a very broken desk as it sat in three pieces or the grandfather clock the two guys had just shifted.

All the collection had in common was that the contents had been formed out of gold.

Gretchen's harsh eyes turned on Flora. "Can your weird Midas powers tell you anything?"

"Did you compare her to the old myth and didn't even get it right for this context?" Quintion questioned. Gretchen shrugged.

"I don't know what you're expecting," Flora shuffled to balance more on her knees, her hand still unwilling to loosen its grip on the golden pole, "but the answer is no. I can't sense anything except that there is gold."

"But it's all real?" Wane asked, throwing the canoe next to the clock.

Flora nodded. "One hundred percent."

"We could be rich," Darlene mused, and Flora watched her stare at one of the small golden bottles nearby. The statement was that of a child, of innocence.

Ziva turned in a circle. "Where did it come from?"

"I can't tell," Flora said.

The idea that this seemingly random pile of *junk* was actually important somehow haunted Flora more than she cared to admit. If it hadn't been gold, the things abandoned here wouldn't have been anything special. She kept staring at it all, trying to find the connection. The more she searched for an answer, the more confused she became.

Flora's grip on the pole loosened and she found herself able to move on, but only towards the pair of running shoes. Everything from the stitching to the laces to the logo on the side were shimmering and shining. Admittedly, the lowering orange sun made the spectacle all the more appealing.

If she hadn't been attracted to gold because of her abnormality already, Flora knew she would've wanted anything here on the beach in that moment anyway.

Sudden noise burst to life from Flora's right, and the entire group froze, then threw themselves back into the trees. Even Flora managed to fight her need for gold and run under cover.

Men filed into the space seconds later. They rifled through the treasures like they might find something hidden beneath it somewhere. The group in the trees took a collective large step back further when the men drew nearer to inspect the clock.

"Researchers?" Chandler grumbled.

Flora managed to shift her attention from the treasure to her companion. With dusk approaching, and fast, it made seeing slightly difficult, but Flora could still make out the heavy pink dusting Chandler's cheeks and the gaunt look on her face. Chandler's eyes were drooping too, and she'd probably had the most rest out of everyone; almost sleeping through meals which they'd forcibly had to wake her for.

The whole time they'd been here, Flora realised Chandler hadn't spoken much. It was as if the island itself was sucking the lifeforce out of her. She was transforming into a ghost of herself in front of everyone's eyes.

"Chandler?" Quinton whispered.

"Where are..." Chandler took a deep breath and tried to force her body upright, but only half-succeeded. "Researchers?"

Ziva scowled, then pointed out to the group of men as they started to walk away. "That's not them," she said quietly. "Those looked like guards, and this is what they're guarding." Ziva indicated to the piles of things they could still all quite clearly see and then to the men in tight suits who held spears in their hands. "So where are the researchers?"

"What were they studyin' again?" Gretchen asked, closing in to make the group appear more like a misshapen circle.

"Don't know," Chandler managed.

"They had someone important with them, someone the government wanted," Wane filled in. "He had some sort of abnormality."

"Right," Chandler agreed. When had her rapid decline started happening? Flora had never seen her like this, but surely she hadn't stepped off the boat at the beach looking this bad? "There was a letter." Despite her state, she managed to roll her eyes. "The only other thing was the letter saying he was being tested here, on this island."

"We never found out what his abnormality was though," Wane added.

"It ain't some kind of a coincidence that we've ended up 'ere together," Gretchen said. "One island has paid off its debts and a bunch of researchers have disappeared with an Abnormal?"

"You think he discovered all this?" Ziva asked.

"Can't have," Chandler said.

"He didn't disappear that long ago and neither did the researchers. This had to have come *before* the missing people," Wane explained. He looked at Chandler. "Do you need to lean on me again?"

"I just need a rest," Chandler huffed.

"How much more rest can one person fuckin' need?" Gretchen whined loudly.

Ziva whirled on Gretchen. "You don't know how she feels right now, so lay off. The suns hot and she's practically *made* of ice."

"She shouldn't be 'ere if she can't 'andle it."

"None of us knew what this was going to entail when we arrived!"

Gretchen's smile wasn't anywhere close to kind or friendly. "Someone's grown a spine after all." She stepped closer to Ziva, almost close enough to breathe on her if she wanted. "Where's the timid girl who shuffled through those big doors a season ago? Where's she gone?"

"Leave her alone, Gretchen," Chandler said, sounding more alive suddenly.

"Or wha'?"

Chandler pulled Ziva back, just to take her place. "I don't care how tired I am, I'll still beat your arse into the ground right here."

"Pretty words from a pretty girl. Do you even know how to fight?"

"Probably *way* better than you do."

"I ain't afraid to test that."

At once, the boys of the group grabbed the girls away from each other. Wane took Gretchen deeper into the trees and Quinton shuffled Chandler off the other way. Neither girl protested much.

Flora looked between them. She had no doubt Gretchen would start a fight but she believed Chandler could end one. She hadn't spoken to either much, but Gretchen definitely came across as having a bigger bark than bite; even from a distance, people could see that. Chandler was still untested though, too new and too closed-off in all aspects.

Darlene glanced up at Ziva. "I thought you said everyone got along?"

Flora wanted to laugh. But she couldn't. Even less so when the men returned to the trove and with higher numbers.

One breath was all Flora got to take before chaos broke loose.

Because as the group all looked at one another, Chandler slipped sideways to the ground, her body crashing out of the treeline and into the sand with a defeated *thump*. Flora could just make out when her eyes rolled to the back of her head. Quinton gasped audibly.

"There!" one of the men yelled, and the entire group began to pounce.

All eyes of the recruits locked together. They backed away from the treeline.

Quinton and Chandler didn't move.

They were paces away, out of reach and desperately too far for even Wane to swoop in and pick Chandler's seemingly unconscious body up. And Quinton seemed reluctant to leave her.

The guards were closing in like blood warriors.

"What're you doin'?" Gretchen yelled at Quinton, not bothering to be quiet anymore.

"Find out where this gold came from," he called back at her, ignoring her question. "And keep my sister safe! Go. *Go!*"

The men surrounded Chandler and Quinton as Flora snatched Darlene's hand.

No one stopped. Those who were free raced through the sand and the trees for their lives, leaving two of their fellow recruits in the hands of men that possessed a hoard of troubled treasure.

CHAPTER NINETEEN

QUINTON

26th Day of Winter 2406

Quinton shifted as much as the bindings around his arms and legs would allow, which wasn't much, but it did alleviate some of the tightness in his muscles. His shoulders screamed from how they'd been pulled back, his wrists bound together while his elbows were secured against the chair. But he couldn't give himself more room.

He twisted his fingers, the rope at his wrists chafing further. His fingers touched skin that wasn't his own. He bit his lip to control the noises of pain as he searched along the *other* skin for a pulse point in the other wrist.

When I said I wanted to come back, this isn't what I meant or how I meant it.

"Chandler?" he whispered. "Chandler? You need to wake up."

Nothing.

Grunting, Quinton stretched his reach further. He felt it, the moment his own wrist popped and the chafing started to become a burn, but he didn't stop moving until two fingers pressed down deep enough into Chandler's arm.

He waited. One second. Then two.

Faintly, there was a pulse.

It was weak, barely there and struggling, but it existed.

Chandler needed help, some form of medical attention. And she needed it *now*. But they were tied together and strapped to chairs, back to back, in a room somewhere dark.

After Chandler had passed out, the guards had rushed both her and Quinton. He'd yelled at the others to run. Thankfully they'd listened or they would've all been stuck here. At least with some of them free there was a chance of a rescue if Quinton couldn't somehow get them out.

Focus, he told himself.

The strength of the rope finally won and Quinton had to drop the grip he'd secured on Chandler's wrist. But he refused to pull all the way back. He looped his forefinger around her thumb as best he could. Even if she didn't know where she was, he did, and if she happened to wake he didn't want her to think she was alone.

Sitting there, darkness and heavy dampness surrounding them, Quinton had nothing better to do than curse himself.

He should've seen the signs sooner. He'd thought Chandler's behaviour was strange. Someone in the group had even commented on it – he'd forgotten who, maybe it was even himself – but no one had done anything.

Quinton also cursed Chandler for not speaking up.

She had to have known her body would've overreacted to the heat, that her ice power would've kicked into overdrive trying to keep her internal system cool. Surely she'd sensed herself burning – whether that be an ice burn or otherwise.

Powers weren't a definite thing. The Abnormality gene that created them wasn't invincible. It could warp. Power itself could warp. In the same way some abnormalities could evolve and twist, some had built in mechanisms to protect the owner from outside forces or themselves.

And that's what Chandler's had done. It'd protected her so hard it had sucked most of the energy out of her in an attempt to preserve her life.

Chandler, he thought, stroking her thumb a little, *why didn't you say anything? Even to Ziva?*

"Your wife has truly passed out."

Quinton looked up as the door swung open. He hadn't given much thought to the room before that moment, purely focusing on himself and Chandler. There wasn't much to see besides them and the door, except a sturdy looking wooden table that stood propped against the far wall. No windows out, no roof hatch in. Just a small box room with a single exit and two prisoners inside.

A man dressed head to toe in light camouflage sauntered into the room with a third chair. He swung it round and sat on it backwards, facing Quinton, propping his chin on his crossed arms. His face was clean shaven and clearly open to the elements if the sunburn across his nose was anything to go by. But his eyes were dark and while his demeanour appeared calm Quinton wondered if it would stay that way.

"She is pretty," the man said. He had an accent when he spoke English, but Quinton couldn't make out his native tongue. "How long have you been married?"

Quinton tried not to scowl. "Not long."

"The necklace gave you both away."

"The necklace?"

"More like the ring gave you away."

The man took a pen from his pocket and leaned over Quinton to get to Chandler. Quinton couldn't see what he was doing, he didn't understand what was happening at all, but nodded anyway.

Ring? Quinton thought to himself.

It took him a moment to remember a very specific emerald ring he'd bought for Chandler on their first mission. He tried not to show confusion. Was she wearing it now, still? He'd seen no sign of her wearing it

"Delicate," the man continued. "Much like your wife."

"She picked it out for herself," Quinton responded slowly.

"She has good taste. But then, so do you by choosing her." The man sat back, his hands back at his side again. "What were you doing in my garden?" he asked next.

"Your garden?" Quinton questioned.

"Don't play with me, boy. I know where you were captured from. I know you were within the borders of my statue garden. What were you doing?"

Quinton had two ways he could play this, and he wasn't sure about either of them being particularly smart. He shifted in his seat. "Oh, the statues are *amazing!*" he declared. "So real. Must've cost a fortune to have made. The arrangement and the normality of objects you decided to turn into ornaments... It's not what I would've expected."

"So you don't deny being there?"

"As you said, you know where you found us. Why would I deny it? There's no sense in lying."

"The arrangement of the statues is unique to *me.* I leave them where they desire to get to. A journey of gold, shall we say, ey?"

Quinton didn't know what to make of that since the objects seemed to have been just scattered randomly. But clearly this man knew something else, which was not a surprise if the 'garden' was his – or so he claimed.

"Me and my wife," Quinton continued, "we were taking a walk along the beach. She saw something glittering in the distance and wanted to see what it was. You know women and their shiny trinkets. They can't help themselves sometimes. Like magpies."

The man threw his head back as he laughed. "Oh, this man speaks the truth!"

"I couldn't leave her to go alone, so I followed."

"A protector."

"Only of her interests," Quinton flashed a small, trickster smile. "We'd barely been there two minutes before everyone showed up, started yelling, and then the next thing we know we woke up here. Or, I woke up here." Quinton tried turning again but the restraints hadn't budged an inch. "My wife, is she alright?"

"She has been asleep for a long time," the man answered.

"She fell in my arms! You didn't see her wake?"

"No one did, no."

"She might be seriously ill! I need to get her to a healer!"

"There is no healer on this island at present, called away elsewhere, and we cannot just let you go. You intruded somewhere you shouldn't have been."

"We didn't know!" Quinton tried to struggle again, both for show and not. "Please. We're not from around here. My wife... If she hasn't woken, there might be something seriously wrong!"

The man leaned back, narrowing his eyes. "We know you're not from around here. Your accent suggests a higher person, ey, like nobility?"

"There's no one noble here," Quinton said, trying not to grumble the words.

Despite all his father's money and power, Quinton never felt like it was noble to have or use. The money had always come from something underhand somewhere, even if by face it appeared to be clean.

"You at least have money?" the man tried again.

"Look, my wife is *sick*. I can talk money all you like but I'd rather not. I want to take her to a healer and for her to get better."

"Which is a lovely thought."

"I'm—"

"We can see you care for her," the man interrupted. Quinton stopped his thoughts and tongue immediately. "But we don't need money. You saw my garden, I have plenty of the paper stuff *and* the raw materials." The man stood again, his body moving fluidly from sitting to leering over Quinton. "There is nothing of harm on either of your persons, we can see that. And we can see your wife desperately needs medical attention. You will be given water and we will return you to the beach so you can find it."

Quinton blinked. "You'll take us back—"

"But don't mistake this. If we find you near my statues again, we will know you had no innocent intent here. We are taking your naiveté as a non-local. We are trusting your word on all this." He bent lower, sticking his face so close to Quinton the smell of long ago smoked tobacco wafted from his mouth. "Do not break that trust. You don't want to know what happens to those who break that trust."

"I won't. *We* won't!"

"Get your wife to the hospital. And I hope to never see you again."

The man opened the door, allowing two similarly dressed men inside in his place. They cut the bindings holding Quinton and Chandler to the chairs.

Immediately, Quinton sank to his knees in front of Chandler to catch her lifeless body. She weighed like stone in his arms but he didn't care, he scooped her into his arms like she was made of air instead. Sweat lined her brow and pink flushed her cheeks. At least she didn't burn to the touch, but she also didn't feel cold.

Quinton brushed a hand over her face, drawing back her hair from her eyes. He'd seen her frustrated and annoyed before, just as he'd seen her happy. Though he'd spent very little time with her, he could honestly say he'd never seen her look so vacant before.

The two that had come in to cut them free appeared at Quinton's side again and glasses of water were handed over.

Instead taking one for himself, Quinton propped Chandler up against his chest and used his other hand to part her lips slightly. Carefully, he poured a few drops into her mouth and watched as her throat gulped.

After a few repetitions, he nearly sighed with relief as some of her flush faded and the warmth of her skin drew back.

Only once the glass was empty did he lift his own to his lips and drink deeply.

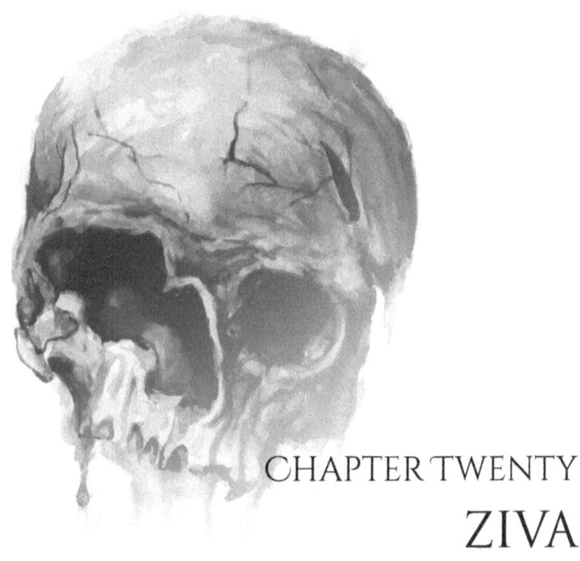

CHAPTER TWENTY

ZIVA

26th Day of Winter 2406

The amount of tracks they left in the sand on the beach might've been beautiful on any other day. But so many back and forth footsteps just showed worry. They'd made it back to the dock where they'd originally all came in, and were circling round in the same vague area.

Gretchen felt the need to keep close to the treeline while Wane stuck more towards the slow waves of the sea. Ziva, Flora, and Darlene were left in the middle between them like children of waring parents despite most of them being somewhere near the same age. But Ziva could definitely sense some sort of tension between Gretchen and Wane.

They'd been that way since they'd reconvened.

There was no real direction they were heading, just forward. It had to be enough. And they made sure that wherever they walked, there were clear lines of sight around them. They didn't want to have another sneak attack descend upon them.

"Who took them?" Darlene asked, her face a blanket of childish innocence. "Who has my brother and... what's the girls name?"

"Chandler," Flora answered before Ziva could.

"Right! My brother spoke about her. Were they close?"

Ziva stopped her endless, pointless walking. "Me and Chandler joined this group later than others—"

"At that big house?" Darlene interrupted, also stopping in her tracks.

"Yeah," Ziva nodded. "We've only been there for one season, so we didn't know your brother *that* well. But we did have an adventure with him."

"I'll say," Flora muttered. Ziva glanced at her questioningly. Flora noticed, and pushed her headband further back on her head to keep her brown hair out of her eyes. But that just revealed the flush on her face that definitely wasn't from the day's heat. "We heard some of your last mission together."

"What?" Ziva spun towards her completely. "When?"

"Dalton hacked into the computer systems of that high stakes party you were all at, right?" Flora dropped her gaze.

"He didn't close the connection," Ziva guessed.

"We couldn't hear, but we could see."

"How much did you see?"

"Enough. Like Quinton and Chandler dancing, how they treated each other like it wasn't only a mission to them, how defensive he got when his parents were involved."

"They weren't around long," Wane said, walking closer. Ziva looked at him and he shrugged casually. "I was watching too."

"Did you see his face?" Flora looked up again, and though her cheeks were still flushed, she had a set look in her eye. "He was watching her the whole time. I don't know if she noticed. I don't think she did. Because even if he didn't turn to face her directly, his eyes followed her around."

160

"That could've been nothing."

"Could it really?" Wane questioned.

"He talks about her," Darlene added. Ziva had almost forgotten she was there. "He's mentioned all of you before, he has! But there's something about Chandler, isn't there? I think Ma noticed it too once. I heard her talk to him about it. He mentioned her powers and how he saw her, what she looked like, how she acted. He spoke about everyone, but he focused on her sometimes a lot more than others."

"Oh," was all Ziva could say.

"It might not be anything," Flora tried to insist. "You were both fresh recruits and everything to you was also new. He could've just been looking after her welfare. Especially around his parents. We've heard some stories over the years."

"They're nasty and 'ateful," Gretchen piped in, finally drawing into the huddle. "Well, his father is at least. And that's only what I've 'eard from Quinton himself. He doesn't tell me much about either of them, but I can read him well enough anyway. They ain't the sort you want to be around much. Quinton's the best of the bunch, almost like he doesn't come from them."

"Right," Flora nodded. "I think we're all well equipped to read people."

"Because we have to," Ziva agreed.

"One fault of the job," Gretchen said. "We see everythin' because we're trained to."

"Whether we want to or not," Wane sighed.

"I want to read people!" Darlene chirped.

On their previous mission, Ziva had sat in a hotel room, several laptops open around her as she'd watched her friends indeed mingle and dance and drink. She'd seen what she needed to, but if she had to look deeper, could she have seen more?

And he caught her when she fell, Ziva thought.

By staying with the presumably unconscious Chandler,

Quinton had condemned himself too. They'd been swarmed by island guards together. That didn't mean anything though. Any of them would've done the same for someone else. They all would've stayed with someone to make sure they weren't left alone. Well, maybe not Gretchen...

Plus, none of this meant what they were insinuating. Or it didn't have to. Quinton could simply care for Chandler the same way he did for Ziva.

No. That wasn't right and in her heart Ziva knew it.

During the last mission, Quinton had raced after Chandler when she was nearly caught in a fire, had begged for her to have a separate medical room and *yelled* at the medical staff to get her there with the best care they had to offer. He had watched her dance too, led her during them, and had made sure she was alright throughout. Not to mention how obsessed he became with both Chandler and Ziva about whether they would stay on at Redwing after that mission or not.

Whatever was happening, Quinton seemed to be drawn to Chandler. Ziva didn't know what it meant, maybe he didn't even know himself. She also didn't know if Chandler felt anything similar, whatever it was. Ziva would ask her when she could. Subtly.

But none of that mattered now. Neither Chandler or Quinton were there.

"We need to get them back," Ziva muttered.

"Don't you think we know that already?" Gretchen huffed.

"Bony," Wane warned, finally joining the others.

"What?" she barked. Without her usual heavy make-up and dark clothes, she appeared less threatening. The stripes of green through her hair however were still some kind of warning, like a frog with venomous bright colourings. "We're just walkin' laps through immovable sand while our team are captured."

"They have to still be on the island," Flora pointed out.

"Do they? It's been *hours*."

"And secret people like taking other people quietly," Darlene added. All eyes spun to her, alarmed. She shrugged. "What? I've seen the part of the films where that happens. Ma doesn't know I'm watching them behind her, but I *know*."

"They can't have gotten off the island," Wane reinforced. "The only way is by boat and we're at the docks."

"Unless they 'ave another way," Gretchen commented unhelpfully.

"How?" Ziva and Flora asked in unison.

Gretchen threw her hands up. "Why do I have to think of every little fuckin' thing? This fuckin' group! I swear you're only here to fuckin' wind me up!"

Wane had covered Darlene's ears just before Gretchen's outburst like he'd sensed it coming. When she calmed down and stomped towards the water, he let go.

"I'll go after her," Wane muttered, following Gretchen to the shoreline.

Ziva, Flora, and Darlene were left looking at one another in confusion.

CHAPTER TWENTY-ONE

GRETCHEN

26ᵗʰ Day of Winter 2406

ant to tell me what that was all about?"

Gretchen didn't know whether to punch Wane straight in his rigid and previously broken nose, walk off into the sea to drown herself, or drag him down on top of her on the beach right there and then. All in the idea of alleviating tension.

Her mind was a mess.

Instead of doing any of that, she stared towards the horizon with determination. "No."

"Ok, well then you'll have to listen to *me* talk."

"No, I—"

"Tough, Bony. I'm talking so you can listen." Wane took an audible deep breath. "A lot's happening around you that you can't control. The world is moving, your best friend left and then came back without telling you, people are trying to get close to you and be your friend, there's been something between us this past season, your original mission has veered off course. And you hate that. You hate everything that's happening now and everything that has been happening. Once something slips from your grasp, you seem to think everything will.

"But that's not how this works, Bony. One thing might go awry. Or many things will. Not everything. Life's not a slope that just keepings falling down.

"You don't seem to know what to do with yourself when change happens though. You're already so closed off, so shut down within yourself. You fold up. The only person I've ever seen you truly let in has been Quinton and even that took time. In all the *years*, I've never seen anyone else get close.

"I thought maybe you'd let me be the next. I'm not. I don't think I will be. And I'm ok with that. But you can't keep staying so inside yourself."

Wane sighed heavily, like the hope that he might've come to be what he wanted to her really was draining out of him. Gretchen saw it flow from him and wash out into the water at their feet. But she couldn't do anything. Her body had frozen up tightly. Even if she did have free range of movement, what could she have done?

He took several deep, steadying breaths before looking up, directly at her, and continued in her silence.

"Quinton leaving, I think, proved to you how alone you are and you hated looking in the mirror or listening to your thoughts to see that. It proved that if he wasn't there, no one was. And what if he didn't come back at all? Would anyone be there?

"I also think that's really why you've been sleeping with me. I'm just a momentary distraction from how alone you've made yourself. Because no one else has done this. You've built these walls."

"I'm not..." Gretchen trailed off, her voice fraying after just two words.

"You can't dismantle it all in a day. I wouldn't expect you to. But I *hate* seeing you so closed off behind those walls, Bony. You've shut yourself out."

"I 'aven't.... I'm not.... I didn't sleep with you just..."

"Whatever we are, that doesn't matter." He paused, searching her face slowly. "We'll circle back to that in time, I'm almost positive. But that's the *least* of the issues here."

Gretchen flinched away from Wane like she'd been slapped. Mentally, she had been. Physically, she felt her hands begin to shake.

Wane reached out as if to touch Gretchen but she dodged him. Sighing, he walked off again.

Tears sprung to her eyes, fast and burning. Gretchen couldn't remember the last time she had cried. She didn't need to remember. She didn't *want* to.

He was right though. Every damning word Wane had said, in that calm and soothing tone of his, was truthful. That's why it hurt so much. Truth always hurt.

And Gretchen hadn't wanted to hear it but Wane had given her zero choice.

The past season she really had seen how lonely her life was. There were many reasons *why* things had gotten that way, but it all ended with the same answer.

Her whole life before Redwing, her trust had been broken; her parents may have been semi-decent, but her friendships hadn't. They'd been the ones to report her to medical staff, the pokes and prods and needles a result of their hatred. And then jobs letting her go because she'd been forced to declare who she really was – even if she did it proudly sometimes. People on the streets lobbed insults and tried to cage her with abuse just for entering shops or trying to walk past once word about her got out. And some of those 'friends' that had remained weren't true, and they continued a bombardment of terror behind her back *and* eventually to her face until she'd had to flee.

Time and time and time again Gretchen had suffered through life.

She'd learned early on that people wanted from her but they would never give back; they would take miles but never give an inch. So she hadn't let anyone even try; building walls to keep her own heart safe had been easy, and letting them stay had been even easier.

Quinton had been an abnormality himself. Right from the start, there had been something about him that had urged her to trust him. Little by little she'd opened up until one day when he'd called her a friend and she realised that was indeed what they'd become to one another. And she hadn't hated it.

But he'd been a single exception.

Then he'd left, too.

And that had proved, to some deep and dark part of her that had never recovered, that no one should be allowed near her.

She kicked at the sand just to dispel some of the anger rising through her body. It burned like fire, waiting to consume her. But she couldn't let it. She *couldn't*. No matter how much she wished it would set her alight.

Gretchen needed to pull herself together. Just like every time, she needed to get herself in line and get to work. Her friend had come back to her and here she was, on the beach, fighting herself over something pointless. What did it matter anymore if she was alone? Who did it effect other than herself?

What *did* affect others was Quinton and Chandler being kidnapped.

If nothing else, Gretchen could allow herself to trust in the knowledge that everyone at Redwing would look out for each other on a base level – that they were all Abnormals and the outcasts of the world would stick together.

She stomped back up the beach to the rest of the group. They collected themselves in silence. Words weren't needed, they were all in agreement. They could make thorough plans later.

They reached the treeline in a tight cluster, though everyone made sure, in some unspoken pact, to not expose Darlene any more than she already was. They surrounded her like human shields. Thankfully, Darlene seemed agreeable to this.

Gretchen wasn't always aware of her powers. But on the rare occasions she was, she could sense every rattle, every movement, every extension of bones around her.

Right now, she could feel those close to her, but she could feel two full skeletons edging closer through the trees. There was more strength, more *life*, to one set of bones than the other.

Forcing her way to the front of the squad, she stopped them with a single raised hand.

Gretchen edged away from them. The two oncoming skeletons were running. Actually one of them was using its full potential, arms and legs all working. The other seemed to be detached from itself.

One more step and Gretchen froze. She spotted a blue blur and instantly *knew*.

Quinton, carrying a limp Chandler in his arms, crashed the small rescue party that'd been halfway to them.

"Quin—"

"We don't have time," he cut in. There were bruises around his wrists, maybe even small broken bones in his left pinky and left forefinger, and slight redness around his nose, but he seemed more worried about the girl in his arms, watching her intently. "She needs water."

"What kind?" Flora asked, stepping up.

"What do you mean 'what kind'?" Gretchen asked. "Is there more than one kind?"

"The kind you drink or the kind you lay in," Flora adjusted.

"I think she needs both," Quinton said. "I can't explain now, but we need to get her to some water."

"The sea is right behind us." Wane said it in a way that suggested everyone had lost their minds in forgetting they were on a beach. "She can lay in that and then drink the water we have in our bags."

Quinton shook his head. "That's too obvious, too close. Is there anywhere we can go that's private?"

Darlene stepped up to her brother's side. "She *is* pretty," she said, looking at Chandler and reaching a hand out to stroke her hair. Quinton opened his mouth but Darlene cut him off. "There's a natural pool a mile from here inland. We can get her in the water there."

"How do you—" Quinton cut himself off quickly. "Never mind. We're going."

"You're trusting her word?" Wane asked, not unfairly.

Quinton ignored Wane and started walking, breaking into something just shy of a run only a few steps in.

Gretchen didn't understand how Quinton and Chandler had gotten free or why they needed water, but she could sense the urgency in how tight Chandler's skeleton was becoming inside her skin. It was as if the bones were fusing together, and Gretchen had only sensed that a few times before. It was never good.

She trusted enough in Quinton to follow him now.

CHAPTER TWENTY-TWO

QUINTON

26th Day of Winter 2406

The water pool and matching waterfall appeared in view just as Darlene had promised. Quinton stared at it for a moment. How his sister had known it was here – not guessed, she'd *known* – he hadn't figured out yet.

Chandler groaned in his arms. Quinton looked down at her and the returning paleness on her otherwise soft face. He wanted to hold her tighter but didn't want to hurt her. She was already so fragile he couldn't risk making it worse. Instead he shuffled slightly to ease her in his grip; it might've made his arms ache more but he would live.

"Someone needs to take her in," he told the group.

"I'm not," Ziva said. She avoided eye contact at her outburst. "I never learnt how to swim."

"Same," Flora admitted. "It wasn't part of my growing up."

"I *can't*," Gretchen whispered beside him. Quinton knew all about her history with water; fights had nearly broken out the first few times she'd had to take a bath instead of a shower back at Redwing.

"I'm strong but not a strong swimmer," Wane said.

"I could—"

"*Nope!*" Quinton cut his sister off. "Not you. I know you can swim but you're too young."

"Too young? You dragged me all the way out here!" she argued.

"No, you dragged yourself." He shook his head as Chandler groaned again, this time fainter. "This is a waste of time. *I'll* take her in if none of you can."

"We'll look for a place to rest," Flora assured him.

It took several minutes of back and forth, passing Chandler to Wane to hold, and stripping down to the bare essentials before Quinton started lowering himself into the clear, sky blue pool of water.

The cold surface touched his skin like a breath of relief from the natural world. If it felt that good for him, he could only imagine what it would feel like for Chandler.

Once his feet touched the bottom rocks, he planted them. The bottom wasn't too deep so his head and shoulders stayed above the waterline, but he knew he'd have to get away from the edge. They were still too noticeable. Just as they would be in the middle. They'd been told to leave and this wasn't them leaving. Not that they could go. They had unfinished business here. There were trees about but not enough cover if someone was to trail after them or come looking.

Quinton eyed the waterfall. They needed to get closer to it. The rushing water would cover any noise and the thrashing would distort their images enough like a shield. It could keep them safe while they regrouped.

"See if we can hide behind the waterfall," Quinton said, looking at the group.

"It'll take us a little while to get there," Ziva said, grimacing.

The pool was expansive. It hadn't looked big but up close it was much larger than anticipated. It would indeed take a while to scout round the edges of it to the waterfall. And it would also take a while to swim across while pulling someone else along.

"We can take a little time to be careful," Flora suggested.

Quinton locked eyes with Wane. "Pass her to me."

Wane sank to his knees, careful not to jostle his precious cargo. "Look after her," he whispered so quietly Quinton almost didn't hear him.

Quinton nodded back and took Chandler into his arms once more.

He kicked away from the edge and started pacing towards the centre of the pool. The temperature of the water didn't heat or decline, staying a nice level. Quinton thought he heard a gentle sigh escape Chandler and stopped, glancing at her.

She laid on the surface of the water; her legs and arms had dropped below the surface while parts of her clung to the top. Her hair floated around her like a cloud. Ziva and Flora had aided in taking off her few layers until she'd been left in a t-shirt and underwear.

Quinton tried to be respectful and not look. This was no time *to* look. But snake and vine tattoo on her arm was also fully on display, and he couldn't help but notice a new one in the shape of a mask on her opposite upper arm. He fought against reaching out and tracing them like delicate pieces of artwork. He wondered if she had more.

To keep his hands and self respectful, he touched her hands and interlocked their fingers before cautiously pulling her deeper in.

They reached the centre of the pool with less fanfare than he'd been expecting. He glanced around for their friends but they'd vanished from view already.

Securing his feet, he noticed the water now reached his neck. He didn't know for sure but this had to be the deepest point, so he hopefully wasn't about to be washed away. He stood on a jagged shaped rock that jabbed and scraped into his soles but he barely felt the pain. He had bigger things to be concerned over.

Looking back at Chandler, Quinton suddenly realised why their captors had assumed she'd been his wife.

Dangling and shining brilliantly from her neck indeed was the emerald ring he'd gifted her during their last mission together. She'd woven it through a chain to hold it there. Despite their captor telling Quinton he'd seen the ring, he hadn't quite believed it could be there.

Quinton gave into his desire and touched the gemstone, running his finger over it while careful not to touch her skin.

Quinton had wondered what she'd done with the ring. He'd thought maybe she'd pawn it off or give it away, taking money and letting go of the memory. But here she floated, the ring around her neck like she couldn't let it leave her. She was *wearing* it. Maybe not as a ring but that didn't matter. She carried it with her still.

Quinton's heart pinched and he couldn't quite explain *why*.

Still smiling, he let go and the ring sank against her breastbone. Then he heard her sigh again.

Chandler's eyelids fluttered.

He lent closer. "Chandler? If you're in there, if you can hear me, kick, scream, call me anything you like, just *let me know*."

Her hand twitched in his.

"Come on, Icy," he pleaded. "Come and tell me you hate me, that I've managed to get you naked after all, that I'm a little bitch for worrying so much when you're clearly fine and there's nothing to pull my hair out about. Anything is better than silence."

But the silence continued.

All Quinton could hear was that his breathing had started to rattle his chest.

A small part of him wanted to shake Chandler. He wanted her to create a fuss over something, anything. He'd told her the truth. He longed to hear whatever it was she wanted to say, however she wanted to say it, and he didn't care about what that was as long as it came from her.

They floated together. This whole momentary peace would've been exactly that, peaceful, if he wasn't so terrified for Chandler.

Quinton knew it wouldn't be a permanent fix until they were off the island. But he had to try. He'd been the one to catch her as she fell and had been with her from then on. He didn't want to think about what would've happened if he hadn't been with her or they hadn't found this place when they had.

Chandler's lips parted and she groaned. Yet still her eyes did not open.

Obviously *something* was working. This was the most Quinton had gotten out of her in hours. He held onto that.

"I'll let you dye my hair whatever colour you like," he promised her.

Another groan.

Quinton sighed and glanced around again. No one emerged from the trees; no enemies or friends were around them.

"Wane told me to be careful before I brought you in the water," he told her, speaking so softly he hardly recognised his own tone and voice. "He cares about you. So do the others. Ziva loves you, I think, like a sister. Gretchen might not care, sorry to say, but she doesn't care about most things." He laughed lowly. "Maybe she'd come around to like you. You're as much of a pain in the arse as she is. The amount of trouble she's given me over the years and you're managing to beat her in a single season."

Another groan. Another sign to keep going.

He stared at the ring at her throat. "I missed you," he finally admitted. It was a truth he hadn't even told himself, not until then, but he'd felt it all along. "I missed everyone but there was something about *you*."

In all his sleepless nights where he'd pictured her face, heard her laugh, danced with her again in memory, he'd never quite figured out what it was about *her*. Even now, he couldn't tell exactly.

He also knew he was being unfair and selfish. They'd hardly spent any time together, barely a few weeks. He'd definitely pushed his limits with being intrigued by her and her abnormality. They knew parts of each other, had trusted their lives at points too, but that was so far from the full picture of them as individuals.

But it didn't seem to matter. Those moments had tied Quinton to Chandler in some way he couldn't untangle and didn't feel like he wanted too, either.

Quinton let go of Chandler's hand gently so he could scoop water up to pour over her cheeks and forehead. The paleness had begun to fade and no blazing blush was rising to replace it.

"*Quinton.*"

He startled at what sounded like Chandler's voice and nearly slipped off his rocky perch.

In a daze, Quinton touched the tips of his fingers to Chandler's face, dragging them down her cheeks and round her pink lips to come to rest on the side of her face.

He couldn't stop staring now that he'd started. She'd looked beautiful before, in that emerald dress at the posh party, and she looked equally as beautiful now. He just wished to see her hazel eyes staring back at him again.

Oh.

Suddenly Quinton *did* know. Everything he'd questioned, everything he'd thought of, came into perfect clarity. It all had answers and made perfect sense.

How had he not seen or *felt* it sooner? How had he been so confused?

But the thoughts of him being selfish and of not sharing enough time together to feel *that*, circled in his mind again. There was no way his heart was right. His brain wanted to tell him that it wasn't. And yet his own mind thought that assessment was wrong.

It didn't matter. None of that mattered right now.

Quinton didn't know whether to scream or stay quiet. In the end, he smiled at Chandler even though her eyes were still firmly shut.

"We'll get you home," he said. "You'll be in your safe space again soon."

"Ice." That was definitely Chandler's voice.

"You'll create your ice again." His smile grew. "You'll be ok. I'll look after you and get you out of here."

"Trust."

Quinton didn't know if he was hallucinating or hearing things or not, but it certainly sounded like Chandler was responding to him. He hoped his theory on the water was working and she was slowly coming back to consciousness. Above everything, he wanted Chandler to open her eyes to see how stunning this place truly was before they had to leave it behind, possibly forever. He wanted her to see the beauty here, just as he was now waking to it.

Ever so gently, Quinton bent forward and kissed her temple. "You'll be ok," he promised. "You're strong and there's so much more to you than what I already know. You intrigue me, Icy. I want to learn it all."

He threaded his fingers with hers again and finally kicked off the rock he'd been stood on, pulling them both through the water once more. But every few paces, he had to turn and glance at the ring at her throat, her face too, before he would return to face the waterfall.

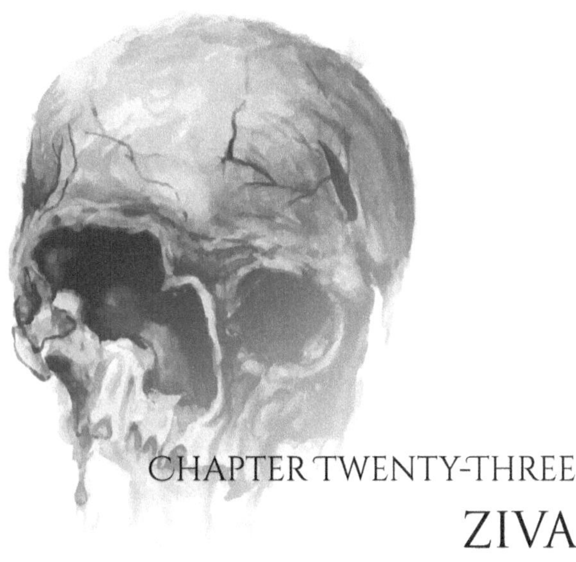

CHAPTER TWENTY-THREE

ZIVA

27ᵗʰ Day of Winter 2406

There existed a space behind the waterfall that could be used as a hideout.

Wane had stumbled across it first, blundering through to it despite possibly being one of the most careful members in the group. Gretchen and Flora hadn't been much further behind him. Darlene followed at the end.

Bags were immediately dropped onto the stone floor. The resounding sound of a sigh of relief echoed along the walls of the cave, and it was impossible to tell who exactly had made it.

Ziva had half-thrown her bag against the wall in frustration. The two people she considered her friends, one her *sister,* had swum here, outside in the blue nature-made pool in order to hopefully save her life. And Ziva hadn't been able to do a damned thing to help.

All her life Ziva had been forced to raise her siblings or care for her elders. Now she was stuck in a position where none of that accidental training was coming in handy. The only thing she could do was keep going outside to rewet the t-shirt they were using to keep Chandler's head cool as she rested.

Quinton had called for help in getting out of the water when night had finally fallen silent. Not even the Island's crickets clicked that late.

Wane had taken Chandler and tucked her into the back wall of the alcove where it felt coldest. Quinton had gotten himself out. Ziva couldn't remember where the t-shirt idea had come from but it'd happened somewhere between Quinton drying and redressing, and half the team falling asleep due to sheer exhaustion.

"Do you need water?"

Ziva flinched at the sudden noise, and she had to focus her eyes in the dark to be able to see Darlene clearly. She was surprised the young girl was still awake at this hour.

"I'm alright, thank you," Ziva said.

"I haven't seen you drink." Darlene rustled something and then a bottle was being passed over to Ziva. "You have to stay hydrated. That's what my brother was telling me. You should listen to him too."

"Your brother's pretty smart," Ziva said as she took a long gulp of crisp water.

"He's an idiot," Darlene contradicted.

Ziva nearly choked on her laughter. "You love him really."

"Those things go hand in hand. Especially with him."

"Thank you." Ziva handed the bottle back.

"Do you have any brothers?"

Ziva half-laughed. "I have enough siblings and family to fill this whole cave up."

"I only have Ma and Quinton."

"I don't know your mum—"

"She's the best!" Darlene jumped in. "She never gets angry

or upset, lets me have sweets on the weekends. She even takes me to the local fair every summer."

Ziva smiled at the young girl, hoping she could see it. "She does sound like the best."

"Do your parents take you to the fair?"

"I haven't been for a few summers... We've all been busy."

Simply, though, that was a lie. Ziva hadn't been to the fair in years because her parents had focused their money on taking the younger ones and travelling to the beach – something they'd never done with Ziva. She knew she shouldn't have been jealous, but sometimes it was hard not to be, especially when she was only there when the adults wanted something from her but otherwise ignored.

"You should get some rest," Ziva suggested, changing the subject.

Darlene groaned like the child she was. "I've *had* sleep," she whined. "Are all missions like this? It's boring. I thought there'd be more adventure, more fun, more *guns.*"

"Trust me when I say you don't want guns," Flora's voice whispered into the space. "No one *ever* wants guns."

"But don't you have them?"

"Sometimes," Flora admitted. Ziva could make out her shape nearby; she hadn't seen Flora wake or get closer despite Ziva's ability to shift the darker colours to lighter ones for her own benefit. "I wouldn't go asking or looking for one though. Any weapon is bad news."

Ziva didn't want to point out that sometimes Abnormals were considered weapons.

"Then I want adventure!" Darlene cried.

"Day," Quinton's voice cut through the space. Now he was awake too. "Every mission is always different, depending on what's required of us. Neither of us were meant to be here on this one. You aren't meant to be here *at all.*"

Darlene huffed. "How long are you going to keep bringing that up for?"

"Until you understand that you shouldn't have done that. So, probably a few years at least."

Ziva saw Darlene roll her eyes and she had to stifle her laughter. It appeared Flora was having the same trouble in her little corner, her hand covering her mouth to stop herself.

"Get some sleep, Day," Quinton said after a moment. "You're grouchy when you're tired."

"Am not," Darlene argued.

"You are," Quinton said in a sing-song tone.

"Am *not!*"

"You know damn well you are," he called back. "There's nothing more we can do tonight. Frankly, I'm as tired as the dead and would go to sleep happier and healthier knowing *you* were asleep too."

"You're not my parent," she mumbled but shuffled off anyway.

Ziva turned back to Chandler. She mopped her friend's brow and noticed how dry the t-shirt was becoming yet again. Was Chandler absorbing the water from the t-shirt to cool herself? Ziva hadn't timed each period between wetting the cloth and having to redo it, but she could've sworn it was around every half an hour, possibly less.

"Can you keep an eye out?" she asked Flora.

"I brought an extra over," Flora announced, replacing the drying cloth with a freshly wet one. The resounding squelch of fabric against skin made Ziva grimace. "Go take some time anyway. I'll look after her for a bit."

Ziva wanted to argue, her mind pushed her too, but Flora was right. She could give herself five minutes. She couldn't remember the last time she'd rested and her bones sighed at the opportunity.

She carefully wove her way around the bodies of her fellow teammates. The cave was deep enough to fit them all, even Wane with his expansive muscles. But the height was lacking, meaning they had to crouch or shuffle half-bent when inside it.

The night and the gushing of the waterfall greeted Ziva at the exit. The whole group hid inside the cave, the waterfall blocking them from sight.

Taking her shoes off, Ziva sat on the tip of the space and let her toes dangle outwards. The spray of water coated her lower legs and feet. She took a deep breath in through her nose. With even the insects tucked away, peace flowed towards her.

At the sound of shifting dirt, she turned around quickly. Quinton's blue hair was distinct and she could make it out before the rest of him.

"Why blue?" she blurted.

Quinton paused, then dropped beside her, sticking his feet out like she had. "I just fancied a change from the red."

Ziva nodded and started to swing her legs. "Didn't you tell your sister you were tired?"

"I am."

"Then why aren't you sleeping?"

He huffed just as his sister had. "Do you ever get so over-tired you feel wired?" Ziva looked at him curiously. "I feel like I've been electrocuted. All my strength has gone, all my energy was zapped in swimming, but I've been given so much *extra* my body doesn't know what to do with it. It's like the adrenaline is lingering and that's what's keeping me up."

"I can try singing you a lullaby?" she tried to joke.

Quinton laughed. "Oh, I'd love to hear that."

"How's your sister holding up?" Ziva asked next.

"She's a pain in the arse, but she's good," Quinton said. "I didn't want to involve her in any of this. I wanted to keep *this* separate from her life. She could've grown up *normal*. And that's horrible because there's nothing wrong with how we are, but she could've been kept away from all this nonsense the world creates."

Ziva forced her gaze on the water in front. "She saw this place."

"Yeah, she did," he sighed, heavily, like an old man tired of life. "And she found the Mansion."

"Has she—"

"No, she's never been tested."

Testing came when a person was suspected of having the mutated gene that led to developing an abnormality. Though the genes didn't often run in families, or if it did it didn't always make scientifical sense, those around Abnormals were almost always forced into being checked in case.

It was often treated like some kind of infectious disease. People were seen to be cursed with it.

Years ago virus' mutated human genes in less than one percent of the population, so technically a disease *had* created the Abnormals. But Ziva had seen evidence since, in a museum during her last mission, that the effects may have always been around. That some genes in older humans, from long dead ago, had mutated way before. So how long had they *really* been around? And why was it only a problem now?

"Katia knew about me," Quinton continued. "She didn't think it was a problem, though." Abnormals didn't supposedly *have* to be documented, plenty could develop gifts without going on records, but not many got away with it for long. "There's always a chance, with anyone, developing it these days. Even if it is technically still a rare thing."

Most of the world's population didn't have an abnormality. Those people lived everyday lives as boring as the next. But it also kept them safe. It kept them thinking they were better than everyone else too. To them, those who weren't different, who weren't *other*, had the high ground.

Somehow, without having any powers at all, those ordinary Humans had the most power.

"Did she not want her daughter to face the scrutiny that came with the label or...?" Ziva didn't quite know how to finish asking what she wanted.

"I think, to Katia, it didn't matter what her daughter became because she'd love her either way." Quinton smiled. "Darlene's plenty troublesome *without* an abnormality. But if she had one, Katia would've loved her all the same. That's the kind of person she is. Her love is unconditional. Always."

Ziva found herself smiling. "She sounds lovely."

"She's a bundle of love wrapped in a Human." He turned his head towards her. "I love them both, Katia and Darlene. They're my family."

"I'm glad you have them." Ziva reached out and took Quinton's closest hand.

"Darlene found me," he laughed. "She blundered in like a storm in the night. You were there."

"And you took her back home."

Quinton nodded slowly, solemnly. "She's young. Too young to be following me around."

"She followed you here, Quinton. I wouldn't underestimate her."

"Oh, I haven't for a long time." Quinton squeezed Ziva's hand.

"Do you think she has an abnormality?" Ziva asked quietly.

"*She* found *me*, in a place that isn't supposed to be found."

"Her mum will still love her." It was Ziva's turn to squeeze his hand.

"She will," he agreed. "And so will I. This wouldn't change anything. It'd mean she's just more herself."

Ziva's heart ached. She wished her family was like that, that their love was unconditional. But they seemed to want for something. They always asked for more, even if it couldn't be given. Only then could she 'earn' respect or love.

"What about Redwing?" she dared to ask.

"I've been thinking about it."

"And?"

"I could have both my families together. But that's selfish. Day, she'd have to leave her mum behind. She's too young to make that choice." He sighed then. "But that's a problem for when we're *off* this Island and not before. I can't let my future worries interrupt my present ones."

"We do have two missions to complete," Ziva agreed, understanding that he wanted to switch up the topics. "Any idea how we're going to do that?"

"No fucking clue."

Quinton laughed and Ziva laughed alongside him. They calmed down after some minutes, the quiet of the night taking them back. Ziva felt at peace, like this was what she truly needed. A moment of laughter rather than a moment of rest. Her heart felt semi-full again.

"We'll find a way," Ziva said once her breathing evened out.

"I think we're close. Flora got us to that 'garden' when we'd been stuck. All we have to do is look at the bigger picture and put the pieces we have together, because there's definitely more going on there."

Briefly, Ziva wondered about Quinton's quartz necklace and his ability to see into the future of those who touched it.

Should she ask to touch it so he could read her future? Would it give them answers to this mission? Or the fate of their friend?

She quickly dismissed it. She didn't want to intrude or force Quinton to, either. His power wasn't exact, futures could change, he'd explained that once, and she didn't want to make him watch if something bad was coming. She didn't want him to immortalise it in a drawing either, something else she knew he did after *seeing*; not that she'd seen his notebook to hand, though there had hardly been the time for it.

They sat together, in a locked silence. As much as the waterfall protected the group from onlookers who may still be searching for them, it also kept them from the world. Right here, they couldn't look out, like they were kept in a bubble to stop harm from reaching them and from them reaching out to it.

The silence was broken by a pattern of footsteps from behind. Quinton seemed to sense the same thing. Both he and Ziva spun away from the water in unison.

"Flora?" Quinton questioned.

Flora approached, arms held high as if worried one of them might strike her. "It's Chandler," she breathed. "She's awake."

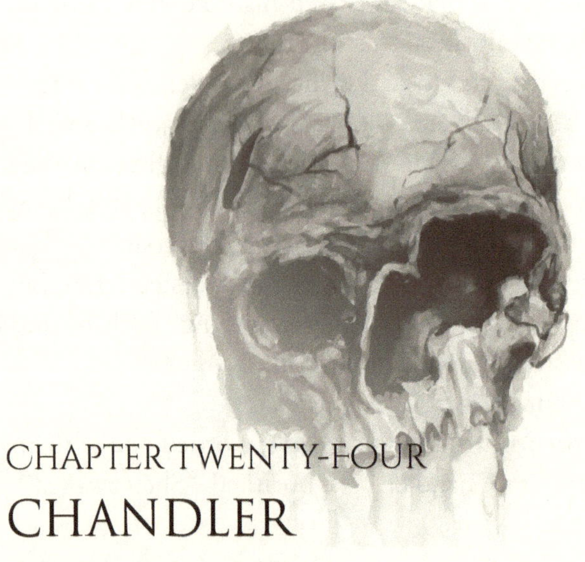

CHAPTER TWENTY-FOUR

CHANDLER

27th Day of Winter 2406

*C*ome *and tell me you hate me...”*
“...you're clearly fine...”
“Anything is better... silence...”
Words sank through Chandler. It felt like she was swimming in a pool of them. Her body seemed weightless; her arms and legs just hanging, her head tilted. She knew her eyes were closed but she could see everything still, like the world hadn't turned itself off to her.

The sky had been painted black, but ice-white words were scrawled across it. Her eyes searched them, reading them over and over. The pool she found herself in transformed to match making it all a landscape that never started or ended, that had no top or bottom or sides, but everywhere met as one.

“Wane told me... careful...”
Some words were easier to make out than others. Chandler

had to properly screw up her face to focus on the distant ones. She laughed when she realised she was doing it.

This must be what it was like to cloud-gaze.

Chandler had never done *that* before. Her mother had always been too busy to stop and stare at the sky, and with Chandler at her side she seemed to always need to go double speed as if Chandler would do nothing but waste time.

Parks were always forbidden places and Chandler could only go outside in her school playground when the teachers had decided she'd completed enough work for the day – she was sure sometimes she had more to do than other kids. Had her mother infected the teachers with something to make them think Chandler didn't deserve to play? It certainly seemed that way.

The only time she remembered being a kid was with her uncle.

As if thinking about him summoned him, his face appeared in front of her. His cheeky handlebar moustache was just as he'd always made it up to be. Raggedy clothes hung off his limbs yet he styled them together in some sort of lumberjack fashion of forgotten years.

"He cares about you..."

Those words zoomed into existence right above her uncle. Chandler smiled at them. Her uncle was quite possibly one of the few people *ever* to care enough about her.

The figure of her uncle nodded.

Chandler stared at her arm, at the tattoo her and her uncle shared. She'd always admired it. So when she'd been old enough, she'd got one to match. Except she had no little kid hanging around with markers to colour it in every time they saw her.

"Ziva loves you."

Ziva did and Chandler loved her too, like long-lost sisters. They'd grown close right from the start and that hadn't stopped. They regularly stayed in each other's rooms at Redwing, sharing snacks in bed while planning what they were going to do the next day. Chandler had been teaching Ziva how to play pool, and Ziva had been sharing about her family's – but not hers – religion, too.

"...sorry to say..."

Her uncle's image smiled one final time before fading with the words. Chandler smiled back at the empty air. Those words were his, a goodbye from him in this place to the real her.

Chandler cracked her knuckles and they sounded like little fireworks with every *pop*. How could they sound so great yet so unreal?

"...as much of a pain... she is..."

Chandler stopped. Her whole body stopped floating in a single spot. The sensation that she was no longer in air but rather in water cascaded along her skin, prickling it. She cracked her knuckles again.

Whose words had those been? No other face had appeared. Not here.

Of course there was no sign of her mother. She didn't need the woman to appear and definitely didn't expect her. If she did materialise, Chandler would've thought she was completely dead.

These images and flashes of words were already convincing her she might be halfway there anyway. The fact that she couldn't feel her heart in her chest just added to the fear that this was her tunnel towards the final end.

But even then she shouldn't expect her mother to show up to some kind of memorial or to say goodbye. Chandler wasn't what her mother wanted. The only thing her mother thought precious was money.

All her life, Chandler knew her mother hadn't really cared for her. She had just been another accessory to gain more from whoever would give it. That included Chandler herself.

But things had always run deeper than that. Her mother's lack of true care came when she'd been old enough to eat and move on her own. Chandler had been maybe ten or eleven the first time her mother had left her home for two days straight, alone. No one had come for her in that time. She knew her uncle would have, but he'd died six months previous, so that left no one to find her.

Growing up, Chandler hadn't minded. Having the little place to herself had given her peace and freedom. But that all vanished whenever her mother returned. The woman had demanded to be waited on, hand and foot.

Chandler was grateful for Redwing and everything it'd given her. And it'd only been a single season since she'd joined. Yet she couldn't imagine anything better, or why she'd taken so damned long to decide to stay there.

Summoned from her thoughts, the clouds above her shifted into the shape of Ziva. Her hair now cut to her shoulders, her curtain fringe shaping her face. Chandler laughed as Ziva swam through the sky like a bird, and the sound echoed.

"We'll get you home."

Chandler scowled. Could she leave this place? There seemed to be no end to it.

"Ice."

Chandler slapped her hand over her mouth. The word had slipped off her tongue.

The image changed, reshaped into something less familiar but still known.

Quinton's white hair appeared first, followed by his smirk. Chandler groaned. What had brought him here? She definitely hadn't been thinking about him. She'd barely *seen* him in the last season, not since he left to be with his family.

A sketchbook flipped open in his hands. His smirk grew as he pulled a pen out of his hair.

Quinton put aside his items and they sank away. Then he himself drew closer, walking instead of floating. He pulled the necklace away from his chest.

Chandler stared and instantly started to reach for it. She'd called on its power before, at his guidance, and clearly he wanted her to again.

The quartz was cold this time; her palm tingled under the weird pressure of it. "What do you want to know?" she asked.

"You'll be ok," he told her.

"I trust you." She let the necklace go. "But why wouldn't I be ok?" Her voice sounded far-away, empty, like she hadn't spoken aloud.

She dragged her gaze from left to right.

Suddenly this place didn't look like it could be a tunnel to anywhere but instead more like a never-ending, never-bending room. How could she be floating through an empty void? How could words write themselves into a black sky that met the horizon as if it wasn't a changing thing at all?

Coldness turned to ice along her skin. The tingle of freezing temperatures caused her gentle search to turn frantic.

Where was she? What was happening?

"You'll be ok," the Quinton figure promised. *"You're strong... Intrigue me..."*

Chandler didn't know what game was being played here, but she wanted none of it.

Her arms shot out from her sides. Whatever she'd been laying in drifted off her body like she really *had* been floating before but now rising above it. She grasped onto the water around her. The temperature plummeted but it didn't affect her. Only warmth could harm her.

She gasped. That was the last thing she remembered. *Warmth.* A cursed thing to someone who needed the constant opposite.

Summer could be managed carefully, it always had. But a summer climate that desperately clung to everything, everywhere? That was like torture.

Chandler remembered the almost personalised torture. It was as if the heat clung to her still, the warmth trying to bury under her skin and kill off the cold for good. She felt her heart's rhythm panic at the idea. *She* panicked at the idea. She didn't want to be replaced by the sun.

"Quinton," she called. He needed to come back. She needed him to tell her she would be ok again, that he saw in his crystal she'd be fine. "*Quinton!*"

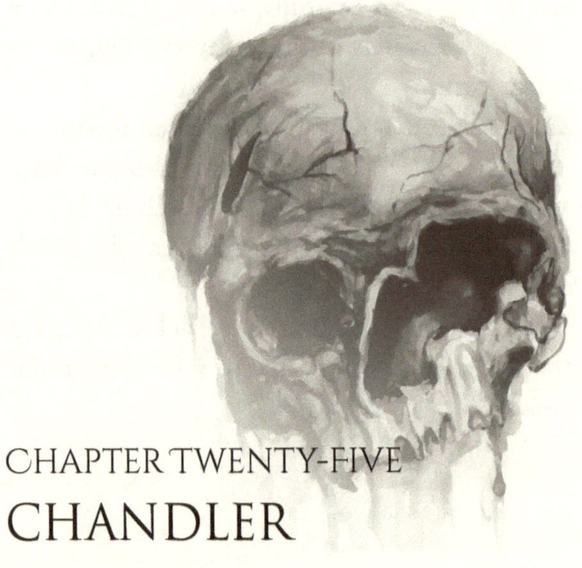

CHANDLER

27th Day of Winter 2406

"Quinton!"

Her body jolted to attention, her spine freezing while her limbs shot about. She sat up like the dead coming back to life. The gasp she took rattled her chest, her lungs crackling.

Chandler's hazel eyes met Wane's small brown ones. He looked her over slowly, carefully. Chandler glanced down at herself. She could tell her clothes were damp, and there was less of them than she remembered. Her trousers were missing and she'd been stripped down to a wet vest-top that clung to her sides and curves.

She coughed and Wane's gaze shot up to hers. A slightly embarrassed flush danced across his cheeks in the dim light. "I didn't mean to disrespect," he said.

"You didn't," she reassured.

"I was just checking you over."

She nodded once. "I know."

He leaned in closer, putting his mouth right to her ear as he whispered, "I won't tell him you called for him." He lent back slightly to look her in the eye again. "He's outside with Ziva and everyone else is asleep. I don't think anyone heard."

Dazed, Chandler nodded, not knowing how to *begin* to explain what'd happened to her or why she'd called out. Wane smiled lightly, like they now shared a secret, which she supposed they kind of did. She thought, not for the first time, about how alike yet different he was from his brothers; the mild manners and all-round polite courtesy wasn't a familial trait.

She changed the subject. "What happened?" Her voice sounded thin, and her throat felt scratchy. "Why am I wet?" She spied all the grey rock around them. "Where are we?"

Wane's face scrunched up. "You passed out, Icy."

"I... passed out?" she scowled.

He nodded. "It's nearly been twenty-four hours. We were worried like hell." Chandler stared at him. "We think it was the heat," he continued. "It tried to take over and your body was working double-time to cool itself. Someone said something about you using too much energy and power."

"You burnt out," came Gretchen's voice. She sounded groggy like she was still fighting sleep. Chandler couldn't see her, but she had to be somewhere nearby. "I've never seen it 'appen before."

"It scared us," Wane said.

"Sorry for the inconvenience," Chandler muttered.

"Should be," Gretchen grumbled.

Chandler rolled her eyes and cracked her knuckles. "So I passed out and you brought me to a cave?"

"That's not..." Wane tilted his head like a puppy. "How much do you remember?"

She tried to think. "I remember... There were trees, and a weird pile of gold *things*."

What were probably Gretchen's snores filled the cave.

"That's where you collapsed, at the sort of garden of gold," Wane explained after a minute.

"Garden of gold?"

"It's what I'm naming it!" Wane declared, looking rather proud of himself.

Chandler let it go. "But what happened?"

"Guards came out of nowhere to capture us for supposedly trespassing. We were trying to run but you fainted. Quinton caught you but he couldn't get you up in time. He stayed with you to give us a chance. You were captured, Icy."

"But I'm here?" She then realised she hadn't been the only person in that story to be taken. "Where's Quinton?"

"He's fine," Wane promised, dropping his voice low.

"Everyone's okay?"

He nodded again. "I didn't think you'd care about people as much as you do."

"I care," she said, not bothering to add the, "*when I let my-self*" part she was thinking.

Because it was true. She *could* bring herself to like others and care for them. It'd happened before. But she was also pretty good at reading people, and since so many people had screwed her over before, she didn't want to get close to others in case they all turned out the same. Some of those cuts still ran close to bone.

Wane's expression softened like he'd heard her thoughts anyway. "Your captors let you go, but Quinton had to bargain with them first. You needed medical attention and they could see that."

"They let us go so I could get help," Chandler realised.

"They made him promise you wouldn't come back," Wane admitted.

Chandler shuffled to lean against the rocky wall. "But we're still here."

"The mission isn't over. Neither of them are."

"And they're more important."

Someone shuffled inside the cave. A little pebble kicked against a nearby wall. Chandler assumed it might've been from Gretchen rolling over in her sleep.

"Well..." Wane cocked his head. "We had to make a decision. You weren't doing so hot. The urgent medical care thing wasn't a complete lie. But we didn't think we could get you off the Island. Quinton had a theory."

She rolled her eyes. "Of course he did."

"And it probably saved your life. I think you owe me a *little* grovelling thank you."

Wane's lips twitched like he wanted to smile, but one look from Chandler shut him down immediately. He shuffled away instead.

The cave they'd holed up in wasn't big. How they all fit inside was some sort of miracle. But as Wane's shoulders touched the furthest wall, it revealed the others.

Clearly the noise Chandler had heard hadn't been Gretchen after all.

Flora's hair was rumpled, her headband slightly further forward on her head than normal as if she'd replaced it in a hurry. In the dark of this place it was difficult to see her freckles or copper hair but Chandler could see her left cheek twitch nervously.

"Glad to see you're awake," Flora said, sounding earnest. "And now that you are, and seem fine, too, I'm going to try and get some rest."

Chandler tried not to scowl. "Right, yeah..."

Flora disappeared.

That left Ziva and Quinton.

Ziva flew at Chandler, arms tightening around her without restricting Chandler's shoulders. Chandler breathed her friend in; Ziva smelt of salt water.

Chandler looked at Quinton over Ziva's shoulder. It was as if her thoughts had summoned him. She couldn't remember his hair being blue, but she must've known; this wasn't the first time she was seeing him. Then she realised what else was wrong. His usual smirk was missing.

"Not happy to see me too?" she teased as Ziva pulled back. She remembered how easy it was to joke around with him, like a routine kicking back in as if they'd done it one hundred times before.

"Oh, believe me, I'm overjoyed," he said, then his face broke out into a big smile. "You gave me *Hell*. Can you not do that again?"

Chandler cracked her knuckles. "I can't promise anything."

"I'll beg if that's what it takes?"

"Interesting," she smiled slightly, "but I still can't make those kinds of promises."

"Typical." He shook his head. "I drag you through a bloody waterfall and you can't—"

"A waterfall?" Chandler glanced between Ziva and Quinton.

Ziva crouched in front of her. She placed a hand on Chandler's head, a comforting pat. "You were burning up and we needed to cool you down," she said. "He had to get you in the water."

"What?" It sounded ridiculous.

"I thought that if your external temperature cooled, your inner would too," Quinton explained. "Getting your body into water was the easiest way, but we couldn't go to the beach. Those people let us go but I bet they would've been watching. The might still be anyway. They could be combing everywhere looking for us."

"But now we're stuck here," Chandler argued. "If they're watching the beaches for us, then how do we get off?" Quinton snorted loudly. She shot him a look. "That was *not* meant in the way you heard it!"

"I know," he said, grinning.

"You're still acting like a fucking moron."

Quinton's grin grew. "Fuck, I forgot how moody you could be."

Ziva groaned. "Don't start where you two left off."

"We didn't leave off anywhere," Chandler told her.

"Our first mission? You both bitched to no end about the other. Quinton, that was more you than her." Quinton shrugged, still grinning, and Ziva shook her head like an exasperated mother. "Just pick up from the middle, then. The bits where you *got along*. Please. Save the rest of us."

"We didn't bitch that much," Quinton argued.

"There's no trying to deny it," Ziva told him. "You got along eventually, but you both took your time to get there."

And then he left, Chandler thought sourly. She glanced up at Quinton. He stood with his arms folded and slight smile on his lips, but he wasn't looking at her.

They *had* gotten along after a while. He'd said some things to her and she'd said some back, but they had worked well together. All three of them had.

"We still have two missions to close here," Ziva pressed on. She'd dropped the volume of her speech and Chandler wondered why until she heard the sound of snores coming from various places in the cave. "*Two*. And we can't leave until they're done. Not just because someone's watching us."

Chandler watched Ziva twiddle her fingers. "Wouldn't it make more sense and be better for everyone if I got off the Island?"

"Why?" Quinton asked quietly.

She looked right at him. "Are you forgetting your whole story about dragging my arse through water to beat near-death heatstroke?"

"I'm not forgetting anything," he said. "Though I wasn't thinking about your arse."

"And that's why I'm not in trousers?"

"We had to get as much skin exposed to the water as possible," Ziva said, cutting in before Quinton could answer.

"Last mission I woke in a medical centre without trousers, and here I am again."

"Trousers are for the normal," Quinton joked.

Chandler let herself laugh once. "But I'm serious. This could all just happen again."

No one had a response to that.

"Have you all finally shut up?" Gretchen's voice grumbled.

"Sorry, Gritty," Quinton chuckled.

"You're not fuckin' sorry," she complained.

"Just close your eyes," he told her. Gretchen grumbled again but it was too distant to understand. "We should all do that. It's been a rough twenty-four hours."

"I've had enough sleep," Chandler said. Her limbs ached from being so still.

"There's nothing to do," Ziva said. "And sleep will heal you more."

"You'll use less power asleep," Quinton added.

"I want to see this waterfall," Chandler tried again. "Then I promise I'll sleep."

Quinton notably shook his head. "Why don't I believe that?"

"Come with me?" she suggested. "You can bore me to sleep."

Ziva coughed though it sounded like she was trying to hide a laugh. "You're doing it again."

At the same time, both Chandler and Quinton said, "Sorry mum!"

The trio broke into a fit of laughter. It really did feel like they were back on their last mission, laughing as they were stuck somewhere with information they didn't know what to do with.

Absently, Chandler touched the ring she still wore. She couldn't explain why, but she hadn't been able to part with it. Something about it had tied itself into her heart, so that's where she wore it.

"I'll take you outside," Quinton said.

Chandler looked at him. "Don't think about pushing me in."

He held his hands up. "I wouldn't *dream* of it! Don't push me in either."

"Damn, there go *all* my plans."

"Please don't tire yourself out to the point of exhaustion," Ziva said. She scooped Chandler up into another hug. "Go to sleep the second you feel tired. I can't watch you pass out again." Ziva squeezed her. "And go easy on him. He saved you."

Ziva pulled back and drew away, probably to her space in the cave. Chandler turned to Quinton, who was already watching her. He smiled.

"Shall we?" he offered, his arm jutting out.

"Like old times," she said, actually taking his arm.

CHAPTER TWENTY-SIX
QUINTON

28th Day of Winter 2406

You really don't need to be out here with me."

Quinton ignored Chandler and sat back where he had been with Ziva earlier, flicking his legs out so the waterfall spray tickled his toes again.

He knew he didn't need to be out here, anyone could've done it, but *someone* had to. Chandler had only just woken up. There was no way in Hell anyone with a decent heart would let her wander about on her own.

Night had fallen.

Quinton tried to spot the pool of shimmering water, but he could only see an endless glimmer of stars. The horizon met the water and reflected it everywhere. Apparently living on a small Island without much smog provided a clear sky every night unless natural clouds covered it.

Quinton wondered if midnight had passed and they were starting a new day yet.

The last few had seemed so long. He couldn't remember the last time he'd properly slept either. Maybe at Katia's? He certainly hadn't slept in the last twenty-four hours. His eyes were heavy yet they'd refused to close earlier and they definitely weren't closing now.

He yawned anyway.

"Go to bed, Quinton," Chandler told him.

Raising his eyebrow curiously, he watched as she shifted a few times, clearly uncomfortable. "There's no way you just told me what to do," he said.

"I'm trying to," she admitted.

"Don't. It won't work."

She met his gaze. "But you're tired."

"Even if I go back, I won't be able to sleep."

"How do you know? Have you tried?"

In all honesty, he *hadn't*. But he didn't need to. He knew what would happen. The aches would keep him awake and so would everyone's snores. Not to mention his brain wouldn't shut down for longer than a minute.

"How pretty is this place in the daylight?" she asked him.

He blinked at her sudden switch. "Very," he nodded and dropped his gaze away from her.

"Did you get to see much?"

"Enough." He smiled.

"Wish I hadn't been unconscious for it." Chandler sighed next to him.

"There's always the morning," he promised.

Chandler let out a stunted laugh. "I think I'd like this place but I already know it doesn't like me."

"It's definitely unfortunate."

"How's your sister taking it all?" Quinton's head whipped round. Chandler was already looking at him. "She's here still, right? I remember her being with you when you arrived. She looks a little like you."

"Oh, she's too much like me," Quinton laughed. "She's coping better than most people would. I've barely heard her complain."

"There's enough to keep her interested."

"What? Between us, this place, and the mission?" He laughed again. "Me and Ziva think she's *exactly* like me."

Chandler scowled. "In what way?"

"We think she might be Abnormal. It's what we were discussing before you woke up."

"Sorry for interrupting." Chandler smiled, and it brightened her whole face.

"You *should* be apologising! How dare you?" His grin matched hers. "I don't know what to do about it though." His face relaxed. "Do I take her home or back to Redwing?"

She cracked her knuckles without looking at them. "Since when did you make a distinction between the two?"

"Since the two of them needed to be distinct."

Chandler raised a brow at him. "Look who's growing up."

A laugh forced its way out of him. "Don't get too ahead of yourself there. I'm still plenty childish." He gave her a quick once over. Even under the shadow of night he could see how *wrong* her skin looked, and despite the waterfall gushing he could hear the wheeze with every inhale. "How're you feeling?"

Chandler pulled a face. "Honestly? Like I've been fucking bulldozed by a truck."

"That makes sense. You dropped like a rock, Icy."

"Ugh, don't call me that," she groaned. "Everyone else has started to but I didn't need to hear your voice say it today."

Smirking, he leaned in closer. "What do you want to hear me say instead?" he whispered. "I'll call you anything you like." He ignored how hard his heart pounded when the words reached his own ears.

Thankfully Chandler saw it as the joke he'd intended to

make it and tried shoving him. Her hands touched him but she barely made a breeze from the movement.

"Tell me when you've had enough and we'll go inside," he told her.

She rolled her eyes. "You're not going in without me, are you?"

"Sorry, snowflake, you're stuck with me here."

"Fuck. And there's no window to jump out of here either."

"That was fun," he agreed.

"The whole mission was alright."

"One of the better ones for sure."

"What've you been doing since then?" she asked. Quinton didn't think he'd ever heard her sound so innocent or curious before. Definitely not about him.

"I was with my family." He swung his legs as he spoke. He needed to dispel some of the energy that was building inside him.

"Did you see your actual mum and dad in that time?"

"No."

"Why not?"

"I wanted to see my mum, but she would just come with *him* and I didn't want that." He might as well tell her. "He's getting more desperate for me to step into his shoes. I talked to him once, called the actual house I was born in, not one of their vacation homes on the chance mum might be home. Dear old dad picked up instead. Then he picked a fight when I denied him, because of course he did. I haven't called since."

"And I'm guessing since they don't know where you are they can't call you either?"

"More like they wouldn't call anyway since I'm the one that needs to apologise."

"For standing up to him? I didn't agree with him before and even less so now."

He smiled at her. "I remember you not being his biggest supporter."

"Bigger supporter in him getting smacked into next week. Now *that* I can get behind."

"When did you get so violent?" he asked.

"Probably around the time I was old enough to understand how the world worked."

"Ah." Quinton could understand that. "Have you seen anyone since joining Redwing full time?"

"No."

Short and sweet, and clearly the end of the line to that conversation.

Quinton wanted to ask, wanted to get Chandler to tell him, but he wouldn't push it. Not here and now. Maybe one day she'd trust him with the story, and as much as he was intrigued by it, why she shut down so hard every time her life before *now* came up, he respected her enough to stop.

"Have you had any more visions lately?" Chandler asked, surprisingly breaking the silence herself. She was doing a lot of surprising things today.

"I haven't used it much at all." He grabbed the crystal around his throat. "There's been no one around to try and use it. Makes me miss Seamus and Doug and their joint stupidity a little."

"The twins are definitely no better now than when you left. Just the other day they woke up extra early and locked Violette in her room so no one had to do morning training."

"But she has telekinetic powers?"

Chandler nodded. "But she's not strong enough to move a bath with four other recruits piled into it yet."

Quinton snorted. "Seriously?"

"They're shitbags," Chandler laughed.

"Did anyone rescue her?" he found himself asking.

Chandler raised an eyebrow. "Took a few hours for the rest of the older recruits to notice Violette was actually missing, but then they got to her."

He nodded slowly. "No doubt she made them pay."

"She made *everyone* pay. She screamed the whole place down when she got out."

"I'm sure she did." Quinton could remember Violette's tantrums well enough.

"We all had to run extra laps since no one would confess to who was behind it. Praxis allotted extra time to morning training for a whole week to prove the point. Seamus and Doug also had to help the Helpers with the laundry for two weeks. And that was only because they confessed."

"Why did they confess?"

"To save people like Helen from having to do their unfair share."

"Heroes," Quinton laughed. "But it's steep price for their glory."

"They took it like champs, really."

"They're always aware they'll get punished. They just don't care."

"Story of our lives," Chandler grumbled, looking away. "Getting punished for stuff we do."

"But sometimes it's fun and worth it."

Chandler nodded slowly. "Sometimes."

A lush breeze swept under the waterfall, sending droplets wildly. Quinton spluttered as a few splashed his face. He wiped them away with the back of his hand.

"Feels like an Island storm might be coming," Chandler announced.

He stared at her. "How do you know that?"

"Water," she said. "Occasionally I can feel it shift or move because I can drag it down and solidify it. That breeze felt like a shift. I don't know if we'll want to be stuck in a cave when it comes."

Quinton opened his mouth to say something else when another gust shot through the space. More water slapped his cheeks and nose, even his eyes this time. Coughing, he wiped it away again. Then he looked at Chandler.

Chandler hadn't lifted her arms at all to shield herself. Instead, the droplets had hit her and she'd left them to stain her skin. They didn't slide or drop off. They simply clung on like little gems.

He didn't know what possessed him to do it, but Quinton started to reach out. His fingers grazed the edge of Chandler's cheek, connecting several droplets together. She didn't flinch, just followed his face with her ever-watching yet quiet gaze.

Pain laced up his elbow and he yelped, flinching back.

He'd forgotten he'd smacked the outer elbow when he'd been climbing out of the water-pool after helping Chandler out into Wane's waiting strong arms. The rock had sliced the skin open and now a red gash lay on the surface.

For such a small cut, he didn't think it would give him so much trouble.

That wasn't the only pain though. Underneath his skin, his muscles ached both from the climb in and out of the natural pool and from the swim through it with all his strength going into pulling two bodies through the water.

In a blink, a small block of ice appeared in front of him. Quinton stared at it. Then he stared at Chandler who looked flushed again.

"What did you just do?" he questioned, slightly harsh with his tone.

"Put it on your arm, Quinton," she breathed, sounding a little winded and wheezy.

"You just used your gift."

"Quinton…"

"That was *far* from your best move! What the fuck did you think you were doing?"

"Don't fucking start with me!"

"You *just* woke up from passing out and you think the best thing you should be doing right now is using your already over-worked powers and more energy? Fucking *brilliant*."

"How fucking *dare you!*" Her voice carried, and Quinton wondered how many people inside the cave were now awake to hear this. Chandler didn't seem to care as she continued. "You don't get to tell me what I can and can't do! I know the extent of my powers."

"Cleary you don't! They caused you to *faint* because you couldn't control them."

"That's something that hadn't been tested before."

"Yeah? And how much else hasn't been with you?"

"You're un-fucking-believable." She shook her head like she was disgusted. Worse than that, her voice dropped again. Calm anger radiated off her and that *hurt*. "Injury or not, next time you can get fucked."

"Icy—"

"Don't call me that. Not when I clearly don't know my limits or my power."

"No that's—"

"I was just trying to help in the best way I knew how. *Awake*, and right now, I know my limits. But not to you, because you know me oh-so-damned-well. I won't bother in the future."

"Chandler—"

Chandler had already clambered to her feet, rather un-steadily, and was halfway back inside. Quinton knew he should've got up to follow, to help, but he was frozen like the ice.

She disappeared from sight, leaving him alone.

Anger ebbed into confusion. What had just happened? They had both gotten so *heated* and so quickly with one another. The calm moments from just before had faded into nothing now. A good memory replaced by something horrible.

Quinton put his head in his hands. He didn't often wish his power could work on him, but right now he did. He wanted to know how bad that looked from outside or if there was something he could've done differently. Probably plenty.

His heart thumped loudly, beating out in annoyance.

More spray from the waterfall touched him, but he didn't wipe it from himself. He thought he deserved to be wet and miserable.

He'd only been trying to say that Chandler needed to be careful, that he cared for her wellbeing. But somehow it'd come out all wrong.

The words repeated in his brain over and over and over. They tumbled around until he groaned loudly.

Shuffling away from the water's edge, he leaned up against the rock wall at the entrance to the cave. He folded his arms over his chest and laughed to himself as his hand registered his necklace. A necklace that weirdly matched Chandler's.

He wondered if she'd take it off now.

They both needed time apart to cool down, then he would apologise. He was in the wrong and she had every right to come for his throat as she had. Even if he'd just been trying to protect her because he cared.

Quinton groaned again. He *cared*. And not just about her *wellbeing*. He was realising that was barely what lay on the surface of what was going on.

Some people might've been onto something when they thought emotions and feelings weren't as great as others thought them to be. But Quinton couldn't imagine not having them. They made him human. A clumsy, bumbling, fucking stupid human.

He tipped his head back, staring at the sky. He'd fix this. His heart needed him to.

He closed his eyes and left them shut.

CHAPTER TWENTY-SEVEN

FLORA

28th Day of Winter 2406

A new dawn dragged the same old problems round again.

The recruits all sat together in a circle facing one another. Quinton stayed closest to the entrance, his back blocking out most of the storm that had started, while Chandler remained deepest in the cave, a freshly wet t-shirt over her body. They seemed to be avoiding making eye contact but Flora watched them jolt with surprise every time it accidently happened.

Oddly, Flora felt refreshed. She'd never slept on a cold, hard floor before but something about it had relaxed her. She wondered if her body liked how basic it was, how uncomplicated.

Sitting like this made her miss her friends back home. They would create a circle out on the lawn and have picnics. Aleema was allergic to strawberries, so there would always be little lemon tarts instead. Dalton would bring the freshly poured lemonade or crisp, iced water. Flora took the role of acquiring sandwiches. The Helpers they asked for assistance from always indulged their wishes.

As soon as she returned home, Flora was requesting a picnic.

"You were right about the storm," Quinton said. Flora's cheek twitched when she noticed that he was talking directly to Chandler, something Flora noted he'd actively been avoiding for some reason until now.

"I told you, I can feel the water." Chandler didn't look up from her hands which she inspected diligently for some reason.

"Feel the water?" Flora asked, for once not willing to let a conversation slide.

Chandler looked up at her. "I can sense the droplets. I want to reach out, or my power does, and change their state to ice."

"That brings us to why we're here on this Island. Our next and bigger problem," Wane said. "What are we going to do about the pirates?"

"Pirates?" Darlene piped up. From Flora's angle, her body had been half-hidden by Wane's until she shuffled forward. "We have pirates here?"

"No," Gretchen, Quinton, and Chandler all said at once.

"They're hording treasure," Ziva said, trying to sound reasonable.

"Pirates," Wane chimed.

"It ain't treasure," Gretchen groaned.

"How is gold not treasure?" Ziva questioned.

"It *is* a precious metal," Quinton shrugged.

"See, *pirates*," Wane beamed.

"There's no such thing in the modern world," Gretchen barked.

"*There's no such thing in the modern world*," Wane mocked semi-decently. "If anything, dear Bony, there's more of a chance now than before. We're proof that anything could happen." His eyes were alive and bright.

"We're also proof to some that some things *shouldn't* happen," she challenged. "And *don't* fuckin' call me Bony!" It was an unfortunate nickname based around her Abnormality most didn't dare use to her face – not unless the person using it were really close with Gretchen and wouldn't suffer pure wrath.

"Do you mind?" Quinton looked between the arguing pair. "A, don't swear in front of my *little* sister, and B, don't start sprouting the same crap Normals do about how Abnormals shouldn't exist."

"Yeah!" Darlene called. "I might be one of you and I definitely *should* exist!"

Flora smiled at Darlene. At least someone didn't see being burdened with a mutated gene as a problem the universe screwed them over with. If only one kid could convince the rest of the world to agree. The terrors and horrors against Abnormals might stop then.

It wouldn't happen, but Flora could daydream.

"I want to leave," Ziva said, trying to get the group back on track. "And to do that, we need to finish this."

Ziva made sense. Flora also agreed; she wanted to leave too.

"How do you propose we do that?" Gretchen asked.

"We confront the pirates!" Wane declared, earning a *whoop* from Darlene in support.

"No pirates," Quinton aimed to reason. "But Gretchen's right. We've already tried one way and it didn't work. What is there left to do?"

"We follow the riches," Chandler said.

"What do you mean?" Ziva asked.

"There's jewels?" Darlene's eyes widened like saucers.

"They're not ours," Flora told her.

"Anything could be ours if we're brave enough," Quinton tried, grinning. Chandler snorted to Flora's left, like covered up laughter. Quinton turned to his sister. "But we're not stealing. Not from here."

"How do we follow the riches?" Ziva asked.

"Our original mission was to find a group of scientists that had an Abnormal with them," Wane said, pointing between himself and Chandler. "They came to realise that that Abnormal could literally sense riches. And so they left their confinements. They went off with their riches smelling bloodhound Abnormal."

"And we're trying to find out how an economy built itself from nothing," Flora added. Gretchen nodded once in acknowledgement.

"The scientists had to have made it here."

"What makes you say that?" Gretchen asked him.

"Because there's nothing to say they didn't." Wane unfolded his legs, then refolded them beneath himself. "If they disappeared or died on their way here," he eyed Darlene warily but she didn't seem effected, "then it would've been worldwide news. It wasn't. We wouldn't have been involved unless it was something world threatening. So maybe the Abnormal with the scientists registered the gold garden pirates here, and *followed*."

Gretchen groaned, loudly and annoyingly. "Yes, but we've been 'ere before. We're talkin' in circles. Again."

"I hate to agree but..." Chandler grimaced.

Wane shrugged. "It was your idea to follow the riches."

"But what do we do about it?" Gretchen questioned. "The whole point is to find the scientists, right?" Chandler and Wane nodded. "And to find out why this Island can pay off its debts."

"That's a lot of *finding*," Darlene commented.

The group continued to talk, but Flora didn't invest in it.

Ever since they'd reached the golden garden, as Wane called it, Flora had a sense that something hadn't been *right*. It wasn't the sheer volume of gold, but rather the lack of it compared to what she'd been feeling there should've been.

Not for the first time, she considered that there might've been more elsewhere.

While the others talked, Flora closed her eyes. The presence of the golden garden lingered in her mind. She could visualise the ornaments, the objects, the *things*. They shone in the sun, and now it was storming the rain pelted them with gloom but they didn't dull.

But that wasn't all she could feel.

Off in the distance, another glow hummed like a live wire in her mind. The more she focused on it, the louder the hum became. She tried to zero in and the hum became a buzz.

Flora opened her eyes again. She hadn't noticed how quiet it'd gotten inside the cave. She glanced up at the eyes watching her.

"Are you alright?" Ziva asked.

Flora attempted to smile. "I think I missed something."

"Missed something?" Wane questioned. "Like what?"

"I was so focused on that garden, I think there's another one. Or something similar," she tried to explain. "It's like a buzzing in my brain. It's a little distance from here but I can feel it there. It felt hidden before, or like I couldn't sense it, but now I'm focused and *trying* to find something else..."

"There's more treasure?"

"Something treasure-*like*," she said, nodding.

"Do you think it's worth checking out?" Chandler asked.

"*Woah*," Quinton raised his hands. "We're already in enough trouble. If those people find out we're *still here*..."

"I wasn't suggesting we *all* go," Chandler told him. "I was just asking if it was worth *any* of us going."

Flora could feel the tension in the air between Quinton and Chandler. Apparently so could the others as they seemed to watch the silent eye-contact match, raptured by it. Flora didn't want to wonder about what'd happened last night when she'd fallen asleep.

It made her think of Preston and the tension she knew she probably leaked when he was around.

It also reminded her of the whispers about Quinton after he'd left Redwing last season.

Over the past few years there were quiet rumours about Quinton hooking up with Violette, some even saying they'd been together. Either way, the tension there needed a knife to cut through. But Violette had issues with almost everyone despite being a superior and supposedly above all the mess of being a recruit.

The rest of the whispers had been about Quinton and Chandler, and Ziva too. They'd barely known each other for a few days before being sent out on a mission together, returning with a closeness no one could explain.

Sure, recruits had to trust those they were partnered with. This job required nothing *but* trust. But a lot of recruits spent time around each other first, even if it was just sleeping under the same roof. *Then* everything else, like friendship, could build.

But Quinton had returned as happy as anything like he'd known the girls all his life. Other recruits had claimed they'd seen him watching Chandler wherever she went. Everyone had definitely seen her rising out of the grounds' lake on a pillar of ice, laughing in his face at his shock.

Ziva was talked about too, but not in the same way Chandler was. There was something different about the girls and how Quinton acted around them. *Especially* Chandler.

Flora thought people were reading too much into not a lot. No one had gone on that mission except the three of them. Only they knew what'd happened.

Flora couldn't ignore what looked like an engagement ring hanging at Chandler's neck though.

That's where the last rumour came from. The whispers said Chandler and Quinton had known each other before all this. Maybe they'd been engaged once. Young and stupid and in love, but it hadn't worked. Now they'd been forced back together.

Maybe all of that happened or maybe none of it did. Flora didn't honestly care that much. Those around her did, but what did it matter to her? If Quinton and Chandler had been together before and now found each other again? Good for them. If they'd never known each other before but had come back friends? Good for them again. If the ring had been Quinton's, okay. If it had only ever been Chandler's, fine.

But the tension they oozed... That was something *real* and far more extreme than anything Flora had experienced or even seen before.

"How did the sensing feel?" Wane asked, cutting Flora out of her thoughts and dissipating the tension around the whole group. "When you searched for the gold, that's your thing, right? How did it feel?"

"There's another gold stash somewhere." Flora reached up and adjusted her headband. "I could feel it. I could feel both. The one we've been to and the one we haven't."

"And?" Gretchen pressed, leaning in. "How can you tell there's something else?"

"Buzzing," Flora said, remembering the hive of energy. "Like a live wire in my brain shot electricity down it when I focused on the other place."

"That doesn't sound as good as you think it does," Quinton said, carefully moving his gaze to study her.

"I'm fine," she assured him. "There's no injury or damage. But, like I said, I think I was wrong before. I think the garden we stumbled onto wasn't the only one. Maybe I was too far from it before, but I can feel the other one now."

"Maybe it was protected before?" Wane suggested. "Maybe the pirates had buried it—"

"No pirates!" Gretchen, Quinton, and Chandler all chorused.

Wane shot them all dirty looks. "Whatever. I think they're pirates," he grumbled. "Maybe the *pirates* unearthed it."

"Why would they do that?" Darlene asked. "Buried treasure is safer."

"What if they wanted to make sure it was still there?"

"Maybe us stumbling onto one garden made whomever was hiding it want to check the other one to make sure we hadn't looted it first," Quinton mused. "Not pirates, but people. Thieves. Criminals. Maybe they wanted to check their stash in case we, or anyone, had found that one as well."

"Pirates," Wane and Darlene muttered.

Flora groaned at the headache this group caused her. *This* was why she missed her friends. Not because they were quiet. They were often far from it. But more because they could cooperate.

But this whole job, not just this assignment, didn't take friendships into consideration. Often people were paired with others they wouldn't automatically become besties with. It put skills together instead. Because that was what was really important to get the cases closed. This was a job, not a hang-out.

"I don't think I can go anywhere," Chandler admitted quietly. She pulled her wet t-shirt from her body and it aggressively slapped right back into place. Flora pulled a face at the terrible sound. "The storm will pass and the heat will return. I'll be a sore thumb out in the open again." She didn't look up. "Worse than a sore thumb, actually."

"I'll stay," Ziva decided. "I won't leave you on your own."

"But—"

"Just like I can't argue with you, you can't argue with me on this. I'll be able to move and change your t-shirts and stuff." Ziva's smile was soft and familiar, kind too. Chandler smiled back, nodding.

"Obviously me and flower-power Flora need to go," Gretchen declared.

"Flower-power Flora?" Wane glanced at Flora, then back to Gretchen. "You come up with that?"

"It's hideous," Flora complained.

Gretchen shrugged. "I'm not just a pretty face." Wane beamed at her.

"Day?" Quinton called.

"You're about to tell me to stay, like a dog, aren't you?" Darlene whined. "I guess you'll be *abandoning me*? Having all the adventures *without me*?"

"It won't be much fun without you," he told her.

"But you're still leaving."

"Yeah, I have to."

Darlene stuck her tongue out at her brother. "I'll have more fun without you anyway."

Quintion laughed, and that seemed to be the end of the discussion. Finally.

Bags were packed and those leaving stood by the entrance. Quinton forced Ziva and Chandler to promise they'd get Darlene away if something happened. Both girls did. Wane then promised, under Ziva's cutesy death glare, that he'd carry everyone out if things their end went south.

If the groups didn't meet up in two days' time at the waterfall, whoever was left needed to get off the Island by any means necessary. That was the deal for doing this.

Everyone agreed.

Flora didn't want to split up despite the headache being together caused. They'd already been forced apart once. Doing so again, this time by their choice, didn't feel any better.

She didn't get to voice her concerns though. Everyone waved and muttered an almost lazy goodbye, and then the leaving party walked out of the cave.

CHAPTER TWENTY-EIGHT

GRETCHEN

29th Day of Winter 2406

It took nearly sixteen hours to get somewhere *close* to where Flora thought the new treasure trap *could* be. If Chandler's little fainting episode had taught them anything, even if her Abnormality did exacerbate things dramatically, it was that no one was above the heat and they needed to rest or drink water. Abnormals were used to pushing themselves beyond certain limits, but there were times when they couldn't.

Tucked in a little naturally-occurring alcove by the beach, Gretchen thumped her head back against it and closed her eyes. She panted and sipped at her water, which was already three-quarters gone. And that was before the return journey they needed to take.

This Island wasn't big. Far smaller than even the UK or surrounding Island nations to it. It probably could be driven across in a handful of hours. But the group didn't have vehicles and had to stay to the shadows.

Several times they'd narrowly escaped the detection of what appeared to be the Island's protective force. They heard one marching group pass, hiding from them on the other side of a few trees, and they'd talked the entire time on what their orders were.

According to the Island force, their entire group was to be 'treated' on site. Gretchen could fill in the blanks on what that actually meant herself.

"Lovely weather," Quinton said joyfully as he slipped down the wall beside Gretchen. He dripped some water into his mouth, more sparingly than she'd done, and swallowed harshly. "I think I could live here, you know?"

"You could probably buy the Island if you wanted," Gretchen snipped.

"I could see it," he nodded. "A nice row of huts out in the shallows of the water. Maybe some diving experiences? *Oh!* What about treetop huts and little campgrounds beneath?"

She scowled at him. "Would you though? Sounds trashy as fuck."

Quinton snorted. "If you think I'd buy an Island to commercialise it, you're the one with issues."

"No, you're definitely the one with issues."

"Really? Because this is the most you've spoken to me directly since I got here."

Gretchen opened and closed her mouth several times, well aware she probably looked like a fish. She slammed her teeth together, grimacing at the sound as Wane and Flora turned to look at her. Her look of annoyance at their attention was enough to send their gazes elsewhere again.

"I've tried talking to you," Quinton continued. "But you've ignored me."

"Like you ignored me for *weeks*?" she complained.

Quinton seemed to visibly deflate. "I suppose that's fair."

"It's more than fuckin' fair."

"But what was I supposed to say?" he asked, though it didn't sound like he was questioning Gretchen.

"Anythin'! A single 'hello' would've been a nice fuckin' start. Can't you come up with somethin' on your own or do I 'ave to spoon feed all of it to you? I ain't doing that for you."

"Bony—"

"*Don't*," she huffed, rolling her eyes. "You've been away for a whole season. I'm sure in a few days I'll forgive you for it. I never can hold my anger around you, and you know it. But let me remain pissed for now. I'm owed this."

"I don't think a 'sorry' would quite cover it, would it?"

"No."

She shoved her bottle back in her bag and climbed to her feet again, brushing sand from her fingers. She stomped over to Flora, who had recently been a more stable person in her life than her supposed best friend. And *that* was the real kicker.

Flora seemed to realise something was wrong immediately. "You alright?" she whispered, shifting closer to Gretchen.

"I'll get over it," Gretchen dismissed.

Wane laughed. "You're a person who thrives with fire inside them, Gretchen." It unnerved her how easily he used her full name, like it meant nothing and everything in one breath. "You never get over anything. You walk around with grudges and words and arguments strapped to you like personal chains."

"I like things that way," she told him. "They're my style."

Flora tilted her head, her eyes running up and down. "I think chains would suit you."

A startled laugh escaped Gretchen's mouth. "What?

"I mean…" Flora backed up a step, her face flooded with heat that couldn't just be from the sun. "It's your look, right? Black, platform boots, green hair. Why not add some other bits in?"

"Have you been lookin'?" Gretchen teased.

"You're hard to miss," Wane put in.

Gretchen assessed the other girl curiously. "You're suggestin' I start wearing metal and harnesses then?"

Admittedly, she'd considered it before. Maybe her wardrobe could do with some updates to coincide with her life changing. But to hear it come from Plain Jane Flora... That was interesting. Gretchen could suddenly see why Quinton found everything and everyone so interesting – there wasn't always just one layer to something.

"Not the time for this." Flora waved her hands in front of her own face. "We need to keep going."

"Way to change the subject, Flower," Quinton laughed, drawing in close to the group again.

"Subtle too," Wane agree, smirking.

Gretchen pointed at Flora. "We're not done with this."

"Please, let's be," Flora groaned, cheeks still pink. She pointed further along the beach to where the Island curved viciously, almost at a right angle to itself. "We need to go that way," she declared, not meeting anyone's eyes. "That's where I feel it."

"And what is '*it*'?" Wane asked. "Pirate treasure?"

"I don't know about *treasure*. I can only sense gold."

"We're wastin' time," Gretchen complained. She wanted to be done and halfway home already.

With nothing else to say, the four of them kept to the trees and traced the edge of the coast along to where Flora had pointed.

The Island tapered into a long point; Gretchen wondered what this curve of sand looked like from the air.

Unfortunately, due to the change in landscape, buildings and shaded areas slipped away, leaving only thin palm trees for cover. The group darted between them, hopping behind tiny trunks separately as they could no way hide behind any together. Since none of them had a 'hiding' Abnormality, this became the best they could do.

They kept each other in sight as best they could and used the basic hand signals they'd all been taught during their tenure at Redwing to communicate.

As the area they travelled grew tighter, the sandy beaches pressing in on both sides, so did security. Several times they had to flatten themselves tightly, stopping all movement immediately.

But that also proved they were headed in the right direction.

Flora halted the entire group with a fast closing fist. Mere seconds later, a whole squad of guards marched past them. Gretchen counted her heartbeats, and realised they matched the rhythm of the footsteps.

It became obvious only three tree-hops later that they couldn't keep going like this. They had to switch it up to get closer to their intended destination. But how?

Gretchen didn't recognise any of the following signals Flora waved about. She'd only ever paid attention to the basics. The rest of the time Violette had been too distracting with her arms – and her breasts waving at the same time – for Gretchen to focus on specifics.

Quinton seemed to understand though.

He shrugged his backpack, clipped it together at his chest, then gripped the sides of the thicker trunk he was behind and grinned directly at Gretchen like a maniac. She wanted to roll her eyes at him but that would've given him too much undeserved attention.

Without warning, Quinton leapt onto the trunk and started climbing.

The leaves far above him barely ruffled as he shimmied his way up. Flora whistled a short note, just once, to indicate everyone else needed to keep moving and Quinton was staying, keeping watch from here. But Gretchen didn't want to take her eyes off her friend.

She didn't even know he could climb trees.

She wondered then if it was possible to ever truly know someone. Maybe people always had secrets. Gretchen definitely did, so why had she not expected the same? Quinton had proved last season he was quite capable of having them himself.

Gretchen moved on without looking back.

As the beach and surrounding area narrowed further, the trees became more sparse. Gretchen listened for signs of life but knew she'd quite easily see anything at this point.

The group stopped again. This time, Flora looked pointedly at her.

Gretchen nodded and focused. She zeroed in on every living thing with bones around her.

A lizard moved ten feet away from Wane, who was around three feet from Flora. The sunken carcass of a large fish lay somewhere in the water nearby, but it wasn't a complete skeleton yet. Gretchen heard the seagull before she sensed the bones. She could even reach out and find Quinton somewhere behind her.

But she couldn't sense anything else.

She opened her eyes, unsure of when she'd closed them, and bright light flooded her vision, making her blink harshly. She met Flora's gaze a few seconds later and shook her head one, drawing an X-shape across her own forehead.

For now, they were alone at the tip of the Island.

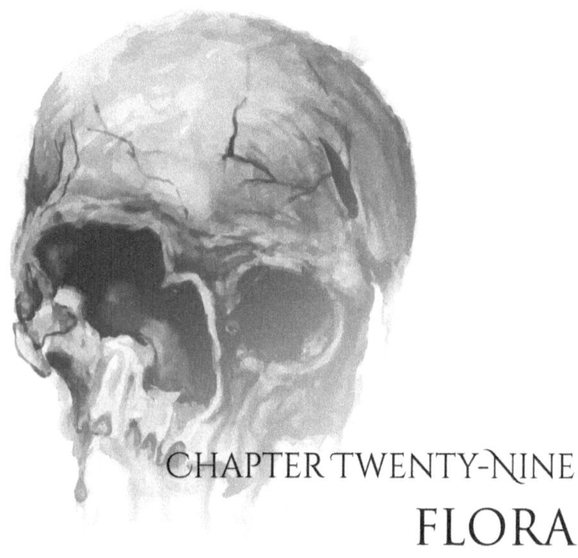

CHAPTER TWENTY-NINE
FLORA

29th *Day of Winter 2406*

Gold feathered through Flora's mind. It tickled her senses, alerting her that it was there. Those sorts of vibrations only grew the closer she got.

Sometimes the amount of gold mattered. Small pieces sent out tiny ripples. They'd be mostly associated with jewellery or gold leaf artwork from years past since not much *pure* gold was ever used in the creation.

Flora could ignore those types easily.

The other kind grew on Flora's skin like an itch. The vibrations would start in her mind, then travel down her arms and spine to scratch. Statues and elaborate frames for artwork caused most of those vicious little attacks.

Those were the sensations Flora couldn't ignore.

Just like at the gold garden, Flora felt herself being pulled along in a trance-like state. Her hearing became slightly muffled and her tongue felt a little scratchy on the roof of her mouth.

The heat of the sun no longer scorched her skin as she reached out her bare hands.

Weaving around the rest of the trees didn't take long.

Flora was acutely aware of the patrols the group had passed on the way here. Though Gretchen had confirmed that no one was currently around them, they had no way of accurately knowing if that would change, or when.

Speed and time needed to be on their side now.

Flora pushed ahead, not paying much attention to where anyone else was. They wore no gold and were of little importance to her. The trance she'd been wrapped into the centre of carried her along. She stepped over loose rocks and fallen, rotten coconuts. She darted between little shells and empty holes in the sand.

She didn't stop until the very end of the thin stretch, where her vision cleared and her brain rewired itself.

How had she not sensed this before? Clearly this gold *hummed* with energy she could almost hear it. It vibrated so fast it sent her teeth into a jittery mess. Yet she'd been distracted by the garden. But maybe that had been the point? Maybe the garden had meant to distract.

Flora took a cautious step closer, and her mind finally registered what it'd first blocked out.

Bodies.

Plenty of human-looking figures were in various positions around what was clearly being displayed as the golden masterpiece. The bodies were crawling or sinking, standing or reaching. And all of them were made of gold. But the signs of pain across the faces were perfectly clear.

"Wait!" Gretchen's voice yelled.

Wane stopped right up against Flora's side, his own hands outstretched like a grabbing child. "But... *treasure*," he whined.

"Don't touch it," Flora told him, creeping closer herself.

Gretchen closed the gap. "What do you feel?"

Flora looked at her. "What do *you* feel?"

"Nothin' good." Gretchen shoved her hands behind her back. "But I want to touch it."

"Don't," Flora warned.

"I ain't a child."

"I didn't say you were." Flora took another, more careful step. "I think there's a type of hypnotic *thing* about this."

In front of the trio was a golden marble podium ornamented by a skull of dense gold.

The jaws were perfectly aligned, teeth all showing. The eye sockets were hollow but glistening. Every inch of bone had been shadowed with the element, and the sun reflected harsh light from it. Flora had to blink faster than normal to counteract it.

"The bone's real," Gretchen informed them. "It's Human."

Wane, who'd crept unnoticed almost up to the podium, froze. "What?"

Gretchen moved to his side. She touched his shoulders and with a howling cry, he sank to his knees where he was. "There," she said. "Now you'll stop moving."

"Did you just *break* something?" he questioned, tears streaming down his face. "Did you just *break me*?"

Gretchen didn't seem phased. "Maybe."

"Bitch," he grumbled, though he didn't sound entirely *upset*.

"Come up with somethin' original to call me, I beg."

Flora ignored them, too narrowed in on her element. She circled the podium a few more times, then looked at the people surrounding it. Weirdly, some of the golden statues appeared to be moving *away* from the skull while others were fully facing towards it.

"I don't like this," she mumbled. "I *really* don't like this."

"We don't have to *like it*," Gretchen told her. "We have to contain it. This is clearly where the gold is coming from."

"*From* the skull?" Flora asked, turning to Gretchen directly.

"Can't you feel it?"

"Feel what?" Flora circled the podium again, never once taking her eyes off the skull.

"The *power*?"

Flora stopped. "I can't feel bones."

"But you can feel your gold."

Flora analysed the skull. It certainly appeared like the gold had overpowered it, claiming the bone for itself. Like a snake smothering its prey, the gold appeared to have slithered over the skull.

She circled it once more, needing to see it all from every angle she could. The silent call to touch it itched persistently. Flora was eager to reach out and run her fingers along the dips and chips in the bone structure, to feel the fluidity of her element and retrace how it'd consumed the entire cranium.

All at once, she stopped. Her eyes locked onto something, the tiniest detail she almost missed.

An inconsistency in a single tooth stared back at her.

And it all clicked.

The gold hadn't been passed to the skull. The gold *came* from the skull.

"Flora?" Gretchen called.

Flora's eyes shot to meet Gretchen's. Using her proper name meant something serious was afoot. "Yes? What?"

"Tell me you can feel it."

"I can't feel it, but I can see something."

"Feel? See?" Wane pressed. "What's happening here? Are you two having a moment? Do I need to leave you alone? You'd have to get me up first. Or is the pirate treasure possessing you both?"

"No possession," Flora promised, still staring at the tooth.

"It feels like the bone came *secondary*," Gretchen tried to explain.

"Is that even possible?" Wane asked, still whimpering slightly on the beach floor.

Gretchen shrugged. "Somethin' obviously is. We still don't know where exactly our Abnormalities came from. Yes, genes and a mutation. That much we do know. And we know there's the possibility we've had a few of those in our lifetime as a Human race. But there could be a case made that us Abnormals have possibly been around for *ages* and no one's realised. In one form or another, we could've always existed."

"Just that one, more recent mutation..." Flora trailed off. She knew what Gretchen was thinking but couldn't voice the rest; that the most recent mutation that threw Abnormals into the limelight, over one hundred years ago now, might not have been the only one but maybe just the most notable because it came with the largest wave.

"An Abnormals genealogy could've shifted?" Wane questioned, catching on.

"Over our lifetime our powers can change and grow, so maybe our entire biological make-up can too?" Gretchen threw back, but not unkindly.

Flora stepped back from the skull at once. "The skull belonged to an Abnormal."

"More than likely," Gretchen agreed. "I'm sensing something from the bone."

"Maybe he was a pirate that was cursed to turn into gold," Wane tried. Gretchen snorted at him. "Like Midas?"

"The myth?" Flora asked, taking another step back. "With us, it seems anything's possible."

Gretchen's gaze turned to the golden people-esque statues around them. "And those people here..."

Flora looked at the same time. Someone in a story had finally had a similar power to her own and she'd clung to it. She remembered the myth well, and how everything Midas had touched, it'd turned to gold. He couldn't control it like she could, but the story was still hers.

"What if the skull can pass on the curse?" Flora asked no one in particular.

"An abnormal's power workin' even after death?" Gretchen said something else too quietly to hear.

"Oh," Wane cut in.

Gretchen peered down at him. "What now?"

"These people," he spoke slowly as if he was still trying to process something. "We, me and Chandler, were tasked with finding those scientists? We think they *were* hunting for treasure." He nodded to a shape.

Tentatively, as if knowing what she was going to find already, Flora walked in the direction he'd indicated. She scanned the body up and down, and then finally saw what Wane had from further away.

A badge pinned to the chest. The name was unreadable, but the style of badge, mixed with the long coat that'd been frozen in gold like a breeze had caught the bottom of it, clearly displayed this person as a scientist. And most Abnormals were well acquainted with those medical groups to spot them easily.

"The skull turns whoever touches it to gold," Flora said, a little short of breath suddenly.

"Midas," Wane's voice echoed.

"And if they touch someone else, then they also turn," Gretchen said.

Flora inspected the bodies to find two statues holding hands. "And items," she added, finding a small notebook dropped to the side of them.

Which was how the Island was paying its debts.

Any item that had been transformed by gold was being sold. And as long as the skull was here, the cursed gold falling around it would be endless, always.

Flora carefully thought about Wane's mission, as he'd just mentioned. Researchers watching an Abnormal who could find treasure had all gone missing. At least they knew where they'd ended up. Somewhere along the line, one of them must've gotten greedy enough to try and take the treasured gold, or the mental stress of resisting the call to it had worn them away until they'd touched it.

"This is a curse to everything," Flora whispered.

If they left the skull, more people would possibly be attracted to it and then transform. Then more items would be shipped out to pay for this Island's ever-growing wealth and status. More people would come here as the Island grew as a resort. And that cycle would continue on.

"What are we meant to do?" Wane asked.

Flora turned to him, then Gretchen. Wane still had tears in his eyes and Gretchen's face wore an expression of pain now itself. Were her internal walls slowly falling?

They all knew what had to be done.

Flora couldn't let either of her fellow recruits break themselves or give in to touch the cursed skull. But it also couldn't stay here on the Island.

She faced the skull. Whatever call everyone heard, Flora could hear it in a whisper, not a yell. She could sense gold and manipulate it sometimes. However, this wasn't just simple gold.

She didn't know how her Abnormality would cope, or if it would even work.

Flora didn't give herself time to second guess her decision. She pushed her headband up, clearing her hair from her face, and took one breath.

She heard shouting behind her, and what sounded like her name. It sounded nice coming from Gretchen. She hoped she'd get to hear it again, maybe when this is all over with some laughter in the tone instead of anger and fear.

One step.

Flora snatched the skull up.

Paralysing pain coursed up her arms, to her elbows. She sucked in a shallow breath as if that could fight it.

Glancing down, she saw the curse begin. She watched as the gold seeped from the skull and layered over her nails, then her fingertips, her hand, and up to her wrists.

She didn't scream. She *couldn't* scream.

As the gold touched her elbows, Flora saw golden stars circle her head and her eyes rolled to the back of her head, blackness finally consuming the bright.

CHAPTER THIRTY

GRETCHEN

29ᵗʰ Day of Winter 2406

"Don't just *kneel there*!" Gretchen cried. "Go and pick 'er up!" She practically shoved Wane towards Flora.

"Won't *we* turn to gold next?" Wane argued.

Gretchen didn't know for sure. "It hasn't progressed past her elbows," she pointed out, indicating to the gold that had slithered like liquid serpents up Flora's arms. "I think 'er abnormality is keepin' it at bay."

"And if it can jump from her to me?"

"I think it has to be direct touch to the gold."

"This is a lot of guess work, Gritty."

Wane was right, this was a lot of guess work. But what else was there?

Silence followed.

Wane stumbled a few times, his fractured knees now undamaged, while his feet fought against the sandy terrain. Gretchen watched, helpless, as he scooped Flora up, carefully avoiding the cursed skull and her doomed hands.

Somehow Gretchen had known what Flora had been about to do before she'd done it. She'd nearly let Wane drop early in her desperation to get to Flora before she'd picked the cursed item up. But her screams had gone unanswered and unnoticed – and she wasn't used to being ignored.

Back on his feet, Wane trudged over to Gretchen and they set off without a word.

Quinton met them halfway back along the beach. He must've heard Gretchen's cries because he was already down on the sand, eyes wide in both surprise and horror. Gretchen wondered if her expression looked the same.

The trek back to the others would be harsh but they would push on without stopping. Flora needed help, and the only help she could get now would be that from back home at Redwing.

Gretchen didn't bother to cover their tracks. She barely bothered to seek out oncoming bone structures unless they were within immediate range, keeping her focus on Flora.

Though her Abnormality revolved around bones, sometimes Gretchen could feel what was happening *around* them.

It wasn't a powerful self upgrade, but it helped her know that Flora's heart was at least still beating. Quite well, in fact.

No one spoke for hours. There wasn't a bird's call or shouts of anger nearby to them. Even the wind seemed to have died in grief.

How could Flora have been so *stupid*? She'd known better than any of them that the damned item was bad news times one thousand. Yet she'd been the idiot to pick it up off it pedestal.

Gretchen stared at the girl Wane carried a few times. Flora's arms seemed to be welded to the skull now, but the flow of gold hadn't travelled further than the tops of her elbows. Her eyes didn't flutter beneath her lids but her throat did swallow once or twice. Because there was no wind, her hair didn't flutter, but when the band threatened to slip out, Gretchen made Wane stop so she could adjust it back in.

Gretchen forced the group to keep going, even as night fell and it became harder to navigate.

Days ago, Gretchen would've penned Flora as a coward. The idea wasn't harmful or untruthful, as she'd always lived behind her friends, never wanting to really be seen or heard. There wasn't anything wrong with being a coward either.

But that'd changed.

Since arriving here, something in Flora had shifted. Gretchen had watched it happen, right from the first moment the girl had stood up to her in their hotel room.

Fuck I miss that hotel room, Gretchen thought.

The first thing she wanted to do when home was soak in a hot bath. Then maybe visit a masseuse. Or dye the rest of her hair green. Or shop for harnesses like Flora had mentioned.

No, she thought as she stepped over the long-buried bones of a bird. *I want Flora with me when I do that. Bet that'll shock her! It's shocking me...*

More than anything, for once, Gretchen wanted *rest*.

She wanted to be tucked in her own bed, back in her clothes with her eyebrows drawn back on, eating chocolate by the boatload. She wanted to kick her feet up in fluffy socks and have someone rub them. She wanted to scurry by people in the Mansion and to be left alone so she could wallow in her own darkness. She wanted to have her best friend back and for them to wear ridiculous facemasks and talk about nothing and everything together.

Gretchen glanced at Quinton. He always knew when she watched him, because he winked and smiled.

Then her eyes found Wane. His smile was much softer, like he'd just seen exactly what'd come up inside her mind. In all her wants, she'd never thought about him. That wasn't to say she wouldn't. He was attractive and there had been some kind of chemistry. But right now, rest and friendship called to her more. So maybe he'd been right, before? Maybe they could start again as friends at the very least?

None of that mattered though if they didn't get their arses home.

Gretchen shifted the group as some skeletons approached, and they headed in their new direction. They needed to get out of here.

Flora sucked in a tight breath in Wane's arms.

Everyone froze for a second and watched as a single inch of gold receded back off her skin and towards the skull.

Eyes met eyes. No one knew what to do.

Gretchen made a point of giving Flora a once over; checking that her heart still beat and then firmly looked away, marching on even harder than before.

They needed to get out of here *now*.

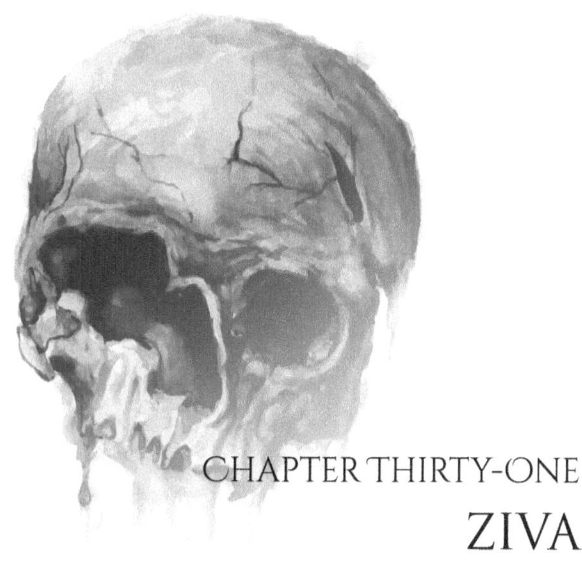

CHAPTER THIRTY-ONE
ZIVA

30th Day of Winter 2406

They waited until dusk fell before heading down to the beach.

Before the group had split, they'd decided that if they didn't reconnect at the caves and waterfall within a certain time, they needed to get out separately. And the other group hadn't come back. Ziva hated leaving anyone, but she was following the orders they'd set together. Strangely, she had no protests from her fellows.

As the stars came to life above them, Ziva realised they seemed dull. She wondered if her power had finally affected her own eyes.

She carried Chandler mostly on her shoulders while Darlene took what little baggage they had. The little girl didn't complain once. She happily skipped down the sand like nothing was wrong. Ziva wished she was still that naïve.

Ziva dropped Chandler into a leftover deck chair right on the waterline. Chandler sighed as the seawater rushed up to sink her feet. The walk from the waterfall cave hadn't taken long, but the day's heat had still taken its toll upon her. Her skin looked *wrong* again, and a faint sheen was along her brow.

"Have you got any snacks?" Darlene asked, sitting beside Chandler on a little bump on the sandy part of the beach. "I'm kind of hungry. And Ma said you can't do anything on an empty stomach."

"Your Ma's right," Chandler responded calmly.

Ziva sat on Chandler's other side and handed over the last of the crackers and a water bottle.

"Thanks!" Darlene shoved three crackers in her mouth at once. "Want one?" she asked around a full mouth. "They're good!"

"I'll take some water?" Chandler asked like it was some kind of inconvenience.

Ziva passed her a new water bottle. "Drink—"

"Slowly, I know." Chandler smiled weakly. "It's all you've been telling me to do, Z."

"Someone has to remind you to be easy on yourself."

"What are you?"

"Apparently, right now, I'm your nurse since you can't look after yourself."

Chandler laughed once, though it sounded pained. "I'm never living this down, am I?"

"Not if I have anything to say about it," Ziva smiled. "We'll have Praxis update your records too, so you can't come to hot places in future."

She groaned. "Take me somewhere cold, *please*."

"I want to go to Snowdonne," Darlene announced.

"It's lovely there," Ziva said. "I think you'd like it."

"Can you help me convince my brother to take me? He said he liked it there."

"He liked Ziva's company," Chandler joked. Since those longs rests, she had much more energy to be more *normal* again. She still wasn't one hundred percent herself yet, but she was far better than the passed-out husk from before.

Ziva smiled at her best friend. "I don't think it was *my* company he enjoyed," she whispered.

"Oh really?"

"Wasn't *me* he danced with or gave a ring to. He didn't take *me* to meet his parents."

"That was part of our mission."

"Dancing wasn't. You two could've stayed on the sidelines, but no, he wrapped you up in him."

"Stop it." Chandler playfully swatted at Ziva. "He liked the intrigue. Nothing else."

Ziva wanted to ask if it was the same for her, and if that was why she still wore the ring around her neck, but she didn't. There would be a time to ask that, among other things, but here and now wasn't right. Not with Quinton's sister eagerly watching them both.

"Where is my brother?" Darlene asked next, handing back the empty cracker bag. "Isn't he supposed to come back for us?"

"He'll be here," Ziva promised. She didn't know how she sounded so confident. Plenty of people were meant to come back for others, but she had actual faith in Quinton doing so.

"Good," Darlene nodded. "He always carries the best snacks."

Chandler laughed. "Are you still hungry?"

"Not *now*. But I will be!" Darlene sighed, the sound far heavier than a child should be able to make. "Are there good snacks where you live?"

Ziva and Chandler looked at one another. They didn't know how much Quinton had shared, or how much he wanted his sister to know about Redwing or his job. It wasn't their place to say anything.

"Sometimes," Chandler said, taking the lead. "Other times its vegetables and fruits and—"

"She likes fruit."

The three of them got their feet with varying degrees of ease.

Quinton trudged down the beach quickly, his heels kicking up sand in his haste. He beelined for Darlene and snatched her arm, pulling her aside. She went without argument. Ziva couldn't hear their voices as they talked.

Ziva didn't understand why he'd pulled her aside until she saw the rest of the party heading their way. She instantly knew something was wrong. When Wane appeared, an incapacitated Flora in his arms, she could *see* why.

Darlene and Quinton rejoined the group a moment later. As Ziva looked at Darlene's worried but unsurprised face, she realised that he'd wanted a moment to warn her of what she was about to see. Ziva smiled, despite the circumstances; Quinton was a good brother.

"Is there a boat we can commandeer?" Gretchen asked.

Ziva pointed out past the small pier. "It's small, but it'll hold us all."

She'd seen the little boat a few days ago when they'd arrived. The paint was tarnished and the name was barely visible, but it still floated and definitely still had an engine. It could get them to the next shore over. And that was all they needed.

"Then we need to leave," Gretchen urged.

They all raced down towards the boat without wasting time.

Ziva loaded in first, taking the bags. Then Quinton came aboard, bringing his sister. Both Ziva and Quinton had to help get Wane on board since he couldn't use his arms, while Gretchen and Chandler had to assist him from their side. Gretchen got Chandler settled and then herself.

No one questioned how Gretchen knew how to drive a boat. She simply fired it up and they were on their way across the waves.

Being in the middle of the sea made the darkness of the night feel more ominous. Ziva wondered if she could control that darkness to bring them a little light. She tried to reach out to it, hand extended to draw in the nighttime, but didn't think she succeeded in her plans when no one said anything. The colour of the darkness clung on tightly and no new colour replaced it.

Defeated, she flopped down in her seat.

It didn't seem to take long before they were docking again; their original Island destination long behind them and nowhere in sight. Quinton unloaded himself and his sister first, then barrelled down the gangway on his phone. Ziva helped Gretchen get Wane back on dry land, then Chandler, before herself.

As a team, they raced past other docked boats like someone had set their shoes on fire.

Call it some kind of miracle or just good luck, but nobody stopped them to question why they were nearly running or why someone was carrying a body with obviously golden hands.

Quinton pocketed his phone again just as a private shuttle to the port pulled up. When everyone was in, he explained that he'd secured not only this shuttle but private seats on the next air-shuttle out to get them home.

The air-shuttle arrived just over an hour later, and they boarded with no issues. Thankfully passes weren't need for identification, Quinton's name getting them ahead once again.

Before they knew it, they were up in the air.

Ziva flopped beside Chandler who was chewing on cubes of ice. Ziva smiled, which only grew to laughter when Chandler politely offered her some.

"Do I get to see where you live now?" Darlene's little voice came from behind.

"I think you will," Quinton replied.

Chandler looked at Ziva and leaned in close. "I don't know if I want to be around for this."

"For what?" Ziva questioned.

"How well or not Quinton coming to Redwing will be, and the result of that for Darlene."

Ziva grimaced, unsure if they were about to have any choice on what they were about to be witness to or not.

One thing was for certain though, they were finally going *home.*

CHANDLER

37th Day of Winter 2406

How was the medical evaluation?" Praxis asked, closing the folder he'd been scribbling in. His hair looked less manic compared to before, like he'd finally had someone else cut it for him, and his beard had become barely more than a shadow.

Chandler scowled. "You know how it went."

"Do I?"

"You probably saw the report before I did. Don't try and say you didn't."

"I saw a piece of paper," Praxis confirmed. "But how was it *for you?*"

Since returning to Redwing, Chandler had mostly been confined to her room. Helpers came and went with trays of food and jugs of iced water, and they even aided her in washing. Otherwise she hadn't been allowed visitors or to leave until she'd been cleared by a professional.

It'd been a lonely and slightly humiliating week.

But this morning the main medical evaluation had taken place, and she'd been cleared. She was back to full health, her heart and lungs running as they should again.

Chandler had taken the chance to seek Ziva out before being called to Praxis' office. The girls had talked about nothing and everything, and what they'd do now that winter had finally hit the estate in full force.

She glanced out the wide windows behind Praxis. Snow hadn't stopped falling in days, though the sun hadn't retreated fully. Chandler smiled as she spotted the lake in the distance and the frozen surface.

"I'll live," Chandler said, remembering her superior had asked her a question.

Praxis nodded once. "Your file will say you are no longer to be given missions with extreme heat," he declared. "Not unless there are extenuating circumstances. There's plenty of other recruits for those missions. But don't think this clears you. Just because you've been given the sign you can leave your room, it doesn't mean you can start doing as you please."

"What does that mean, Sir?"

"For the next week, you'll still be excused from the morning training."

"Yes!" Chandler cried happily.

Praxis' eyes narrowed on her. "But only for a week," he said. "You will be watched in that time whenever you eat to make sure you are consuming as much as you should, and if you are making progress in daily life to regain your colour and strength back. That means things like climbing stairs without wheezing at the top of them or needing a rest after changing your bedsheets. If you make progress, which you should be working towards, *then* you will be cleared by me."

"And being cleared by you means?"

"That you can be chosen for missions again."

"Ah," Chandler sat back. "So one week?"

"One week," he confirmed.

"But I might not get picked for months or years for something else."

"Depends on the mission and what skills might be required for it." Praxis moved the file, which Chandler presumed was hers, on top of another on his desk. "You should be clear on that. It might've only been a season, but a season is more than enough time to understand what we do here." He leant forwards. "What I don't understand though, is why you didn't pull out of the Island and come home at the first sign of trouble with your health?"

Chandler cracked her knuckles, the popping calming her. "I told you in my—"

"Report," he finished for her. "But was that all you had to say?"

Chandler might've left a few details *out* of her debrief when questioned. Like omitting how she'd passed out, telling them that she'd merely been on the cusp of collapse instead. And if Praxis wasn't questioning that, then that meant the others had also given half-truths too. She didn't want Praxis to know just how close of a call it'd gotten for her, even if it could save her in the future.

But why would the others have lied for her? Especially someone like Flora, who seemed so by the book, and Gretchen who didn't appear to like anyone. By leaving it out, were they somehow helping her with something she didn't know about?

"Is that it for today?" Chandler asked, rising to her feet.

"That's all the remaining questions I have," Praxis confirmed, though he still watched her carefully.

Chandler headed for the door. As her hand touched the handle, she paused. "Are we allowed to visit our families?" she asked quietly.

Praxis seemed to study her harder. "Why?"

She shrugged noncommittally. "I might want too."

"Is this about your mother?" he asked. "Or father?"

Trying not to flinch at the mention of him, she said, "Does it matter?"

"Everyone is different when they leave their families to join here. Some remain in contact through letters or calls. Some cut all ties. I wouldn't claim to know if there was a right or wrong answer." Praxis finally leaned back and dropped his gaze. "We would advise against direct meetings in some cases. We know your files and we know your lives."

You don't know everything, Chandler's mind chimed.

"But after the recent incident with a certain *member* of the team here," Praxis continued, unable to hear Chandler's thoughts, "I will stick by the 'no right or wrong' rule. So, yes, if you wish to visit your mother, you will be allowed to."

"Before Ziva and I started, you said we would have to make a choice to remain here."

"I did."

"You said we'd have to give up our families and couldn't go back to them without losing this place in return."

"Or something similar, I'm sure." He looked up at her again. "This job isn't easy. The less we're tied or split between lives, the better. Here, we have more at stake then out there."

"But you let Quinton go and come back."

Praxis' mouth quirked at the corners. "I did."

Chandler watched him give nothing away, and she nodded. "It's just curious."

"*You're* curious as to why."

She cracked all her knuckles one by one. "It just goes against what you told us."

"And things in life always go against other things. I'm allowed to change my mind or bend the rules on things if I want. As are you if you wish. I'd rather you bend the rules than break them, just as many others here do." The laughter in his voice floated away. "If you wish to see your mother, no one will stop you. No one will stop you at the doors or gates, and no one will refuse you re-entry."

"Right. Good."

"And I don't need to remind you to be careful?"

"You don't," she said. "Thanks."

"Now, get out of here. It's a lovely day outside."

Chandler nodded once and left the room.

She wandered through the mansion, to the kitchen, and the small door there. She threw it open and leapt out into the winter wonderland that was indeed waiting for her.

Crystals of pure white hung off windowsills and nearby bushes. Her steps crunched underfoot as she traipsed down the path someone had made an attempt to dig out. Chandler ran her hands through several leaves to capture the ice, and made them swing around her body for a few moments like pieces of a chandelier coming together to state she was the centrepiece.

She couldn't deny how *good* it felt to be back here and in near full health. Just being able to breathe without worrying that the ground would start spinning again was a weight lifted. Controlling ice again, drawing water from the atmosphere to change its state, left her smiling.

This was who she was and how she was meant to be.

Returning home, and realising she did, in fact, call Redwing home, had made her realise how much she didn't miss her life before. She'd barely thought of her mother since leaving her.

But she had thought of her father.

The man she'd been named after had been a mystery her whole life. He was gone, supposedly from the world itself, but Chandler had realised over time how much her mother lied and wondered if this was just one more big lie.

Passing out and nearly *dying* had made her think about what she wanted. She wanted the truth once and for all, and then to put it to rest behind her for good. She had a new life here now. That was what she'd really been thinking about.

"Well someone looks happy."

Chandler stopped, reshaped some ice into little spikes mid-air, and turned. "You shouldn't sneak up on me," she warned. "Not on ground where I have the upper hand."

Quinton raised his gloved hands in surrender, and grinned. "I wouldn't be so stupid," he claimed.

He was dressed appropriately for the weather; big coat and scarf and gloves to complete the look. He even wore a hat that covered his blue hair though little strands poked out from underneath.

"Why are you following me?" she questioned.

"I was out here on a walk, same as you."

She dropped the spikes and they fell gently into the soft snow at her feet. "Why don't I believe that?"

Touching the crystal that hung around his neck, he said, "I might have this to help me, but I still can't see myself. There was no way I would've known you'd be out here."

"You still can't see yourself?"

"It's only happened to me once."

"And that was because of me."

"Building yourself up to be a big star there, aren't you?" he laughed. He indicated to Chandler's necklace, which she'd forgotten to tuck into the inside of her t-shirt. "Seems I'm a big star in yours, too."

She touched the ring. "I couldn't get rid of it," she admitted.

"I told you you didn't have to get sell or give it back. It's yours, for as long as you want it." Their gazes locked and Chandler saw something there that she couldn't explain.

She dropped the ring and it clanked against her chest. "How's Darlene?"

"That was going to be my next line to you," he laughed. "Are you sure *you* aren't the future seeing one?"

"I'm fine," Chandler waved off, and it was true. She'd never felt so good, probably because she'd never felt so bad.

"Good. And Day's fine too. She has her own room and everything now."

"Is she staying at Redwing?"

"Her mum's coming here to discuss the possibility."

"Her mum? But this place is cloaked?"

"I called her when we got back, to let her know Day was fine and she wanted to see for herself even though she's run off plenty of times before and has always been fine."

"Still, it's understandable." Chandler wished her mother had cared like that.

"Violette is going to meet Katia in the nearby town," Quinton explained, his voice shifting back to normal after mentioning Violette. Chandler still found herself curious why he so obviously disliked her so much, but quickly shoved the curiosity away. "Then she's coming here to discuss things with Praxis."

"But what does that mean?"

Quinton shrugged. "It could mean anything."

"Do you want her to stay?"

"So I can be close to her, yes. But I also don't want her involved in all this. This life is a lot."

"We can't always control other people."

"No." He stepped closer then, right into her space, looking down at her with a wide grin. She noticed the slight flush of his cheeks and tip of his nose. "Know what I can control?"

She raised an eyebrow. "What idea is this going to be and will I hate it?"

"You won't hate it."

"Can you promise me that?"

"Actually, I can."

"Make your promise to me then, Quinton."

"How much do you like tea and cake?" He paused, the flush deepened, and then so did the smile. "And Ziva, too. She's part of our little trio."

"Oh, we're a trio, are we?" she laughed. She wondered if he was getting cold. Just because she couldn't feel the temperature didn't mean things weren't bad. It had to be cold enough for the snow to settle like it had. "We both like tea and cake."

"Shall we find her then? I'll take you both to our little café for a treat and you can fill me in on what I've missed."

"Is Gretchen not keeping you up to date with the news?"

"She has her own business to sort out right now."

"Does she?" Chandler cracked her fingers.

"And it's none of my business until she's resolved it. Just like she doesn't pester me when I have things I need to sort." He frowned but with a smile. "Well, she doesn't pester me *much*."

"You have things to be pestered about?" Chandler teased.

"Like everyone else," he admitted, then smiled at her softly. "Less now."

"Because Darlene is being sorted?" Chandler guessed.

"Right," he said slowly. Quinton switched things up quickly though and put the back of his hand to his forehead, closing his eyes. All of it was dramatic. "It hurts to admit that I'm as Human as the rest of you with my problems when *clearly* I was born to be superior."

"A superior arse."

Quinton dropped his hand and grinned. "Have you been looking at my arse? And you think it's superior? Icy! I'm impressed."

Chandler started to walk off. "I'm going to get cake without you!"

"You wouldn't leave me out here in the cold by myself."

"I'm about to."

Within seconds he'd caught up to her, and he was laughing loudly. They walked on together.

Chandler looked over at Quinton when Redwing reappeared. "But shouldn't we be treating you?"

He met her gaze again. The white background made him stand out even more so than normal. He was so bright in a place where the colour had faded for the season. There was just him.

"What for?" he asked.

She looked at the path ahead and cracked her knuckles. "As a 'welcome home' thing."

"You can treat me to whatever you like, whenever you like," he said joyously.

"That sounds like I have options on what I can do."

"I want to know what you're thinking!"

"Probably nothing you'll like."

"Oh, I don't know about that," he winked. "But this time, this treat is on me."

"I'm not turning down free cake," Chandler said, opening the door first. "Not if you're buying."

Quinton laughed and nearly slipped over. Chandler caught his arm and helped him to stabilise on the iced step. They smiled at each other.

Chandler really did feel like she was finally home. A place she'd never had before, and with Quinton back, it felt even more like it *should*. She felt right, and everything else did, too.

CHAPTER THIRTY-THREE
FLORA

37ᵗʰ Day of Winter 2406

"I won't lie to you. I don't know if they'll ever change back," Maggie said rather dejectedly. "You might be stuck as you are."

"Forever?" Flora asked, already sensing the answer.

"You might."

Flora waved her golden hands back and forth. "Oh."

"Don't let it ruin you," Maggie told her.

"How can I not? If they won't change back, then *I'm ruined*. I'm not normal."

Maggie's smile was sad. "You may not want to be reminded of this now, but you were never *normal*, Flora."

"But I could hide it before!"

"Did you want to hide it or were you forced to?" Maggie groaned as she got to her feet, patting down the cushion she'd squashed. "No difference is one to be ashamed of. Whether your

Abnormality was hidden or not. And who's to say it won't ever leave? It's already regressed back to just your hands. You never know. It might become nothing more than a special painted fingernail one day."

"But I can't touch anyone in case I pass it on."

"Wane carried you back, and he never turned into a decorative lawn piece."

"I didn't know what I was doing! I wasn't conscious."

"Yet your body knew enough to stabilise it." Maggie sighed.

"He also never touched my arms or hands! And no one else did either."

"If you're worried, then don't touch anyone. And if you do touch someone, and are still worried, make sure it's someone you don't like very well."

Flora laughed unexpectedly at the utter absurdity of it, and Maggie smiled at her again. The old woman patted her leg, just once, before Flora could warn against it. Maggie met her gaze and winked, letting go again and leaving the room.

Flora thumped back into her pillows. She'd been on forced bedrest since returning to Redwing. From what little information she'd collated from the Helpers – the only people who'd been allowed into her room until today – Chandler had been given the same treatment.

The curtains on her windows were wide open. She'd asked them to be left like that, day and night. She'd watched the snow fall and rest outside on the grounds and had tried to count how many birds flew by.

Maggie was right. Though Flora's hands still suffered from the touch of the golden skull, it'd receded from her elbows to just below her wrists. She could easily and freely wiggle her fingers now and if she touched something, like her pillows or blankets which she couldn't avoid, they didn't turn into solid gold lumps.

But try as she might, the gold didn't leave her flesh.

After arriving back home, Flora had woken briefly enough to be able to let go of the skull in a thick container. She wondered if that, too, had formed itself into a solid golden cube. She also wondered what Praxis would do with it since no one could touch it outside of her.

She'd seen no one, not even her friends, since returning. She desperately wished to see them, to hug them, but what fate would she pass on? Could she pass on the curse or did her body contain it? How much control did she really possess?

It hurt to think about how she might cause harm to the people she cared about. So, despite the restrictions having been lifted that morning, Flora hadn't called for Aleema or Dalton to come visit yet and it was mid-afternoon already. She wanted to be absolutely certain she wouldn't jinx them too.

The more painful thoughts came when she considered Preston. For all the love she had for him, how could he ever return it now? She was certain they'd been about to kiss before she'd been pulled away. But he wouldn't want her now. She'd changed, and not, in her mind, for the better. Whatever he'd wanted before, he wouldn't want now, not as she was.

A knock came at her door. Flora peered at it but didn't call out. There was no need since it already swung open.

The last person she expected to see was Gretchen, yet there she was.

Gretchen had redyed the neon green parts to her blonde hair, and her eyebrows were neatly drawn back on her face. She'd dressed in black – a skirt and fishnet tights, thick knee-high boots, and black mesh top – which would be perfect for a nightclub or party, yet she could pull it off at any time.

"Hello?" Flora said, uncertain.

Gretchen closed the door and produced a bunch of soft coloured flowers. "These ain't from me," she expressed quickly. "They're from Wane."

"But you're the one delivering them?"

"He's in his debrief with the big P."

Flora nodded. "Have you had yours?"

"Went by an hour ago," Gretchen said. "Where can I put these?" She waved the flowers.

Flora indicated to the bedside cabinet. "I'll find something to put them in later," she said, then glanced back at Gretchen who was putting the flowers down. "Why hasn't anyone had their debrief before today?"

Gretchen stole the chair Maggie had just been sat in. "P wanted to make sure everyone was fit and healthy first."

"But you guys weren't hurt?"

"Who knows what goes on inside that brain of his."

"Why are you here?"

Flora hadn't meant to ask, let alone blurt the question, but it was out in the air now. Gretchen raised an eyebrow, looking like she was fighting back a grin.

"I came to see if you were alright," Gretchen said. "Someone said you'd not had any visitors yet? Even Icy's up and about, gone out to have *tea* or some bullshit. Are you in here mopin'?"

"Moping?" Flora scoffed. She'd never do such a thing.

"Because you know you've been cleared, right? You can leave this room?"

"I know."

"Then why haven't you? It's been hours."

"I—" Flora cut herself off.

"You're mopin'," Gretchen finished. She sat back in the chair, grin on her face like a cat facing down a mouse. "There ain't anything wrong with wallowing in your misery. You're entitled to do so. We all 'ave our moments. But you've got to get up at some point. You can't live in this room."

"I can," Flora argued, realising quickly she sounded childish.

"If you want," Gretchen shrugged. "Ain't much fun though."

"And I don't have to get up."

"Oh. You've gone past mopin' and have dived right into the deep end of the pool to pure self-loathing. Got it."

"I'm not—" She cut herself off again and sighed. "Did you come in here just to tease me?"

"I told you why I came."

"Since when did you care if I was alright?"

"Around the time I realised you weren't completely useless."

Flora looked to the ceiling and then back again. "That's not the compliment you think it is."

"I didn't want it to sound like a compliment."

"Then what—"

"You're wasted in 'ere," Gretchen cut in. "You're a good Abnormal with more skills than you think. That Island, that *skull*, I think it made you realise that. And you're terrified."

"I'm not terrified."

"The whole time you've been 'ere, you've hidden behind someone else. This mission proved that you shouldn't 'ave been. You're plenty capable to stand on your own two feet. Realising that? It's scary."

Flora *had* realised that. She *was* useful and had done a lot of the work. Without her, two missions wouldn't have been completed and ended, and maybe more would've suffered. Maybe more *people* would've suffered.

That didn't mean she had to admit it though.

"Look at my hands," Flora raised her golden fists at Gretchen, "What am I supposed to do with these? How am I meant to be helpful now?"

"You're helpful however you're helpful." Gretchen shrugged again. "I can't get all deep with you. That's not my thing."

"Isn't it?" Flora lowered her hands to her side. "You came in here, bringing a gift from someone else, to check on me. You're trying to give me this little pep talk. You pestered me on the damn Island before all this to get it together. Now, again, you're telling me to pull myself up and stop moping."

"So you admit you're mopin'?"

"Why does that *matter*?"

"Why do golden hands matter?" Gretchen countered quickly. "You can't go back to hidin' again. You can't just choose somethin' else to use as an excuse to stop."

"Says little miss confidence."

Gretchen snorted ungracefully. "I ain't that."

"Sure you are. You're practically *made* of it."

"Is that what you think?" Gretchen leaned forward then, her arms pressing into Flora's bed. "Alright. How's *this*? Until this morning, I've avoided Wane."

"I—"

"You know we'd been sleepin' together?"

"No, I—"

"I couldn't commit to more than that. I couldn't admit that to him either. You might've heard our little *argument* on the Island?"

"You two walked away before—"

"Wane said it was because I was using him as a distraction for how my best friend had left and I had no one else, that I latched onto the next person who was ready to give me a little of their time. That I was lonely. That I was desperate for any sort of attention from someone remotely decent. And the worst bit in all that? He was *right*.

"I hate change and I have made myself lonely. Shuttin' people out is surprisingly easy. I've tried to protect myself and only made things worse for myself. I'd like to blame my past, but mostly my parents. But they're not 'ere right now to answer to how they treated me or to blame for what's happened since leaving them."

Gretchen paused, only to grin wildly, but not kindly; it was the grin of a wild animal on the loose. "The confidence you say

I have? It's false and an illusion. It's a *lie*. There's nothing to me really except a little mask I wear in front of everyone else. What you see is what you get because there's nothin' else to me. I have no depths or widths or *person*. So, like you with your friends and now your hands, I hide behind what I can so people don't see the *real me*. Because the thought of being known is *terrifying*.

"There's no confidence to me. There is just me."

Gretchen spread her arms out wide like she was saying to Flora 'here I am'.

Flora blinked quickly several times. She didn't know what to say. *Was* there anything to say? 'Congratulations for opening up' wouldn't be right and Gretchen definitely wouldn't appreciate it. But staying silent also didn't come off as a good thing either.

"Then we both have to get back out there," Flora said. To her own ears, she heard how hollow her voice sounded. She could also feel how wet her eyes were.

Gretchen grimaced. "Don't start cryin' on me. I can't handle that."

"I won't," Flora promised, laughing a little to break up the tension. "But why are you telling me this?"

"Honestly? No fuckin' idea."

"Oh, right."

"More than likely because I know how you feel. I can *sympathise*. But this doesn't make us friends. We ain't close to that."

Flora nodded. "Of course not, no."

"I'll kick anyone's arse who doesn't like you, though. Fuck them."

"That's a lovely offer?"

"Mostly 'cause I'm looking for a fight now."

"Can you leave me out of that bit? I'm *not* looking for a fight."

"I'll think about it."

"Think harder. I *really* don't want to be part of it."

Gretchen smiled slightly. Out of everything, having a little heart to heart with Gretchen was at the bottom of Flora's list of considerations. Yet a weight had lifted from Flora's shoulders and the dark clouds in her mind had begun to shift away.

Maybe things were different, but they didn't have to be all doom and gloom. A change had come over Flora, but maybe it wasn't all bad.

She looked down at her hands. *Some* of it wasn't great, but she could live. Things might just be okay. Different, but she'd move on. She had people around her, and maybe, weirdly, somehow Gretchen had become one of them. Even if neither of them would voice it, it hung in the air around them both.

Flora looked at Gretchen, and smiled.

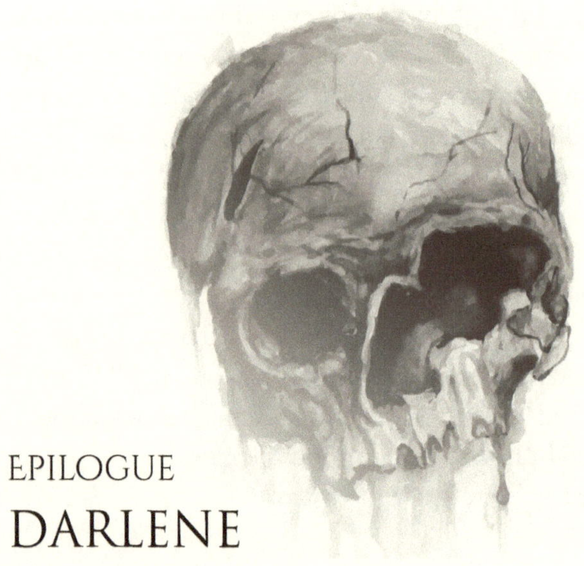

DARLENE

37th Day of Winter 2406

Darlene didn't understand what was so special about this little café.

It was built in the middle of the road and stuck up high on stilts. The outside colours were boring. It took loads of steps to get up to it since the lift was broken, which made her legs ache. By the time she reached the top, her lungs hurt badly.

The door did open with a little bell though, which was fun.

No one turned around to look at her when she entered. She slipped into a nearby chair at an empty table and unwound her scarf. Just as she put it in the next chair, her brother slid into the seat across from her.

"What are you doing?" he asked. He'd already shed his coat and hat.

"Following you," she admitted.

"I can see that." There was humour in his eyes. "Why?"

Darlene pouted. "You left without me."

"To catch up with my friends."

"Oh! Which ones?"

Quinton sighed, and then waved his friends over. In a single minute both Ziva and Chandler sat down, filling the little table of four.

Darlene had hoped to go a little longer without being noticed, but it seemed her brother didn't miss a trick. He always seemed to know where she was or when she was listening in. She needed to get better at hiding that.

"Would you like something to drink?" Ziva offered a menu.

"Do they have hot chocolate?" Darlene asked her brother directly.

"With marshmallows and sprinkles," Quinton confirmed.

"What colour sprinkles?"

"Pink or chocolate ones?"

Darlene gasped. "Can I have both?"

Quinton dramatically rolled his eyes. "If you get a sugar rush..." He sighed. "I can ask if you can have both, but if you can't?"

"Then the chocolate ones!"

"Anything else for the queen of the table?"

Chandler brought her hands up to her mouth and fake whispered behind it. "Your brother's paying."

"Then I want sandwiches and cake too!" Quinton raised an eyebrow and Darlene smiled. "Please?"

"Full afternoon tea?" Quinton asked.

Ziva folded her menu. "Sounds good to me. Are you sure you're alright paying?"

He waved her off. "I said I'd treat my favourite girls."

Darlene cheered loudly, making several other customers turn to look at their table. Ziva laughed at her, as did Quinton. Chandler remained quiet though, looking at her menu, but Darlene saw her eyes weren't moving.

Quinton got up to order. Chandler tucked her menu away and Ziva started asking Darlene lots of questions about her favourite things. Darlene didn't mind. She liked telling people her favourite colour or how she wanted to grow tomatoes like her Ma did.

Thinking of her Ma, Darlene wondered when she'd arrive. She was meant to be coming up to the Hidden House today to discuss Darlene's future. Whatever that meant.

Darlene knew Hidden House's real name was Redwing, but it didn't suit it. When she'd searched for her brother the first time, she knew he had to be hiding from her, like a game. So seeing a house in the middle of nowhere *shimmer* like a lake, she decided that was the place. And she'd been right.

Now she realised the house was much more than something hidden. Lots of people lived there. She wondered if she could live there, because she didn't want to leave her brother. But she didn't want to be without Ma, either.

Quinton came back to the table. "All ordered," he announced.

Darlene sat up straighter, thinking of something suddenly. "Can I see your necklace?"

"Mine?" Quinton asked.

"Not now. Yours looks boring."

Her brother laughed. "It's not. It helps me see the future."

Darlene's eyes widened comically. "*Really?*"

"When we're back at the house, I'll show you? I'll need my sketchbook too."

"You draw?" How did she not know this about her brother? "What do you draw? Can you draw me as the queen you said I am?" Quinton laughed.

"He's really good," Ziva confessed. "Chandler has one of his drawings in her room."

Quinton glanced at Chandler. "You kept that, too?"

Chandler smiled at him. "I had it framed."

"I want to see your necklace, please," Darlene said, hand open and waiting. "Chandler?"

Chandler looked at her little hand. "Mine?"

"I can see it hiding beneath your jumper. You always keep it there." Darlene scowled. "Why are you hiding it?"

"How can you see it?" Ziva asked.

"Because I can tell when something's hidden," Darlene explained, shrugging. "Anything not in plain sight but exists, it shimmers. Like water!"

"And you can see my necklace?" Chandler asked.

Darlene nodded enthusiastically. "Because you want to keep it hidden."

"You might be like us," her brother told her.

"Is that a bad thing?" Darlene asked.

Quinton smiled. "Not to me."

Darlene turned back to Chandler. "Please? I'm asking nicely. Which Ma and my brother say I have to do if I want things. I have to ask nicely."

"But we've also said you can't have everything all the time, even if you ask nicely."

Darlene rolled her eyes at her brother, and he stuck his tongue out at her.

Chandler drew the necklace out, smiling between Quinton and Darlene. "I don't take it off," she said.

"Oh." Darlene leaned in to see it anyway.

"You never take it off?" Ziva questioned. "Not even to shower? What about the stone in the ring? Aren't you worried it'll come out?"

"A little," Chandler admitted. "But..." She said no more.

Darlene was aware her brother kept looking at Chandler, and with an expression Darlene had never seen before. There was even a faint smile on his mouth. Darlene screwed up her face at the look. But when his eyes turned to her, she widened her eyes and focused on only the ring.

"It's pretty," Darlene decided. "I want a ring like that some-day. Do you think I could buy one or will someone get me one if I ask nicely?"

"I'm sure you'll get one," Chandler said, tucking it away again.

"Your brother bought that one," Ziva told her.

Darlene scowled at her brother. "You bought Chandler a ring? Are you marrying her?"

The group laughed. "It's a long story," Chandler explained.

"It has something to do with what we do," Ziva added.

"My parents think I'm marrying her though," Quinton said last.

Chandler's attention went to him. "They still think that?"

He shrugged and swiped his blue hair back with a hand. "They think we're just taking our time, but we'll get there one day. I can tell them otherwise?"

"Is this keeping them off your back?"

"For now, yeah. It's making them think I'm being an adult so they're staying off my behind about the business."

"Then leave things as they are."

Darlene's eyebrows narrowed in the middle as she watched Chandler smile at Quinton, and at how he smiled back. His face seemed *different*, and she couldn't work out how or why. But she knew something hidden had come up; the edges of his mouth were shimmery.

She didn't have time to question it, as food was brought to the table, distracting her with the joys of sugary things.

Ma had been taken into the office with the big boss of Hidden House, while Darlene had been forced to stay outside it with her brother. He held her to him like a bodyguard.

She'd tried to shove him off but he was much bigger than her and sadly stronger too.

"How much longer?" she whined.

"I don't know," he answered unhelpfully.

"Why don't you know? Do you know anything?"

Ma had turned up at Hidden House minutes after Darlene had arrived back from lunch. She'd been gripping her stomach, so full she wondered if she might burst open. But upon seeing her Ma, she'd forgotten all about it and had rushed her for a warm hug.

Now she was waiting to hear what the big boss man said.

Darlene liked it here. She had her own room, her own space, and was getting used to waking up in the night to not entirely unpleasant piano music.

As she went to ask her brother what would happen to her room, the door opened. Ma walked out, smiling. That had to be good.

"Ma?" Darlene asked.

Her Ma scooped her into a hug and then knelt on the floor in front of her. "What do you want?" she asked.

"What do I want?" Darlene questioned.

"Would you like to stay here with these nice people?"

"My room!" she cheered, then pouted. "What about you?"

"I can stay too," Ma told her. Darlene cheered again.

"Katia?" Quinton asked, using Ma's real name. It sounded strange to hear.

Her mum stood up, but didn't let go of Darlene's still gloved hand. "Praxis says I can stay," she said. "I have to earn my way becoming a Helper, but since Darlene is still so young and they think she might be..."

"I'm big enough!" Darlene agued. "I made it here on my own before!"

Her mum glanced down at her with a smile. "Which is why you need to stay here. You might be just like your brother."

Darlene grinned. "I can see into the future too?"

Her mum laughed; Darlene had missed making her mum laugh. "Not the future," she said. "But you might just have a little gift of your own."

"Oh! What's going to happen?"

"You need to be tested."

"Will it hurt?" Darlene shook her head. "I don't want it to hurt."

"I don't know. But I'll be here," her mum promised. "I'll hold your hand."

"Will you hold my hand too?" Darlene asked, peering up at her brother.

He nodded. "If you want me to hold your hand, I will."

"And these tests will give me a gift?"

"They might tell you what gift you have already," her mum answered.

"They're letting you stay to help her," Quinton realised, looking directly at Darlene's mum. "I don't know of any other families that are allowed to do that."

"I'm special," Darlene grinned.

She heard her Ma and brother laughed.

"I'll be here for you *both*," her mother promised.

"She needs you more than I do," Quinton told her. "She's young, Katia. She'll need all the help she can get."

"I'll be here to help her through all of it."

"And after?"

Her mum squeezed her hand. "We're staying if they prove what we think we already know," she looked down at Darlene, "if that's what you want?"

"This isn't an easy job," Quinton warned.

"Life out there isn't easy," her mum reminded him. "But here, she stands a better chance. She can have a life and a family. You know what it's like here. Praxis explained it to me as best he could. She might never get picked. And if she does, then I'll deal with it. We all will."

"She might not get picked for years."

"He's promised she won't until she's at least sixteen. Same as someone else here? Helen, I think he said?"

Darlene watched her brother's face. "Do you want me to stay?"

"You'd find me even if I left again, wouldn't you?" he asked.

"I would!"

"Then I better keep you close by." Quinton smiled. "Yes, I want you to stay, Day."

Darlene beamed. "You get to have both your families together!"

Quinton laughed and snatched Darlene up. He started to race for the back garden, her body wiggling in his arms. She shrieked the whole way there, and grew even louder when she was thrown out into the snow. He threw himself down next to her.

She'd get to keep her brother and her Ma together.

And she'd find all the shimmery things everywhere with them both.

End of Book Two

ACKNOWLEDGEMENTS

For this book, I have a few people to be overly grateful for.

And I need to thank those specific humans here.

Hannah. First as always. You've never stopped believing in me or let me dull my craziness for a single second. You support my every wild idea and yell at me (in a good way) with every project I start – no matter how many variations of the same thing or drafts I show you. Your love for my work and, more importantly, for me is everything. You really are my best friend, the pastel to my dark, the ghostiest little fiend.

Kirsten. The cheers and countless streams of support you always bring are appreciated and mean everything. Every message feels like a "Hello, I see you!" With every little step I take, I know you're clapping for me, just as I do for you. And of course I know how much you love these characters – mostly Quinton (I built him specifically for you, of course!)

Book squad – Mae, Faye, Amy, and Nic. What a wild ride life has been since YALC'23. We sort of all crashed together and have stuck. But over the best reason. You all have been infinitely kind and supportive of these bookish dreams. May 'the sibling-hood of the travelling YALC spork' never die.

Sydney, Enchanted Ink. All of you have helped bring, yet again, another one of my silly stories to life. Working with you every step of the way is amazing and I couldn't ask for a better team of help.

Joe. Best for last. I talk at you sometimes so much about my books and the little ideas I have, and I occasionally wonder how mental you think I am. But then you smile and encourage me to keep going, and I just know that even if you do think I'm slightly deranged you have my back one hundred percent in whatever I do. You haven't just walked into my life, you've run full force into it. Your care, kindness, support in anything, and love for me literally means more than the world. You are the nuisance to my nonsense, and everything good. You simply are the best boyfriend (yes, even when you tut).

ABOUT THE AUTHOR

LAUREN JADE CASE

is a writer from a seaside town in England. She loves writing and reading fantasy, but also sci-fi, dystopia, and occasionally crime/ mystery. Sometimes she just stares out the window at rain and storms with a candle lit beside her.

STARLIGHT is her debut novel and the first in a trilogy.

BEARER OF MASKS is a completely new book set in an entirely new universe, with *TREASURER OF SKULLS* as the next instalment.

Twitter: @ LaaureenJaadee

Instagram: @ LaaureenJaadee

TikTok: @LaaureenJaadee